King Cameron

David Craig

Whittles Publishing

Published by
Whittles Publishing Ltd.,
Dunbeath,
Caithness, KW6 6EY,
Scotland, UK
www.whittlespublishing.com

ISBN 978-1870325-17-2

Printed by Athenæum Press Ltd., Gateshead, UK

What power there is in a popular disturbance! How quickly it changes the whole political situation! The night before there had been a curfew, and people had been frightened anyway, but now the whole town was strolling about and hooting at the soldiers. A people transformed – can it be so near to breaking through the crust of this half-century, into a completely different atmosphere?

Solzhenitsyn – *The Gulag Archipelago*

Many of the people, incidents and other items in this story are real. Where a fact existed, I have never knowingly substituted an invented item for it. I therefore dedicate King Cameron to James Hunter, Kenneth Logue, John Prebble and Iain Johnston of Lochmaddy, who found out so many of the facts, and to the people of Sollas, both the dead and the living.

VOICES OF THE WILDERNESS

Treading water between Uist and Vallay
We faced a horizon blue as wild hyacinth,
Yellow and white as eyebrights. Behind us
The houses of old Sollas humped like graves.
Never a window-light on Taransay
Where seven slave-ships moored in the Sound
And scoured the boys from the beach.

Under us, buoying us, the breakers' last energies
Pulsed among the tangle, lifting it easily,
Carrying food to the foraging mouths
Of the undersea populations,
Streaming landward laden with leafage,
Storm-splintered stems and fine detritus,
Bearing fertility to the machair meadows.

Generations of flowers have followed the clearance,
Tides of anger and heartbreak spent on the beach
(Fires of driftwood, broth of seaweed and nettles).
Their gleam has dulled into the sand,
Their houses heaped like shingle-drifts,
Their crying blown to sea in the gale
On which the *Tusker* tacked to Canada.

We can still hear it under the layers of the music,
Petals droped from the black rose of Ireland
Which is always falling, rising, replacing, falling,
Curving its fragrance around the atmosphere
Like the foundations of the towering cumulus
When the hot turbulence has died into space
And a fine shroud is drawn along the Islands.

Prelude

Six miles east of Edinburgh the blond fields of oats and barley sunned themselves under a sky of mild blue. The woollen fog from the Firth had risen and withdrawn as the sun heightened. Now it hovered in looming areas out to sea, like an array of white ghosts. They might come back. As the land warmed, a breeze stirred from seaward, bringing the savoury stink of herrings curing to mingle with the dry, mealy smell of ripening corn.

Peter Lawson, a carpenter, sat on the back of his cartload of wood and let the horse find its way to Tranent along the dusty yellow road. Somewhere behind him hooves thudded, came nearer. His horse stopped suddenly and backed up, tilting him off. He looked up from the dust. Soldiers – two – three – rearing above him on black chargers. 'Here's another,' said one. The dark eye of his pistol gaped.

'What's ado? I've dune nae hairm.' The pistol tilted. 'Leave me be!' He flung round sideways for the shelter of the cart and the bullet hit him in the right side just above his foot-rule. Slam – slam – slam – his dimming brain registered three more hits before it collapsed.

Half a mile south, James Moffat, a brewer's labourer, walked over to see his aunt with a basket of new potatoes. The hedge beside him burst in a shower of twigs. A dragoon in a green uniform plunged through on horseback, drew his pistol from its holster, fired at him and missed. He ran desperately, like a hare, between the barriers of the hedges. Hooves clattering on stones behind him. A horse beside him, a bare-headed soldier leaning over, grinning, saying, 'Damme, I've dropped my helmet. Will you pick it up?' As Moffat turned, and saw the helmet on its side on the road and stooped to get it, bullets hit him in the neck and spine.

James Kemp and his brother William were fourteen and twelve years old. When news came of trouble in Tranent, they ran from the farm into town to see the fun. It was like a fair day, the press in the street, a buzz and roar from somewhere ahead. But here was a line of mounted soldiers. As the boys stopped and looked, a shout of command came and each soldier drew a sabre. Fourteen naked blades, glinting in the hazy sunshine. James and William turned and ran till their breath scorched their chests. The road shook with horses. Bullets whizzed above their heads like bumble bees. William fell down the bank, crunched into the standing corn, and lay there for two hours in a sweating daymare. Where was Jamie? Should he gang hame noo? He could hear nothing above his head but the barley whispering and the singing of a skylark. Late in the afternoon he crept home like a cat. Soon after, Jamie was carried into the farmyard on a hurdle, stabbed through the chest, the upper half of his head nearly cut off at the temples.

Peter Ness, a sawyer, went from Prestonpans to Tranent with his mate John Guild, to get his wages from James Thin the forester. He always paid them in John Glen's inn. But it was impossible to get near the place today. The Deputy Lieutenants were in there, it turned out, drawing up the lists of men conscripted for the militia and hearing individual appeals. Hundreds of men and women had crowded round the place, shouting for the Deputies to come out, to surrender the lists, to get back where they belonged. A hail of cobblestones clattered against the front of the inn and Ness and Guild saw people climbing up onto the roofs and tearing out tiles to fling. A swish and rattle: down the Millgate a troop of mounted soldiers had drawn their sabres. Ness took fright. 'C'wa man, we'll a' be murdered if we bide here.'

'If we rin aff, they'll hunt us doon. Staund still and they winna touch you.'

But Ness took off in a panic, through an open house-door, out at the back, over the wall of its kail-yard, and off down the beaten earth path between the corn fields. Six dragoons sighted him and galloped after him, whooping like hunters. Fifty yards – forty yards – Ness staggered and fell, and crouched, covering his face. 'You damned Scotch bugger,' said a voice above him and a bullet hit his head, destroying him. Another made his corpse shake. Then the dragoons turned back towards town.

Stephen Brotherstone and his wife Margaret were sick with worry. A crew of wild lads had come yelling round the house that morning and jostled and chivvied their two boys into going to Tranent from Pencaitland.

The Deputies were meeting – the cavalry would be there – they might see some gunplay. At dinnertime the boys were still away and Stephen and Margaret went to look for them. At 2 o'clock a troop of mounted soldiers appeared on the rise ahead, riding briskly. The Brotherstones looked at each other, terrified, and half-fell through a gap in the hedge. They hugged the ground, holding their breaths. Had they been seen? The hedge above them cracked and snapped. Bullets shredded the leaves. One caught Stephen in the shoulder. As he screamed, a dragoon broke through the hedge and slashed at his stomach. Blood poured – Stephen lay in it, paralysed.

Margaret was shouting now: 'Leave him! Leave him! Get off! Don't touch me!'

'You damned bitch!' the soldier shouted back. 'Get to your kennel or I'll –' His sabre hissed like an adder just above her head. After two hours she managed to get a cart to carry her husband home – most of the farm doors were barred, the people too terrified to come out. Soon after she got home, her husband died without speaking.

William Laidlaw and Alex Robertson, farm servants, ran into the same troop further down the road. They walked on towards them, unconcerned. Then the dragoons were driving at them, the horses' chests shiny with sweat, their nostrils flaring, the soldiers waving their swords and shouting, mad snarling shouts. Robertson and Laidlaw ran like rabbits into the corn, plunged into its golden thickets, turned and yelled, 'Have mercy – dinna do it – have mercy.' A horse reared above Robertson, filling the air with blackness. He flung up his hand to shield his face and a sabre slashed it off at the wrist, He fell, blacked out. When he came to, Laidlaw was lying beside him on his face, cut up and holed, already stiff.

John Adam, a miner, was going home from Cockenzie colliery, where he worked for John Caddell, coal-owner and Deputy Lieutenant. He felt blithe in the sunshine, glad to be above ground again. Three boys came running, white-faced and staring. 'Gang roon! gang roon!' they shouted. 'Keep awa frae Tranent! There's sodgers firin' anal' As Adam turned and ran with them towards his father's village of Macmerry, a horse neighed behind them, metal clashed. The three flung into the ditch and one of the lads (William Tait, a journeyman tailor) wormed through the hedge stems and hid under a cart.

'I've dune naething.' That was Adam's voice. 'Leave me be! Oh mercy, mercy –'

'There's your mercy.' A bang, deafening. A brimstone smell of powder. A groan – a mindless gasp of pure pain. 'Blast you – what are you yowling at?' Thuds and a splash. A quick scud of hooves. Then utter silence. When Tait dared to look out through the hedge, he saw Adam face down in the ditch, the water scarlet, his back and shoulders torn as though a bull had gored him.

Eleven dead were counted by sunset, men, women, and boys, in Tranent and the surrounding countryside. Next day and the day after, when the reapers went into the fields with their sickles, they found six more, in the ditches and trampled clearings among the barley.

The Lord Advocate, Robert Dundas, wrote that he was not surprised 'that some of these soldiers once let loose upon such a dangerous mob, as deserved more properly the name of an insurrection, should go beyond the strict line of duty, and do more than what in a cooler moment they or their officers would have deemed necessary for quelling such a tumult and dispersing the rioters'.

The people of Prestonpans had already resolved 'That although we may be overpowered, and dragged from our parents, friends and employments to be made soldiers of, you may infer from this what trust can be reposed in us if ever we are called upon to disperse our fellow countrymen, or to oppose a foreign foe'.

Part I

Mainland

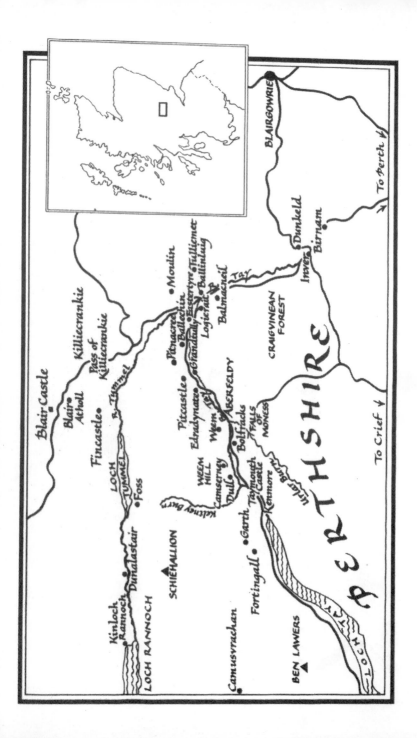

Chapter 1

The News

Thin blue smoke poured straight up from the freshly mortared chimney of the McCullochs' house in Weem. It tinged the air with a smell of herbs and whisky. Old Donald had put three more peats on the fire. His daughter Mary said it was all he was good for – using up fuel that others had cut. She was a scold – whenever she was near him he felt in the wrong and wondered anxiously what it was he ought to have done. But between them, he told himself, they had made this nest comfortable. He looked up with satisfaction at the panelling of the new box-beds – comfort and decency for all three of them, while others in the village still slept on the floor like beasts. And the stone seats beside the fire would be replaced with benches, once Cameron brought the rest of the spare timber he had promised from the linen mill he was building for the Flemyngs at Aberfeldy.

Cameron made him uneasy with his dark, closed look, the way he stopped and thought silently before he answered you. But he got things done, he was a weighty man to have in the village, no doubt of that. Old Donald touched the peats with his fingers to bring more of the dry brown fibres above the flames. His thick fingers with their horny nails that stood away from the flesh took no harm from the heat. He wanted to feel warmed through to his spine, to have the comfort steal into him like strong ale. It would soothe away the worries that ached in his head, even on this hazy gold morning of early September, with a fine harvest coming and plenty of work for the young men in the new town.

A clack of shoes in the road outside. High-pitched shouts. He looked up startled, his eyes fire-dazzled, trying to focus on the door through the dusty levels of sunlight from the two small windows. It flung open and slammed back against the wall. Mary burst in. She stared at him and seemed not to see him. She sat down on the floor and took great heaving breaths as though she had come up a hill with a burden beyond her strength.

'What is wrong with you?' her father asked.

'The lists,' she said through her big breaths, which were trembling now. 'Robertson – has made up – his lists.'

'Lists – what lists?' The old man was taking refuge in confusion. She glared at him and her impatience at his frailty began to neutralize her fear.

'You know very well what lists – marking down the young men for the wars.'

'Will Donald be named?'

'He is twenty-one, is he not? And not married?'

'They may not call on them. They surely have enough already.'

'You know nothing.' She stared in anger at the old man's face, at his eyes which goggled anxiously at hers, then roved off when she met his look, his lips which caved in on his gums and mumbled and tightened as though he was always eating. Did she have to shoulder his fears too? Had he no strength left at all to feed into their little supply? 'If his name is there, he is in mortal danger, and if the French war gets worse, they will be taking them all.'

'They may not be sending them abroad –'

'That is what they promised when James enlisted.' Her heart cramped now as she thought of her husband's folly in plumping for the easy money, as it had seemed, after three bad harvests – his airy promise to come home soon – his failure to return after his regiment had been disbanded in Madras and left to make its own way back round half the world. 'That is what they promised Morag Mackintosh and big Mary, and Sheila Stewart, and Flora MacGregor. And they are all widows now. James was a fool, but Donald will be a pressed man and a slave. And so will a hundred others from hereabouts. No no no!' She rose on to her knees and looked as though she was praying, but her eyes were fully open and the clenched look on her remarkably white face with its mannish black eyebrows suddenly reminded him of her dead mother. 'We will not lie down under this.' She said it with an almost questioning tone, as though listening to the sound of her own defiance to gauge how real it was. But her hands were gripping into fists.

'What will you do?'

He looked scared and she pitied him. 'Och – give them a dose of Archibald Menzies's medicine. A bit of a ride down the road and a chance to change their minds.' She giggled unexpectedly. 'There will be a good crowd at church tomorrow, that is for sure. Where is Donald?'

'Gone after rabbits, up the hill.'

'He would be better doing a day at the mill.'

Her return to mere domestic grievances was a relief after the nightmare about the army. He felt hungry, and went through to the cool room at the back for a bowl of sheep's milk and some bits of potato. When he came back, she had gone. From the front door he could see her walking along the road past the graveyard with three of her friends, their heavy skirts swinging.

As he sat by the fire softening potatoes between his gums, he felt pleased with himself. If they took a whirl at the minister, he would have a fine sight of the fun. Two days ago when they had carted out Menzies the minister and Fleming the young teacher from along the road at Dull and danced round them like children at a Halloween fire and stuck them up on horses, facing backwards, and paraded them past the door and down the road to Aberfeldy, he had flung a soft carrot himself and caught the man on the side of his face. He had deserved all he got – was that what ministers and teachers were paid for? to draw up the militia lists and condemn the young men to the barracks and the camps, to swamp fever in the Indies and their legs and arms blown off? Young Donald – his eyes were clear black-brown, like a lochan stained with peat, his hair was curly like a bull's poll, and he had been a lovely lad until his father went away, clever with his hands, whittling pieces of wood and glueing them to make little windmills and watermills. The wheel he had mounted on a bit of rod from Stewart's smithy still turned freely in the burn at the side of the kail-yard. If he was taken for the army, the light in their house would be damped out forever. Who would reap the corn and the flax, or milk the ewes? Mary would work like a slave, but a woman could not take the animals to market, though he knew of widows living alone, soldiers' wives mostly, who farmed on in a rough way by themselves, their cattle straying and mixing with the herds of others, their oats still standing in November …

Old Donald chuckled in himself as the scene in the road came over him again. The horse had stopped, held its tail out stiffly, and dunged a yard beneath the minster's gaping face. A young lad had called out, 'See what the beasts think of the Act!' And another had capped that: 'Aye – send a dollop of it down to London!' They had spirit enough for anything. They would need it, to match the military. Down in Tranent, which was somewhere near Edinburgh, and anything could have happened there –

but old Donald had had this from Cameron himself, and he got newspapers by the carrier's cart from Dunkeld – some miners had sworn not to serve, even if the King called on them, and the Volunteers had chased them into the cornfields and played havoc with their sabres …

That was a bad dream – like the 'Forty-five again. He had brooded himself into a black dwam, and when the door opened again he started violently and spilled the last of the milk on his legs. Young Donald was grinning at him with his new look of mockery.

'Where have you been?' The old man was trying to imitate his daughter's sharpness. 'Your mother was after you. The hay you left lying last night will spoil when the rain comes.'

'Rain? The sky is clear as glass. Grand weather to be after the girls or the rabbits.' Young Donald leaned his long-barrelled small-shot gun in the corner by the door and then his face darkened over. 'What did she want?'

'She thought you would be working. There is the timber to pay –'

'There is nobody working from here to Killin. Do you know what they have done there? They have taken Fergusson the teacher, while he was nailing up the lists, and stripped him and tarred him –'

'Donald – you would not do that! They will put them in the gaol for that!'

Young Donald coolly considered his grandfather's staring look of fright and answered him deliberately: 'No – I would not dirty my hands on a bit of a teacher. But they will never get the Killin lads. They are off into the hills and they will hide there as outlaws till the Act is lifted.'

'Would you do that, Donald? Would you hide if you had to?' The lad looked suspicious. 'Have you been hatching something up with *her* – to stow me away?'

'She only wants you safe –'

'She wants me safe from Jean. Well – if she had taken kindlier to her a year ago, we might have been wed by now, and I would have escaped the list.' He glowered at old Donald, as though to brand the accusation on to him too. Then he looked suddenly sulky like a child. 'Tell her, if she comes back bothering about the hay, she can turn it herself. Unless she's too busy flinging mud at ministers.'

CHAPTER 2

The Conversation

Angus Cameron looked incredulous, permanently. His friend James Menzies the wine merchant, in whose house he lodged, had said once, infuriated after a two-hour argument, 'Angus – do you believe *nothing* completely?' After thinking about it, Cameron replied, 'James, I was told a good thing once, by the sawyer at Bunarkaig. I used to help there as a boy. "Angus," he said, "if anybody ever says anything to you, think to yourself, How can I disagree with that? And if you cannot, well then you might believe it." And that is the best thing I ever heard.'

They sat in the parlour, on the evening of Saturday, September 2nd, waiting for Menzies' man Allan Stewart to come back with the news from Blair Atholl. They were disputing strategies for the resistance and drinking red wine from France – sour claret, which had proved hard to sell. The room had the look of a tattered nest – piles of newspapers were stacked against the walls, empty stone bottles stood about with dust on their shoulders like soldiers after a battle. The hearth was drifted up with cinders that had been left uncleared when today's fire was lit. Mrs Menzies had died five years before, killed by malaria and stomach trouble from their time in Bengal. Menzies himself had a yellow face with a stained-looking flush on each cheekbone, and when he felt a bout of fever coming on, he drank to drown the symptoms.

Now he looked over at Cameron, taking stock of the quizzical lift of his right eyebrow when he looked out below his black fringe, the downturn of his mouth under his long curved nose, and began to recapitulate his argument with care, uncomfortably aware that Angus might think he was trying not to sound drunk.

'Consider, Angus,' he said. 'They have seized the Session Books at Auchtergaven, and Kirkmichael, and Logierait, and – and many another

11

place. So the lists cannot be drawn up. So the Act cannot be applied. That strikes to the root.'

'The root? We wheedled the book ourselves out of that gullible weakling Fleming over at Dull. But Menzies had had copies made already. They are crafty. We must be craftier.'

'Och, craft … they need frightening. The Auchtergaven men broke in at night with their faces blacked and knives in their hands. Old MacCormack wet himself –' James laughed and spilled wine. 'He must have been terrified.'

'Terror is all very well, but it breeds revenge. I say, discredit them. Menzies and Fleming will never forget that two hours riding backwards, with every soul from Dull to Aberfeldy having a good look at their humiliation.'

'So they'll want vengeance too.'

'But nobody will join them in it, because nobody respects them. They are butts now. But old MacCormack is a victim. Blackfaced men with knives! They sound like pirates, or ruffians. A few wild men playing a violent game. And when the big men, the Lord Lieutenants and the Colonels of Volunteers, when they get violent back, how do we resist? We are many, but we are unarmed. Like the Tranent folk.'

'We can soon change that.'

'Well … There are fifty muskets in the Duke's armoury at Blair Castle. How do we get them? Only by going there in thousands, outnumbering his tenants, talking to *them,* until they feel their power, and disarm their masters. And how do we muster thousands? Our people will never come out unless they understand the reasons for all this stir. But once they *know* … You can keep a people ignorant but you cannot make them ignorant –'

'Tom Paine?'

'Who else? Do you think I could rise to such wisdom?' This sounded ironical but James could not fathom which way its edge was turned – was Angus actually mocking Paine, his chosen prophet, or merely depreciating himself? Angus was too deep – you never knew … Ruffled, and pent-up in his urge to plump for some outright and decisive plan, he grabbed the poker and hit the smouldering coals. A red one jumped out on to the floorboards and they began to smoke. Menzies threw his wine onto the coal, it fizzed, and a reek of bonfires filled the room. Cameron was shaking with laughter, looking on and making no move to help. Steps clicked on the stones outside and Allan Stewart came in, out of breath, his red hair darkened and sticking to his forehead. James at once poured him wine from a fresh jug and refilled his own glass and Cameron's.

'You're early,' he said. 'I hardly expected you before midnight.' 'The Faskally boatman brought me across the foot of the loch and I came straight over the hill to the Brig of Grandtully.'

'So he is friendly?'

'They are all friendly on that side.' Stewart's eyes were alight and he was drinking the claret down like water. 'It is like Hallow-fair from Ballinluig up to Blair. I went for a sup to Widow Duff's howff, of course –'

'Of course.'

'Well, where else would you go to meet up with the Duke and his followers?' (The 'Duke of Lennox' was John McLaggan, a horse dealer from Grandtully.)

'And was the Duke on his feet or his back?'

'I think his head was clear enough, for all it was going round. You know he is known to everybody –'

'As a rogue.'

'And a singer, and a clown with plenty of good stories to tell folk while he wheedles out their money. His sons have been to every place and farm along the Tummel. Every family with a young man knows they may lose him to the war, and they are as furious about it as a swarm of bees. Or Alex and Donald say they are, and I believe them. They are all outside their houses, staring along the roads, waiting for something.'

He stopped talking, still breathing hard, and held his glass out frankly for a fill of wine, like a child asking for milk. James poured, then held the spout of the jug over Cameron's glass. Why was he saying nothing? asking no questions? Surely this was the news they had most wanted to hear.

'Angus?' he said, but Cameron was looking past him at Allan Stewart, sceptical and intent.

He said at last, 'So what plan has come out of all this buzzing and swarming?'

'It will suit you, Angus,' Stewart said, laughing and unabashed. 'They have done their homework too – they have it down on paper. A letter for the Duke of Atholl.'

'Saying what?'

'I would have brought a copy away but they wanted them all. They ask the Duke to do away with the Act, because it will turn the Atholl

Highlanders into slaves, and if he will not, they will fight to the last drop of their blood.'

'With targe and claymore and a roar and a rush downhill?' Cameron's voice dried up their excitement like a dose of paregoric. 'Does MacLaggan want them to charge against the muskets, and make a Culloden in Strath Tummel? Does he know what has happened in Tranent?'

'Come on, Angus, he said no such thing.' Menzies was querulous, an ache in the head was interfering with his thoughts. 'They will confront the Duke –'

'Will he let them up the drive? If more than forty-nine go up there, he will read the Riot Act.'

Allan Stewart had flushed with discomfiture at the defusing of his story. 'He will have no option but to meet them, man. You should see them – they were ringing the Castle round when I came away, and making themselves fires for the night on Cnoc na Lude across the Tilt. If the Duke looks out from his eastern windows, he will see crowds of flames dancing among the tree trunks, a hundred fires and a dozen folk round every fire.'

Cameron looked steadily at him for a while until Stewart turned his head with a little toss and swallowed down his wine. Cameron got up and went over to the back window. In the north their own wooded hill rose up. It showed as a black absence of stars in the lower sky. No fires here yet. Above it the Plough was tilted and he followed the line of the two stars at its end until he found the Pole Star. His thoughts were running north and west, up into Lochaber, the oak woods and pinewoods at the foot of Loch Arkaig which had cradled him in his boyhood. It would be peaceful there. But the Act threatened his people too…

James looked at his back for a full minute, then asked, 'Are you wishing it was like that here – fires on the hill?'

'Well, it is not,' Cameron said without turning.

'But it could be?'

'Oh aye – all sorts of things could be. Fair rents. Fair leases. No king, no throne for him to sit on –'

'Now you are the dreamer.'

It has happened in France, Cameron felt like saying, and then the thought of the gulf between France and Scotland came over him so dauntingly that he suffered a backwash of despair. Lochaber … He thought of the autumn day fourteen years before when his father had taken him through the hills towards Morar. He had been pestering him for a while for stories about the grandparents he had never known.

At last big Angus said, 'Very well – let us go and see the old place – if we can find it.' They had walked by Murlaggan at the head of the loch and up Glen Pean. Midges drawn by the smell of their sweat swarmed round their heads and young Angus began to regret his curiosity, but his father's face was set and dark in a way that froze out complaints, or chatter of any kind. Long before they had passed the watershed and were looking over into the jaws of the mountains at the head of Loch Morar, young Angus felt he had strayed into a foreign country. The black mouths of the peat hags reminded him of stories about ghosts and murders. Suppose they lost the solid path between these pools? The ground quaked as they walked on it. He looked back. All landmarks that he knew had long since sunk out of sight beyond the rise. And they had all that way to travel back .... But now his father was slackening the pace and looking round him.

'Is this it?' The moor looked empty. Big Angus stared at him as though he was not there. It was a long ago, young Angus thought. Maybe he has forgotten. They trudged on again, their feet following a vein of beaten earth under the thickness of the heather. Ahead, a low cairn of granite boulders rose clear of the moor. And another. They were shaped – they were the shells of cottages, each one reduced to its ground plan, one course of massive stones, roughly masoned, with rounded ones at the four corners. Big Angus was pointing along a stretch of turf between the shells.

'There is the street. And there–' He stopped and seemed to struggle. His hands rose into the air and clenched, as though he was wrestling a bullock by its horns. 'That is my father's house.' He pointed. 'My mother was born there.' He pointed at a shell on the far side of the street. 'They fired the thatch –' His hands gripped and whitened. 'They fired every house and they ran the men down like deer. The women and children had gone off to the caves –'

'Did you not fight?' Young Angus felt hot with rage and wrong. His father was more than six foot and could toss the caber further than any man in Bunarkaig. He could have laid in wait for the soldiers and split their heads and –

'Fight? Some of us knew what that meant by then. The bold spirits stood and made a show until the muskets cut them down or sent them fleeing. The rest of us crouched under the bank of the river.' He pointed across a meadow overgrown with rushes. 'When we put our heads up, we saw the fires, and the swords slicing away. When they had killed three sheep and roasted them in the middle of the street and ridden off with the rest of the flock, and the cattle and the horses and the hens, we buried the dead – we were at it for most of a day – and then we went off east into Arkaig. And now I am sorry I came back. But you had to know.'

Young Angus thought, You were a coward – no you were not – what else could you have done? He grew up that day, and never again saw his father as a being who could do anything and was never at a loss. His mother looked nervously at them as they came in long after dark – she was obdurately against the recalling of 'the bad old times' and she would neither ask them what they had seen nor let them tell her. It had been his first and only history lesson, and throughout their hungry and needy years in Bunarkaig he never lost the sense that they lived under threat, that government was pitiless, and that some day they would have to fight again for the right to live at peace in their own place.

He surfaced from his thoughts and turned back to the room. James was slouched back in his chair with his mouth a little open. Allan Stewart was starting to clear away the mess of jugs and pots with a deliberate clatter. Sensing the need to gather the loose strands of the evening into one firm fabric, Cameron said, 'Tomorrow then – we go to hear Archibald Menzies preach at Dull.'

James was staggered. 'We have taken care of him already. We had better torment our own man next.'

'No,' said Cameron, wishing that James would think harder and spoil less for a mere sporting occasion. 'James MacDiarmid will be expecting us, so we will let him stew a bit. Allan here can keep an eye on this place, and handle ambitious little Robertson if he tries to nail up his damned lists. I think we should cover Dull, and see whether the man there has had his wits cleared by the smell of fresh shite under his nose.'

Chapter 3

The Sermon

The Reverend Archibald Menzies, minister to the stony and muddy village of Dull, was not exactly the pride of his parishioners – he had little chance of being that, since he had been chosen by the laird, not elected by the people. But they took some wicked pleasure in his fame as the most extraordinary vocal artiste in the whole Synod of Dunkeld. He used the complete gamut of his voice, from a growl like a dog warning its master that it has a sore foot to a high, exalted monotone which he kept for perorations; and when he was using the words of an Old Testament lament, Isaiah or Zephaniah, to make a piteous effect, he had been known to put his head back and yowl like a tom-cat.

The congregation usually watched him with a perverse relish which he mistook for devout attention, but this Sunday afternoon there was palpably an added curiosity to see how well he managed to live down the shaming comedy he had enacted on horseback a few days before. As he made his way down the path from the manse between the round-shouldered granite gravestones, his face looked pink, as though he had recently shaved in scalding water. Some people at the church door caught his eye and smiled and bowed respectfully but others looked away and exchanged glances with grinning friends. As he put his foot on the doorstep, a young man seemed to jostle him – it was young McCulloch from Weem, the sulky handsome lad with the curly head – why had he come hanging about here instead of hearing his own man preach in Weem? To stir up mischief, no doubt, and to eye Jean Bruce, the blacksmith's daughter – they had been seen strolling about in the gloaming more than once, laughing quietly together and holding hands. But there were other interesting visitors from down the strath – Cameron the builder, who came late, and sat in a pew near the back beside Donald Stewart, the blacksmith from Grandtully. Soon the door was closed, leaving outside, among the gravestones and round the Cross, a small and growing crowd who lingered on with a sense that the entertainment might not be over.

A psalm droned and swelled. The minister read a lesson from Job, chapter 2. When he came to the words, 'Then said his wife unto him, Dost thou still retain thy integrity?', Cameron began to wonder if Mr Menzies was identifying himself with Job, and when he ended ringingly on 'Shall we receive good at the hand of God, and shall we not receive evil?', the suspicion was confirmed. Clear yellow sunlight shone through the window-panes, making a pattern of diamonds on the plasterwork. Children in the congregation watched the diamonds slowly grow squarer, less elongated, as the sun moved down the sky. Another psalm. The shuffling and rustling of bodies settling again into the pews. A resigned silence congealed over the rows of people and the Reverend Archibald Menzies gripped the edges of the lectern, closed his eyes and raised his face to the ceiling, then looked down at the serried faces and spoke.

'I will speak to you today on a text from that book, the Book of Exodus, which is so replete with wisdom concerning the leader and the led. The Book of Exodus, chapter 16, at verse 6.' He paused to let the devout look up the passage in their Bibles.

'And Moses and Aaron said unto all the children of Israel, At even, then ye shall know that the *Lord* hath brought you out from the land of Egypt:

And in the morning, then ye shall see the glory of the *Lord;* for that he heareth your murmurings against the *Lord*: and what are we, that ye murmur against us?

And Moses said, This shall be, when the *Lord* shall give you in the evening flesh to eat, and in the morning bread to the full; for that the *Lord* heareth your murmurings, which ye murmur against him: and what are we? your murmurings are not against us, but against the *Lord.'*

Mr Menzies' exposition was fluent. It swelled, diminished, and swelled again like an oratorio. At times his voice went through its paces almost independently of the sense. When he repeated the text (which he did frequently), 'And in the morning' would boom suddenly and dozy members of the congregation twitched, wondering if they had missed something. What they had missed was an elegant argument in which Mr Menzies cast himself as Moses, the much-wronged and sorely-tried shepherd to the Israelites, and his session clerk and schoolmaster James Robertson as the faithful lieutenant Aaron.

'For Moses and Aaron knew, they knew full well,' said Mr Menzies in a sorrowful coo, 'that their lot was a thankless one. But equally,' his voice surged, 'they knew that the Lord would provide. And they were not mistaken, for He did provide, and provide abundantly: quails and bread, "and he that gathered much had nothing over, and he that gathered little had no lack; they gathered every man according to his eating." But were they satisfied? I fear not, for indeed "they hearkened not unto Moses", they murmured against him, and against Aaron, which is to say, they murmured against the Lord, for was it not the Lord Himself, speaking and working *in* Moses, who had brought them out from the land of Egypt?' And so the words turned back on themselves, phrases reappeared, seeming to confirm other phrases, merely repeating themselves, clicking into place with a semblance of logic which nicely disguised the truth that all these words were nothing but a glittering fabric which hovered above the ground, unwinding endlessly, slipping between the fingers, beguiling like a mirage, taking on whatever shape the conjuror wanted, and leading nowhere.

Cameron now expected a glancing reference to Exodus 32 and a figuring of Aaron the idolator as the rebel and troublemaker who seduced the honest Israelites with the golden calf of dangerous principles. But if Mr Menzies had thought of this he must have been keeping it for another Sunday. Evidently he had decided to finish on a note of grave and reproachful dignity. 'For those were troublous times,' he said on a downward-curving cadence, 'and such times have come again, but take heart: for "when Joshua heard the noise of the people as they shouted, he said unto Moses, There is a noise of war in the camp. And he said, It is not the voice of them that shout for mastery, neither is it the voice of them that cry for being overcome: but the noise of them that sing do I hear".' He finished, face raised and eyes closed, and at once gave out the final psalm.

Mr Menzies had enunciated 'them that sing' with noticeable pleasure in the resonant properties of the words. Looking at his glistening face, his cheeks and forehead like apple-skins, Cameron wondered what fired him most at this moment – self-satisfaction? or a true pleasure in poetic language? Whichever it was, he did live well. He was entirely suited to enjoy the hospitality at the Castle, to relish Sir John's venison and cranberry sauce and compliment him on the beauty of his larches. I am envying him, thought Cameron sardonically. Outside, single shouts sounded – a threatening growl from several voices together – hens squawking. Startled faces turned as they sang, then turned back and looked at the pulpit. Mr Menzies said the benediction, it seemed at a deliberately dragging pace. Everyone filed out, pushing a little, finding it hard to maintain their Sunday solemnity. The graveyard was packed with people, more were arriving down the farm lanes and along the main road from east and west. On the boulder that lay against the rough stone stump of the Cross two men were standing, waving torn papers and conducting the crowd in a chorus of jeers. Cameron caught sight of young McCulloch from Weem, standing beside Jean Bruce with his arm round her waist. He shouldered towards them and asked, 'What is going on?'

Donald McCullochi was jubilant. 'Oh, three of the Duke's boobies from Blair Castle came riding up with bits of paper – some rubbish about the Act. So the lads here knocked them from their horses, and stripped off their breeches' – Jean Bruce giggled and he paused to cuddle her and kiss her cheek – 'and sent them back to Atholl. Their horses are in the park – three good ones, too.'

'What do these papers say?'

'Who can tell? They are in English,' Donald said contemptuously.

Beside the Cross one of the men had torn a paper into little bits and scattered them, to a groaning catcall from the crowd. The other man shook his head, held up his paper, and shouted out, 'Can anybody read this?'

'Give me a look at it,' Cameron shouted back. Faces turned, bodies gave way a little, and he went up to the Cross and took the crumpled sheet. He scanned it – it was little more than a text of the Act. He reminded himself of the details and exulted as he saw what he could do with it.

'Here is a polite letter from the Duke of Atholl,' he said loudly, waving the paper. 'And you know he rarely bothers to address us. But now he wants our young men, so he is gracious. They want six thousand,' he paused, 'not more, a mere six thousand. They are to serve as long as the war lasts, and a month on top of that, they are to serve in Scotland only' – someone cheered – 'or so it says, and you can ask Widow McCulloch, or Widow McGregor, if they have heard that anywhere before. The parish schoolmasters are to make up the lists, and I am sure they will oblige. Every man from nineteen to twenty-three is liable, except for married men with two or more children, and sailors, and apprentices – whoever heard of apprentices as old as that?' he jeered, and the crowd jeered with him. 'And except for ministers, of course – we cannot do without *them;* or schoolmasters – the Lord Lieutenants will need *them* to draw up more lists and sign away more lives when the six thousand have bled and died in France, or Spain, or India.' A hoarse, angry noise came from the crowd and faces turned to look at Fleming the teacher, who was standing near the manse under a yew tree. 'Objections to be heard by the Deputy Lieutenants – all honourable men, I am sure, and well above military age. They have sons, no doubt, but most of *them* will be in the Volunteers already, and I see that they too are exempt. Each district to be balloted to produce its squad for the six thousand, and if the ballot brings up your name,' he paused again and saw the hundreds of eyes fixed on his, 'then you must go off to the Army, or else pay £10 to hire a substitute. So there is the Duke's special message for the people of Strathtay. It will have to be answered, so we had better talk about it in the shelter of our homes, and in the morning we can send and tell him what we think.'

There was silence at that, an air of waiting for more. But presently the crowd loosened into smaller groups and a good many people went off into the village or set off for outlying farms. Fleming the teacher had gone into the manse as soon as Cameron finished. Cameron found Donald Stewart and set off beside him towards Weem, which lay among its woodlands in a light blue haze of evening smoke.

'Will we meet in the morning, then? And had the Grandtully folk best come up the glen and join on at Dull?' Stewart was thirsting for action, his colour high. But Cameron felt spent with the effort of the past hour and would say only, 'Let us see if anything went on at Weem.' And it had: James Menzies and Allan Stewart were full of it. An unprecedented crowd, with quite a few strange faces, had gathered round the church door before the afternoon service. John Robertson the schoolmaster had come 'trotting along from the manse, looking full of himself and with not a word to say to anyone'. He had brought out his lists, four sheets, and had got them half fixed to the door when Allan knocked him aside and tore them down and then spent an hour, with James's help, going down the names and telling the young men to their faces whether or not they were listed. A great anger had heated up, one of Robertson's new windows had been shattered by a stone, and the womenfolk had made a move to drag the teacher out and throw him in the river. But by then he had taken refuge in the church, and the service must have been little more than a conversation between him and old MacDiarmid, because not another soul had dared to run the gauntlet and go inside when the clock struck three.

CHAPTER 4

The Signing

The conference in James Menzies' house that night was brief. Cameron would not drink, feeling his head hum already with the gathering pressure in the village and with his compulsive second thoughts about his speech. He knew he had simplified the matter when he said the six thousand would be sent abroad to the War – simplified it and coloured it blood-red. To make an effect? Like Menzies the preacher? Was he himself as calculating and vain as that? But surely it was right to warn the people, to make them feel their plight. It was a time for fierce tactics, not for scruples. But the scruples would spawn in his head, giving a cynical taint to his image of himself. He sighed tiredly, as though he had been working for a full day with stone and timber, and tried to listen to James Menzies, who was well away, drinking whisky with Allan and simmering with the news from the west, where the lists had been torn down from the church doors at Fortingall and Kenmore, and from Blair Atholl: the Duke's factor had had to meet a crowd of more than a thousand and the Duke had signed a paper swearing not to impose the Act. James seemed in a fever. He was stoking the fire unnecessarily until the flames raced up the chimney.

'So – should we beard Sir John at once, and serve him our ultimatum? Come on, man – the folk are ripe and ready.'

'I would wait a day or two,' Cameron answered reluctantly. 'But they will not ask me.'

They did ask him, however, and they came in hundreds for the purpose. He felt he had scarcely fallen asleep, he was dreaming of a black river, with no banks, yet there was something there, a source of light that he wanted to reach, which he could not reach against the cold drive of the current... He woke in a sweat – voices – a dog barking. Someone entered the room and he recognized Allan Stewart's voice.

'There is a crowd here, asking for you.'

'What time is it?'

'Not sunrise yet. But near it.'

Cameron got out of bed and dressed, feeling unreal. He expected a few dozen people. But the ranks and clusters of them stretched uncountably into the darkness. He turned to James in amazement and saw that he was enjoying his surprise, as though it confirmed one of his arguments. Keen wafts of pine resin sharpened the air. Torches were bubbling out flames and streaming smoke. A man coughed and Mary McCulloch's voice said, 'Snuff it well in, Dugald. It will clear your chest.' The few people who were visible looked like a crew of spectres as the shadowed hollows in their faces shifted with the wavering of the flames. Instinctively the two men were looking for faces that they knew – Mary McCulloch and her friends, big Mary as tall as a man, red-haired Flora. Cameron recognized several of his workment from Aberfeldy and warmed to their comradeship – he had talked little politics with them (in the aftermath of the big treason trials, caution had seemed advisable) but he had passed on his newspapers and one of the men came from Lochaber like himself.

People were stamping their feet and putting their hands in their armpits against the chill of an open, starry night. One person looked at another, grinning or expressionless. Few were talking. The current of force in them was eddying slowly round – it had reached a level stretch after whatever rush had carried them here. No weapons were to be seen but a good many shepherds' crooks and plenty of rough sticks cut from birch or alder.

Cameron felt called upon to act. But why him? He wanted the choices and decisions to be clear. But in this new raw situation that was flooding up round them, nothing could be clear, not yet. He turned to Menzies and said, 'Who all is here? Aberfeldy and Weem, but who else?'

'They say they have gathered in all who would come out from the north side down to Pitnacree, and the south side as far up as Kenmore.'

'The Grandtully crowd? The "Duke's" army? We will need them. We will need everybody.'

'The word has gone up every road and track. Look – they are still flocking in.'

A ripple of new arrivals was making the front row press forwards. Cameron and Menzies were squeezed back nearly into the house, and big Mary, finding herself hard up against Menzies, took his arm, cleared a space with a sideways butt of her hip, and twirled once round with him. 'Come away, James!' she said loudly. 'This is better than a ceilidh.' He twirled her again, hands clapped a rhythm, and faces glowed briefly as pipes were lit. Cameron turned back into the house for his cloak and tried to order his thoughts as the last fogginess of sleep evaporated in his head. If James was right and they could count on contingents from every part of the strath, they would be a force indeed – a mass big enough to frighten the most assured gentleman. Would the others make for Castle Menzies? Where else? You had to trust folk. They knew their business, more or less. They knew the owners, the well-to-do, the grandees back from Jamaica and Bengal who sat here now behind tall walls and drew their rents. Down beyond the fork where the Tay joined the Tummel another world began – the world of government. The axis that joined Edinburgh to London – that was the lightning-rod of power. Sir John Menzies was part of that, by his marriage to Atholl's daughter, and Atholl dined and intrigued with the Lord Advocate when he went to Edinburgh for the season. Each of these men occupied a bastion. Well, they had penetrated Atholl's bastion and he had had to meet 'his' people man to man, and man to woman, on a level, with no intermediary. Menzies the old bon vivant had not a fraction of Atholl's strength, he would not dare to turn them away, and if he did they would go in there with sticks and clubs and – As Cameron felt his anger rising, he swallowed it, took up his own cherrywood stick from the corner, and went back outside.

A pale yellow lustre was growing low down in the east, making feathery silhouettes out of the black stands of trees along the bends in the river. Faces turned as he came out and sleepy people started to get up from the low walls and boulders at the side of the road. James nodded to him as though for confirmation and then said loudly, 'Let us go to the Castle –' He became aware that the further reaches of the crowd were out of hearing and shouted at the top of his voice, 'Let us go – along to the Castle – and let us see – what John Menzies – will do about the Act!' Scattered cheers answered him, big Mary gave a 'Heeuggh!' like a dancer, and the whole throng began to move along the road westwards, past the dark silent façade of the inn, the equally silent church and manse, towards the gates of Castle Menzies.

Sir John Menzies had a recurrent dream, especially on the nights when his young wife would not have him in bed beside her, or he had been drinking late, and he slept in the side bedroom, which was tall and narrow with two pistols perched on nails in the wall. He dreamed, each time, of his plantation in Jamaica – banana palms leafed like green fountains, bright orange papaws clustered at the top of their naked stems, a noise of surf quickened the air with its rustling freshness. All the animals were dying. A cat lay outside the front door, one of its eyes protruding in a grotesque bubble with the iris leering darkly from its rim. Butterflies as big as birds fell down from the branches, wings flopping limply. A golden oriole lay on its side in the twilight of a banana grove; a column of ants was passing to and from the bedraggled corpse. A thud of chopping – movement between the tree trunks – a labourer was coming towards him, one of the consignment of convicts he had ordered through a merchant in Bideford, he had his machete in his hand, he was not menacing, he held out his spare hand in a strange appeal, lifting his face, which was crossed by deep scars, wounds across his eyes had puckered them right in so that he moved like a blind sleeper, closer and closer – Sir John woke up sweating, surprised to find himself alone, and then remembered: he had been drinking with his cousin Alexander Menzies of Bolfracks, the last bottle must have sent him under. His head was swinging and throbbing like a bell. The bell *was* ringing – absurd! Was there a wind to swing the great plantation bell which he had brought home and hung on the oak beside the east gate? He got up in his night-shirt and looked incredulously out at the twigs of the stately chestnut tree in front of the castle. They were motionless. Someone at the bell – why did his factor and nephew Robert not go out and stop them? What could be happening? In a spasm of irritation he pulled a cloak over his nightshirt, took down a pistol from the wall, and went downstairs into the chilly, stone-smelling darkness of the ground floor, looking for servants.

As big Mary pulled heartily at the pleated rope of the bell, a loud murmur of voices and footsteps sounded along the road west. The dawn light showed a crowd of men and women with a pack of dogs running beside them. Cameron and James recognized none of the faces. The men wore short kilts of grey homespun, their hair was flowing or knotted at the back, most were bearded: the uplanders had arrived from the Glen of Keltney. Now, surely, the whole of Strathtay was going to turn out. Looking down from a small window in the lodge house, the factor Robert Menzies was terrified to see the throngs of people, like herds of cattle milling at a tryst. Amongst them he saw, with a further pang, Joseph Stewart, the laird of Foss beside Loch Tummel. What on earth – ? As he watched, a young lad suddenly stooped behind Stewart and made a piggy-back, another lad shouldered him, and over he went, falling heavily while people nearest roared and laughed. He was a prisoner, then? Thunderous knocks hit the door downstairs, the bell clanged and clanged. 'Lock the door behind me!' he said to his wife. He went out on to the landing, opened a window, and called out to the crowd: 'What do you want? who are you?'

'We want you, dearie!' a woman shouted. Above the laughter a man's voice carried and Robert Menzies recognized the wine-merchant from Weem.

'We have business with the laird,' James Menzies shouted above the bell. 'So get him down here.'

'I do the laird's business. But not before the sun is up. Come back at nine o'clock.'

A roar greeted his effort at authority and dirt spattered him, making him blink and cower. If he could see the culprits! But it was hard to pick out faces that he knew in the swaying mass of heads.

'Put on your breeches and get your master. Our business is personal with him and if you get between us –' The factor waited for the threat but a tall cloaked figure standing beside Menzies had pulled his arm to forestall him.

'Take off your nightshirt and come down like a man!' – a catcall from the body of the crowd. Hooves sounded. To his left, along the drive, he saw the grey-haired minister from Weem arriving at a gallop. The gatekeeper opened half the gate to let him through. Before he could close it the crowd swarmed past him in their hundreds and set off towards the castle at a trot.

James Robertson, teacher at Weem and Session Clerk to the Reverend James MacDiarmid, was wakened by the minister in the dim bluish light of dawn. He slept on a straw pallet in the low attic space at the Widow Macintosh's and these days he hated to wake up. Sleeping was no better – fleabites tormented him, fears plagued him like bad dreams. His colleague Fleming's humiliation on horseback had made him dread the same thing for himself. And the ordeal of putting up the lists – he could still feel the brute weight of Allan Stewart's shoulder jolting him aside, the smell of whisky on his breath, and then the twilit hours lying low beside the minister

27

in the church, waiting for the hubbub outside to die away. He shuddered awake. Mr MacDiarmid's long yellow face and white hair were close above him.

'Robertson! Robertson! Are you not awake, man? Half the parish has been roaring past your door.'

'You will wake Widow Macintosh –'

'She is not here, you fool – she has gone off with the mob.'

'Where? What –'

'They are off to the Castle, where else? They will be mobbing Sir John by now. I will ride there and maybe pass them among the trees. You follow as fast as you can.'

'Me? What –'

'You know the business.' The minister's wintry face looked acid with disapproval. 'These people are all mad to escape the Act. Well, we have a duty to draw up the lists, and manage the ballot, and by God we will carry it out and support Sir John, or else there will be madness and misrule here for evermore. Now – dress yourself and come.'

He went out and Robertson heard the hooves of his garron clopping on the road. He got up and dressed as though in a trance, and set off for the Castle with the hangdog look of a condemned man.

In the smithy house at Dull, Jean Bruce had lain silently under the covers until her four little sisters and brothers had stopped fidgeting in the oppressive atmosphere and her parents had started to snore. When she heard the shrill call, like an owl but human, she slipped out and joined her lover in the little barn beside the byre. She and Donald had started to take risks – they wanted each other so much that the reality of other people had dimmed for them, half the time they felt cloaked in invisibility. And now that Donald's name was on the militia list, the thought of being parted obsessed them and they made love as though each time was the last time. Just now they had been utterly careless about the noise they made in the hay. The open night sky had not yet cooled the air, they were sweating, yet they still lay close together and the soft milk-and-blood smell of her breasts soothed his nostrils. But the worry surfaced again.

'If you go for a soldier' – she had said it fifty times – 'it will stop us getting wed. And if you go to England –'

'There are other things could stop us marrying.' He was disinclined to disturb the well-being of the moment.

'Only because I am very young. And father likes you. And *they* married young enough – mother was sixteen when she had me. But you do not sound bothered …' Anxiety was making her touchy, unsure even of him.

'Not bothered!' He was stung to speech. 'Who will have to march and bleed, and live on filth? Who will lose his legs –'

'And sleep without his girl –'

'My family have been through all this already. Where is my father? Rotting in India, or Africa? Where is he?'

'He should never have gone.'

At that he turned his face round and glared at her. 'If there is an army, men will go off to it, if they are poor.'

'I know – I know.' She cuddled close to him again, to soothe away the friction of disagreement. 'But they will never take you, Don – I will hide you here – no, I will hide you up at the old shieling hut – or we could run away west into Rannoch –'

'There are forts everywhere. But the islands might be safe …' So they romanced for a time, whispering on the edge of sleep, until a noise of footsteps, first a few and then large numbers, came from the road outside.

'What is that?' Jean startled awake.

He was listening. 'The Keltney people? Making for the Castle? Look – the sky is lightening. We had better join them.'

She shook his hand. 'Donald – if you go straight there, folk will know where you have been.'

He laughed. 'I will say I was catching a stray.' He put his arm round her waist and kissed her hard. 'Jeannie – if you come, I will meet you among the crowd. Otherwise – tonight, and I will give the call. Jeannie –' They kissed again and then he was gone, running after the uplanders to catch them at Camserney mill.

It was like a drovers' camp in front of Castle Menzies. The light of the risen sun was glittering now on the tall glazed windows of the central part and glowing like honey on the yellow walls. Perfection, thought Cameron – dominance and wealth most perfectly crystallized in dressed stone, sleek plasterwork, trees planted in a picturesque frame. It looked as though nothing would ever shake it. Behind some of the panes pale blurs of faces could be seen watching – womenfolk and servants. When people in the crowd pointed and called, the blurs disappeared. Down on the grass and on the bare earth under the chestnut tree, dozens of people now squatted at their ease among the sheep and their droppings, drinking from skin water-bottles and smaller stone ones of ale or whisky. Most people had stayed on their feet, expectant and alert, and frankly curious to size up the laird's domestic arrangements while they had the chance. Women were remarking on the window hangings – 'You could hang my whole downstairs with one of those red curtains,' said Mary McCulloch, 'and have a length left over for the beds.' A good many boys and girls had joined the crowd now and shouts of laughter broke out as a few of them came out from the gate in the kitchen-garden wall, their hands full of ripe peaches, their chins dripping with juice.

On the edge of the gravel near the front door, Cameron and James Menzies conferred with Allan, Donald Stewart the blacksmith, and John Stewart the pedlar from Newbigging, who seemed to have been everywhere in the past twenty-four hours. The factor had gone into the castle, 'to get his orders from his master,' as Cameron put it. The men were hotching for action, but what response could be dragged out of those granite walls and that oak door? Cameron was resolved on one thing. 'We will not waste our time chopping logic with that underling. We talk to the laird only.'

'The old man will never come out.'

'Last week he might not have. But now that Atholl has given way and condescended to meet the people –'

'He is a diplomat,' said John Stewart. 'But this man here has a temper.'

'His factor will be feeling it now, for letting us through the gates.' James Menzies laughed. 'I would like to have seen him holding us back with an old sword in his hand.'

'Pistols, more likely,' said Allan, 'and a musket or two. Remember the old man is a sportsman – good at killing, and at chasing slaves. He is cornered now – maybe he will come out red-eyed like a bear.'

'So long as we get him out' – Cameron was still cagey. 'We talk to him only – do you agree? And we keep him prisoner here till he signs. Have you the paper?'

Menzies felt in his pocket. 'Yes, it's safe.'

The low thick door had swung open. As the factor came out, it shut behind him and they heard the bars and chains go on. Robert Menzies was nervous, his eyes flickered everywhere, but he had his message pat.

'Sir John will meet a spokesman this afternoon – if you have anything particular to say. But now you are to leave his land peaceably –'

A murmur rose in a crescendo and drowned him out. The people at the front were shouting at him, the news of his message was running through the crowd like a grass fire. Somewhere a bagpipe skirled.

'Tell the laird,' James Menzies began, then raised his voice so that he could be heard as well by the crowd as by the factor. 'Tell the laird,' he shouted out, 'that we will have him out here, to hear us for himself – that is what we came for and we will stand here till we see him. We need his name, in his own hand, on a paper against the Act. And if he stays behind that door' – the mounting gale of voices behind him was lifting him as he spoke, he wanted to jump on the factor, grab his hair and swing him against the door like a battering ram – 'we will fire the roof! and smoke him out!'

A pulse of pressure from behind threw them against the factor, he turned and jumped for the door, beat on it, it opened abruptly, and he fell inside. Cameron turned and rose on tiptoe – the Grandtully crowd had arrived in force, the 'Duke of Lennox' in the lead, he was striding across the grass with an oak-tree branch slanting across his chest like a sceptre, its green sprays nodding on his shoulder. A piper marched beside him, the patched black bag of his pipes under his arm, the chanter blowing a reel. The Duke was revelling in the occasion, his toothless mouth curved up in a great leer like the mask of comedy. When the boys saw him, they ran towards him, calling out shrilly 'Up the Duke!' He swung his sceptre at them and they ducked, shrieking. Shoals of people were coming up the drive from the west gate – Cameron recognized faces that he knew from the sawmill at Kenmore. Amongst them walked a gentleman in an expensive greatcoat, his arms firmly held – another hostage. Good tactics, whether planned or not – the more gentry were pinned down here, the fewer were left to muster the Volunteers or ride off with news to the Deputies at Blairgowrie.

Dust hung in the air now, making it yellow and the sun orange. People coughed. Someone had fainted and a woman was loosening his shirt and running water over his head. Up in the chestnut branches girls and boys were clambering about, hitting at the spiked green conkers and knocking them down on to the heads below. Somewhere behind the east wing of the castle glass shattered. Menzies had better come out soon. As Cameron surveyed the crowd, trying to make a rough count, he saw some women cracking stone bottles against their cudgels, stripping off their stockings, and packing them with shards and handfuls of gravel from the forecourt.

In the hall of the castle Sir John was reasoning with a group of servants while Lady Charlotte had hysterics under the portrait of a clan chief of the sixteenth century – an armoured and bearded warrior who looked down with an imperious black stare. At one side the Reverend James MacDiarmid was standing in his dark clothes with the conspicuously expressionless demeanour of an undertaker's mute. The servants wanted to flee, by a back door.

'McDougal, calm them down!' Menzies barked fiercely at his butler. 'This is a castle, not a cottage, we could sit here in safety for a year.' Glass cracked and splintered in the passage through to the kitchens. A maid jumped and began to scream shrilly on the same note as her mistress. 'Robert' – he turned on his factor – 'you should have made it plain –'

'Nothing is plain out there, I tell you. It is like hanging day in the Grassmarket. You should see their eyes.'

'I will not parley with a rabble.'

'Bring Menzies of Weem in here, then. What else can we do?'

'You said he was obdurate. Who else is there? Are they all cottars and tinkers?'

'There is that tall sharp fellow from the new factory – Cameron. They say he made a speech at Dull.'

'A speech! A farrago of treason. We will have no speeches here. Come on – let us beard this lot and send them packing. The half of them are on my rent-roll anyway.' He looked with displeasure at the frantic figure of his wife and said tersely to the housekeeper, 'Mrs McDougal, have you no smelling salts? Or you might try brandy – it cures most fits. Come, MacDiarmid. Robert, open the door.'

A funeral silence had come over the gathering. Hundreds of eyes stared fixedly as the laird stepped out onto the gravel and stood for a moment with his chin jutting and his mouth pulled down, like a general reviewing his troops. Behind him the minister stood as straight and shadowy as a cypress tree. Two servants came out, labouring under the weight of a kitchen table. The factor showed them with fussy gestures where to set it. They went back for chairs and then the laird, the factor, and the minister sat down weightily, like judges. Cameron could sense James Menzies fidgeting and breathing beside him and he wondered if he had had a dram. Then James spoke up.

'Good morning, Sir John. Mr MacDiarmid – it is Monday now, you know. Are you here to bless us?'

'I am here in duty bound to assist Sir John.'

'Oh, he will need that. But where is little Robertson, to do your writing for you?'

'The Session Clerk has been informed. He should be here by now.'

And he was – a small figure in a drab coat, lurking at the side of the crowd, speaking to nobody. MacDiarmid waved him forward with a commanding sweep of his arm and he came and sat at the end of the table.

There was a pause while everyone present wondered how to proceed. Abruptly the laird smiled, looking from face to face along the front row, and said, 'Well, well – it is a fine morning for it. Shall we –'

But James had mentally worded his speech a dozen times and would not be forestalled.

'You cannot pretend not to know our purpose,' he began, so loudly that the laird's head went back. 'We are all here as free men – not tenants, and not plaintiffs or slaves but free people who are determined to remain so. Now this Act will bind six thousand of us – I am not speaking in my own interest, I am well past the age – but this Act will empty the glens of the young active men – and how can they marry if they are in barracks and camps in England, or in France if you send them there – you say you will not ...' He was wandering now, his voice had dropped as he struggled to keep his thread and a restlessness at the back of the gathering broke out in shouts of 'Speak up! What did he say?' and then 'Where is Cameron? Tell Cameron to put the case.' Angus looked at his friend. James's face had reddened with confusion but he managed to give him a nod which said 'Go on.'

Cameron half-turned, to speak as much to the crowd as to the table, put his head back, and spoke slowly, pausing between his sentences. 'Sir John Menzies, and Mr MacDiarmid, represent the important people of this place. They have the power to send the rest of us into the ranks of the army, if they like, or into prison or the colonies. But if we are free citizens' – he paused on the word, feeling it alien but unable to think of another – 'if we are not slaves, we must have liberty to say "No, we have no dispute with France – we have business here at home which matters more than anything else on earth – we will not learn to play with swords, or blow out brains with bullets." Now, we cannot speak to the government, but we can speak to *you*.' He turned and let his eyes lock with the laird's, the minister's, and the factor's, each one in turn, while they stared back and tried to look perfectly blank. 'You are sitting here because you have the power, and if that is true, then you can use it as well for us as against us. I hope you do not approve of this Act – if you do, there is not another man or woman in all this country who does. And you must know that, because we are all here. Count us.' He paused again. 'Now, we are *asking you*' – he stressed the word with some irony – 'we are *asking* you to join with us in a petition to the government for relief from the Act. What do you say?'

The laird had been studying Cameron with unwavering attention. Now he looked down at the table top, then sideways at his colleagues and back at Cameron. 'I have listened to you, Mr Cameron,' he said finally, 'and you have spoken for the people of Tayside. I believe, however, you come from somewhere else?'

Cameron smiled at that, a tight smile with his mouth closed. 'Yes, I come from Lochaber, and the Lochaber people, if they were here, would be at one with the people of Breadalbane. I can say that because I now belong to them both. Now, can we do *business* ?' The last word came out fiercely and the force of it set off a low noise from the crowd, like surf on a beach.

Menzies half turned as though to consult the minister, then said abruptly: 'You may petition if you like.'

'But will you join us? And will you?' Cameron leaned towards the minister, who straightened his back still more but said nothing.

Sir John was sitting perfectly still, his hands pressed between his knees, his forehead red under his wig. 'A petition can be proper enough,' he said very deliberately. 'But what will it say – have you thought of that?'

'Oh yes,' said Cameron, 'there has been plenty of thinking. We will have words for you in a minute,' and he turned round to the crowd. 'Have we leave to write down what you are all agreed upon?' he shouted in his loudest voice. 'Can we do that?' There was a roar of assent and the gathering began to stir and kindle into easier feelings – neighbours muttered to each other and laughter came from the Grandtully part of the crowd. Cameron was speaking to the people nearest him, gathering suggestions, prompting, trying to draw in James Menzies, who looked sullen after his poor showing. Finally Cameron turned back to the table and said, 'We have agreed on a text. Will you hear it?' The laird nodded and Cameron said curtly to Robertson the teacher, 'Take this down.'

'What will I write with? or on?' The man was bridling at being treated like a minion.

'I have paper here – properly stamped. I suppose there are pens in the castle.' They were brought and Cameron dictated slowly, cheers punctuating his sentences.

'We, the country people of Tayside in Perth, living between Fortingall in the west, Foss on Tummel in the north, and Logierait in the east, do solemnly petition your Worship to exempt us from the Militia Act, passed in July this year, 1797, for it would submit us to hardship and bondage, which we believe to be no duty of ours.' He paused, and this was taken as a signal for a round of cheers and shouts. 'Is that enough?' he asked the front ranks of the crowd.

'Go on – make him sign,' a young man shouted back and Cameron recognized young McCulloch from Weem. Robertson had caught up with the words and passed the manuscript, still wet, to the laird.

'Give me the pen,' said Menzies. Silently he corrected a word, silently he endorsed it. He stood up, stony-faced, and was turning to the door when James Menzies held up his hand and said, 'Wait – wait – that is only half the business.'

The laird frowned. 'You have your petition –'

'We have that, but we need our safety and liberty as well. You must commit yourself, and so must all the gentry, to take no vengeance for today's work. You must keep the soldiers out of here.'

There was a loud cheer at that. The laird waited for it to finish and said scornfully, 'How can I do that? That is in the hands of the government.'

Cameron was demurring too. 'Wait, James – what is the use of making him pretend to powers?'

'Whose side are you on?' Menzies snapped back. 'We need security.'

'Of course we do, but it must be plausible. If it looks forced, it will count for nothing.'

Angus and John Stewart were restive now and young McCulloch was jeering openly. But Cameron would not budge. 'There is only one way to decide,' he said, and jumped up on the table, making Robertson flinch. 'Here is the issue,' he shouted out. 'Do we ask Sir John to restrain the soldiers – which he cannot do – or do we bind *him* not to pursue or hound us for this action? If you are for the latter, shout out Aye. What do you say? Do you say Aye?' There was a great shout of Aye. 'Or do you say No?' A few calls answered him. 'The Ayes have it.' He jumped down and began again to dictate. 'We hereby solemnly declare that we shall use no forcible means to apprehend, confine, or imprison any person assistant whatever who has appeared at Castle Menzies or elsewhere, or in any part of Perth on prior days. Further that we shall petition government for an abolition and nullifying of the foresaid Act from the records of British parliament; that the members of parliament for this county shall present this petition, or any annexed thereto, to the two Houses of Parliament, and to the Privy Council, during the prorogation of parliament –'

Menzies was seething and he broke in on the last words. 'This goes much too far.' He stood up as he spoke. 'They will never believe this – they will know it was extorted.'

'Very well –' Cameron trumped him instantly. 'Add this: "and this we shall do of our own free will and accord".' He smiled straight into Menzies' smouldering look and said, 'Will you swear to this?'

'Swear? Swear? And how am I to swear?'

'Sir John' – Cameron sounded appalled – 'is there any God but one? Swear as you usually do. Now, Robertson, add this: "of our own free will and accord – as we shall answer to God." That is very fine. I think we have it now. Robertson – fresh ink, and we will round it off in style. Sir John – your name first – you are the leader here. Where is Joseph Stewart of Foss?' The young man was passed through the crowd, looking haggard, and he signed without a word. 'And who is that?' Cameron pointed at the hostage among the Kenmore crowd. He in his turn signed: 'William Stewart of Garth'. Cameron turned back to the table: 'Mr MacDiarmid – you have had a heavy responsibility for the Act – we had better have your name too.'

Donald McCulloch was grinning to his friends. 'It is a poor thing,' he called out, 'when ministers turn recruiting sergeants!' MacDiarmid took the quill and signed, his face like a paper mask. The Grandtully piper, sensing the climax of the gathering, had filled his bag and set off on a steady marching tune. The Duke held up his branch like a banner and began to lead the way along to the east gate, but a large part of the crowd stayed in a half circle round the group at the table, as though waiting for the victor's crow in the cockfight.

'Clear the grounds!' the factor was shouting. 'Clear the grounds!' Young McCulloch raised his cudgel and lunged at him. The factor jumped back. McCulloch laughed and turned away. Cameron folded the paper and gave it to James Menzies. 'Let us meet outside the gates,' he said, 'and draw up the day's work.'

'And take a vote on it?'

Cameron seemed to ignore the dig. 'There is enough to do,' he said, and let out a long breath. 'We had better get some horses.'

CHAPTER 5

The Reel

Before the crowd could drift off, Cameron got up on the massive stone gate-post and called on them to swear an oath. The words drew on his memory of a secret meeting he had gone to at the end of his first year in Glasgow. It had looked like a melodrama – a little group in a candle-lit attic, holding up their arms with fists clenched and swearing to do or die. But they had meant it, and he was eager now to bring everybody together in a fine, hard point of resolve, in case zeal slackened and died away in the holiday atmosphere of this soft, comfortable afternoon. The hills themselves looked asleep, the heather glowed dust-blue in the hazy light, and the people, after a night of little sleep and hours of walking and standing, now looked stunned as they sat on the grassy banks, leaned on dykes, or lay on their backs in the hayfields, munching oatcakes and drinking the last of their water. Some little groups were going off to west and east, but most hung on with a sense that the next thing now demanded to be done.

Cameron raised his right hand, clenched his fist, and spoke in a relaxed voice. 'Very good. We have seen to one of them. But there are plenty more. There is Alexander Menzies of Bolfracks.' He pointed across the river at a squat grey house on the far bank with a stand of trees behind it. 'And further down there is Hope Steuart of Ballechin – a hard man to crack, no doubt. And Alexander McGlashan of Eastertyre – you know them all, and they know you, and by now they will be expecting us. Well – will we disappoint them? Will we?

People kindled a little. Some shouted, 'No, no,' and a woman called out, 'Come on then, Angus – let us go and have our dinners at Bolfracks!'

'I am hungry too,' he answered her. 'Maybe some of these nice gentlemen will offer us meat. But first things first. Are we all resolved to finish this day's work?' He looked from one tired face to another. A few had turned on their sides in the hay and cradled their heads on their arms. 'All right. We have started well. But if you are truly resolved, then pledge it now, swear an oath – come on – let us see all hands raised – come on now – every hand high …' The little army was stirring to its feet, movement ran from front to back of the broad crowd like hackles rising. 'Let me see your hands.' Hundreds of arms were standing up stiffly now like bristling branches. 'Let us bind ourselves now by this oath – say it with me. We do swear –' He paused, and a murmur followed him with some clearer, harsher voices audible amongst it: 'We do swear –' He went on: 'Never to swerve,' and they said it together, 'Never to swerve – from our present path – till we have cleansed the country – of this oppressive Act. And we do swear – never to betray – the name of any friend.'

The collective voice rumbled to a close. Cameron jumped down from the granite post and walked over to his little committee. They were looking at him with an air that mingled irony and respect. He felt like justifying himself, at least to James. But other things mattered more. Another castle to be stormed. For the sake of a scrap of paper. His sudden lapse of morale took him by surprise, like a qualm in his stomach. No food since broth and bread last night. It was mad to charge on like this. But momentum was the thing – self-doubt came sneaking in as soon as they let up. Why wait for horses? There would not be a horse for everybody.

'James,' he decided, 'station yourself here – let five hundred folk come past, then come yourself. Allan – the same, then follow after James. We can wade the river at the shallows. Gather on the terrace under the house. Donald – take the tail of the crowd.'

And the swarm of people flowed down the path, stumbling on stones where a burn ran in winter or after thunderstorms, between the silvery wands of rowans with their clusters of blood-drops and the quivering tapestry of the alders, down into the Tay which ran from the west like molten iron, too flashing bright to look at, and over the Tay, wet to the waist; the girls and boys who had not gone home were prancing and shrieking when they fell full length. But one greyhaired uplander disappeared into a hole below a boulder and was pulled out by the hair and carried back towards Keltney on a stretcher of cut branches.

Up the slope, at the top of his semi-circular steps, Alexander Menzies was waiting for them in his best silk coat like a dandy at a ball, with a straightfaced young man standing by his side. James bowed ironically and offered them the document; Alexander Menzies pretended to think about it for a full five minutes and signed it with extraordinary flourishes that made the pen splutter and seemed to say, 'Very well, I will humour your ridiculous ritual.' James was remembering the young man now, William, the laird's son, a surgeon in the Army; here was trouble. The young man scanned the paper, held it out, and as James's fingers reached for it, dropped it, eyed him, and said in a carrying voice, 'I see you are mad, but does even a lunatic suppose that one of His Majesty's officers would bind himself to oppose the law and refrain from arresting criminals?' They went for him then, Alexander and Donald McLaggan, the Duke's two sons, dragged him from his father's side so that his head bounced on the steps, lifted him bleeding, like foresters keeping a dying deer clear of the hounds, and started to carry him down to the river 'just to cool him off' but Cameron ran and gripped Donald's shoulder and shouted, 'If you injure an officer it is treason on top of sedition,' so they carried him back and laid him carefully at his father's feet.

Cameron was thinking ahead now. In an hour we will be at Aberfeldy, at the Flemyngs' house at Moness, how can I besiege my employers? Why put my head into the bear's jaws before I have to? So he divided the people, half to scour the right bank of the river down the forested links and narrows as far as the meadows above Logierait and force a signature from every proprietor, half to come with him to the north side; they would all meet at Haugh of Ballechin after the sun had set and plan for tomorrow. The McLaggans had put grass halters round the necks of a few of Menzies' horses; Cameron rode on one; from the back in his dark coat he looked like a preacher leading away the faithful to a field communion.

James Menzies and the McLaggans, riding on horses, led the rest away on the long climb of the hill to Dunskiag, a gaunt treeless place where the owner lived without a woman and three great staghounds with long coarse hair slavered to get at them, wrenching their chains. They did not waste time there but headed downhill, taking the shepherds' road that slanted luminous green between clusters of birches, their shadows stretching ahead like gawky giants so that the children jigged to make the shadows jump and curved their fingers from their heads to give the giants silhouettes like devils. The Flemyngs would be away, no doubt, 'at a banquet in Perth', and they were; a butler spoke to them from an upper window and asked them would they kindly leave a message so they marked the house with dirt and rotten potatoes while the servants rushed to bar the shutters over the windows.

The last of the sunlight was diffusing through the trellis of oaks and evergreens in a yellow sparkle; single rays pierced through like stings; in the gloaming Aberfeldy was a ghost town. The laddering and scaffolding round the half built mill reared up emptily like the skeleton of a forest. All their energies had run low now. James was wondering, were they pirates doomed to plunge forever after another quarry? His head throbbed with drink and sunsmite and the bony bouncing of his horse – time to rest and replenish. He led his army round by Anderson's howff. Anderson seemed to be the only person at home; he sold them jugs of ale, small beer for the children; James's credit was good for a stone jar of whisky and one of the Duke's men was detailed to carry it on his back in a wicker frame. They might have become becalmed there as their heads ballooned with the drink but the Duke told his piper to rouse their feet with a steady march, 'Murdo Mackenzie of Torridon', and they headed off downstream towards Grandtully past the standing stone, the quiet watcher, while damp black shadow massed in the river-channel as though the night came from there.

On the far bank Cameron had outstripped them, his army mowing steadily down the strath, winning signatures at the house of Cluny, at Clochfoldich and Pitnacree, by the solid slow avalanche of their numbers, massing quietly round each house, hammering three times on each door. By this time every gentleman knew what was expected of him: Cameron never dismounted, he leaned from the saddle and passed the paper down to the angry, helpless proprietor and took it back signed.

The west windows of Hope Steuart's place at Ballechin flared with sunset, as though fires blazed inside it. Cameron passed it by, the man could stew in his choler for a while, and when the dark came on and his servants and womenfolk grued at every owl-call or salmon-splash from the river, his defiance would burn lower and he would give his name.

While most of the people rested in the river meadow, shivering as the layers of fog brimmed round them, Cameron and a few strong runners made for the Tummel above the confluence, crossed it, and found the people of Atholl and Tulliemet overflowing the howff at Widow Duff's, supping broth, chewing mutton, throwing ribs to the dogs. They had made sure of the few proprietors between there and Dunkeld; the Duke of Atholl's authority was weaker here; tomorrow would be the hard day when they made a drive up to Moulin and Faskally: perhaps they should go and terrify them now while darkness made them lonely? That took care of Strathtummel; Atholl would get up in the morning to find half his country crumbling under his feet.

Cameron turned back up the Tay, glad that the harvest of names was nearly home. The darkness ahead was flickering, shapes of trees appeared and vanished, cheering surged like surf – here was their other army – James and the Duke were standing on a rock conducting the dancers, who were reeling in eights, linking and whirling between the bonfires. The two young McLaggans were taunting and prodding at a trio of hostages, Thomson the constable, Bisset the minister, and the old soldier Major Alexander McGlashan of Eastertyre; they stood in a huddle with their eyes staring, while young McCulloch staggered up to them and shoved stalks of bracken into their hair.

Cameron went and spoke to James angrily, in a quiet voice, What were they doing, holding a ceilidh? Or making their people safe against the Act? James laughed, 'Look at them, Angus, look at the people, they are rampant now, this is better than 'Forty-five, nobody is dying, no royal fop is leading us into the bog. Give us a word, Angus – go on – make these "gentlemen" swear the oath! They will never forget it! Neither will we! For once they are dancing to our music.'

So Angus got up on to the rock and held his fist high and told young McCulloch to stand the hostages on a knoll where everyone could see them and called out the oath above the drone of the pipe: 'We do swear – never to swerve – from our present path – till we have cleansed the country – of this oppressive Act. And we do swear – never to betray – the name of any friend.'

The Major and the minister and the constable repeated it after him in low voices, the crowd gave them a round of applause, the reel was over. They tramped along to Ballechin among the ferns and sheltering oaks, smelling the cheesey smell of cows among the mist. Hope Steuart had felled a tree across the track, two men with cudgels were standing sentry behind it, they dropped the clubs and ran when the whole wood came at them, the darkness between the trees turned into people, people everywhere, herds and thickets of them surrounding the low tower-house.

Hope Steuart had leaned two loaded muskets against the doorjambs; he turned to pick one up but the Duke's two sons were on him, twisting his arms behind him. He struggled and roared out, 'I see you, James Menzies, I charge you with sedition,' and the Duke roared back, 'We charge *you* with tyranny, trail him round the house, lads, show his servants who is the master now.' They carted him like a scarecrow, his heels scoring the gravel, but he was as stubborn as a pig in a cart, he would never squeal without a hard prod; Donald Stewart the blacksmith had to grip his wrist to make him sign the paper.

CHAPTER 6

The Building

Donald McCulloch came back from 'the reel of Ballechin' long after his mother, and when he got up at last next morning, the cold porridge had been thrown out to the hens. He pretended not to mind. His mother and grandfather were eyeing him as he emerged from the bed and he felt the nag of their expectation that he would go off at once to earn a day's wage at Aberfeldy. He pulled on his boots in silence. Bits of mud fell on the floor.

'Where were you, then?' his mother snapped at once. 'Along at Dull till all hours?'

Her ill-humour was nothing but a habit. 'You have a habit of ill humour' – his thoughts spoke themselves before he could stop them. But she probed on undeterred.

'I saw you both at the Castle, then I lost you.' He hated her way of alluding to jean but never saying her name.

'I sent *Jean* home before we crossed the river. The McLaggans were spoiling for a fight and I thought the lairds might have the mettle to retaliate.'

'Oh, he takes care of her then,' old Donald jeered to Mary, trying to side with her. But she wanted no allies. She could think of nothing but her son. She was consumed with gauging his mood, foreseeing every move he made, hag-ridden by the spectres of all the troubles he could bring down on himself and them.

Donald felt the pressure from her and stared from one to the other, letting them feel his defiance and distaste. 'What am I doing here,' he said at last, 'between two old scolds?'

She easily matched him. 'Go away to the army, then – you will be your own man there.' She had said too much. Old Donald looked at her,

43 />

43

shocked, and her son straightened as though lashed and flung out of the house.

Across the bridge in Aberfeldy more people than usual were standing about on the dried mud of the half-built streets. Beside the stone shell of the Flemyngs' new mill, at the back of a piece of ground it now shared with a new carpet factory, long-haired cattle were browsing desultorily among mudded grass and stacks of timber. Drovers had pastured their herds here for many years but their customary right had vanished when Flemyng bought the ground and it was a daily vexation of Cameron's to move the animals out from among his materials and even from inside the unfinished walls.

'Come on now, mind my beasts,' a drover would say, standing up among the folds of the plaid in which he had spent the night and putting on a practised tone of wheedling grievance. 'Look there, they are startling and snorting now – you have frightened them and they will not eat before the journey. No no, they will never make a price in Perth now you have terrified them,' and Cameron would have to spend a good few shillings to make the drove move on.

Now the grey dew had gone from the grass, pats of dung steamed where the cattle had been standing, and Cameron, in his shirt-sleeves with a cloth tying back his long black hair, was supervising the winching up of timbers for the roof. He had an audience: perhaps twenty people had gathered round the site, idly expectant, smoking and calling out. As the men at the windlass rope heaved and a long timber started to rise up and swing, the wheel on the pulley squealed like an injured dog and the man stationed at the top of the wall took a stickful of thick grease from a pot, leaned out, and worked it into the axle.

Cameron pretended not to see young Donald till he was close beside him, then turned in mock surprise and said to him, 'Well well, Donald – we had given you up. Now, suppose I have taken enough men on already –'

Donald laughed. 'If there is no room here, there is plenty up on the hill, and where do you think I would like to be?' But he took off his jacket and went round the back to work with the sawyers who were cutting joists to a length. The work hummed on for a while. After an hour James Menzies came across the bridge from Weem, aggrieved at Cameron for leaving him to sleep late.

'And where was Allan Stewart?' asked Cameron innocently.

'Ach, where was anyone last night?' James retorted, and he went over to unlock his warehouse and take delivery of a cartload of barrels from

Dunkeld. As Cameron turned back to the mill, he saw a small coach coming along the Grandtully road with a pair of deerhounds loping at its wheels and a man on horseback behind it dressed in an expensive tweed cloak. The Flemyng entourage, he said to himself, now what will he find fault with today, and what news will he have heard? The coach trundled briskly past, browning everyone with dust; the deerhounds checked and growled thunderously at the town dogs until James Flemyng called them loudly to heel. He reined in his horse beside Cameron.

'Mr Cameron –' he began.

'Good morning, Mr Flemyng.'

'Good morning. The work goes on again, I see, now that the – holiday – is over. I trust the "holiday" *is* over?' He was looking past Cameron at the mill, eyeing each workman in turn as though to memorize his face, then looking back at Cameron.

'We are ahead of ourselves, Mr Flemyng, as you know. The mortar is set before the frosts, and the roof will be on well before the snow.'

'It must be, Mr Cameron.'

'It will be, Mr Flemyng.' Their gazes locked for a second and then Flemyng followed his wife up the road towards their disfigured house among the birch trees.

McCulloch had watched the comedy with his most provocative look. 'Well, Angus, how do you think they will like the new decorations to their house?'

Cameron was unamused. 'Let us hope his butler was too drunk to remember faces,' he said shortly, and turned back to the work. By noon eighteen joists had been nailed into position against the roof-tree but they were short of nails and little Willie McGlashan had been sent off to Grandtully to order a load from Donald Stewart's smithy. They all took a break then, to eat their oatcakes and drink jugs of beer from Anderson's. Sandy McGlashan, the windlass man, climbed down the ladder and came to sit beside Cameron. He was small and agile, bowlegged and with a rubbery face that squirmed in on to his toothless gums as he chewed.

'Bolfracks had a rough time, then?' He was eyeing Cameron sideways.

'Oh, he knuckled under, but the young man made a great show of being a soldier and the McLaggans went to cool him down.'

McGlashan was sniggering. 'I heard that too. Oh aye, it was a bad day for the house of Bolfracks – no doubt about it – very bad – oh aye. High time they had a fall, eh?'

'No doubt it is.'

'Oh aye, high time and past time. Menzies of Bolfracks is a stony devil, so was his father. I know that – none better – I do.' The man was hotching with his story and Cameron had no need to prompt him. 'Now – if we are going to roast the lairds, and get some rights at last, do you think we can win our lease back from old Menzies – do you think so, Angus?'

'Your lease, Sandy? I thought you were a townser.'

'A townser? We have only perched in Weem, and now here. My grandfather was born at Farrochil, on Bolfracks Hill – we would still be there – but was my father to slave at carting stones from the Menzies's quarry for old Wade to build his damned bridge? He was a farmer, not a labourer – why should he put his plough-team between Menzies' shafts to drag his damned stones for him? Well – he would not, and the laird turned him out for it – he turned him out and sent him off and we have had no land since and he put nobody else into Upper Farrochil – he only wanted it for himself. He was a magnate, Angus. Like his son today. They coin money at Bolfracks. But we will have them out now, eh? They will never stop us now.' As his excitement steadied, he focused on Cameron again and waited, simmering, for his opinion.

'Sixty-five years ago, Sandy.' Cameron's voice came slowly. 'A long time for a claim to run.'

'Well, I have a long memory. Especially for a grudge. Will I take your jug to the howff, Angus?'

'No no, I have no head for it today.' Cameron wanted time to think; he was in a turmoil of emotions; he felt for Sandy's grievance even while he was blenching at the man's mad certainty that a day of reckoning was near. And underneath these feelings he felt some hot, dark stirrings in himself. What were they? A desire to retaliate – against whom? Against landowners whose own fathers had had to flee from the Crown's killers in 'Forty-six? Yet here, on the verge of the Lowlands, most of the gentry had hedged their bets; some had even entertained the Butcher as he progressed triumphally from one massacre to the next and had then bought over the gutted glens and stocked them with the great sheep. He looked round the littered site, at its dried browns and darkened greens, and considered the men who were sitting round quietly talking and blowing smoke at the swarming flies. He did not know of one who had anything to thank the Flemyngs for, or old Menzies at the Castle. Since the busy fencings and ditchings of the previous thirty years, the men who farmed the best land had flourished all the more; they could afford the rents for the greater acreage under the plough. But the families in the little awkward places, at the heads of the small glens, on boggy ground that would not drain – they were nearly helpless, they trembled on the threshold of destitution, impaled on the horn of the one-year lease, uncertain whether it was worth going into debt to improve the ground and knowing that, even if they did, they could still be turned out next term day and their place annexed to the holding of a better-off neighbour. Not one of these men here came from a lower-lying farm (except Donald McCulloch, and their place was only a slip of ground between the steep hill and the road). When the mill was finished, a few of them might get work in it (but the Flemyngs wanted girls for it because they would work more days). The rest would have to go off as wage-labourers to the Lowlands. Or to the regiments. The deathly regiments.

He stood up and stretched, yawning to squeeze the bad thoughts out of his head. Sandy McGlashan was not yet back from Anderson's. He walked over to the timber stack along with a sawyer called Iain Logan whom he knew well – they were both friends of Donald Gillies at Camserney mill. As Cameron started to pick out wood to finish the forward half of the roof, Iain said to him quietly, 'Sandy McGlashan is not the only man with troubles. You know my brother's sawmill at the waterfall above Moness? The Flemyngs would close it if they could. James Flemyng has been at my father, complaining about dirt in the water and the noise of the saws and axes. It is not that at all. He wants the place. And it is only a patch! With a damp, rotten house on it!'

'Is the water dirty?'

Logan looked at him almost scornfully. 'You could drink from it, except after a spate. The Flemyngs can think of nothing but fences, and these fancy trees' (he meant Sir John's larches). 'I would have put a torch to their damned house yesterday, if I had had some tinder. He sends his factor up to terrify my father – after dark – when I have gone over to Camserney with Alastair. I tell you, one night, if we knew he was coming, we would wait for him round the back and pitch him down the falls!'

'And hang for it?'

'Angus' – he dropped the timber he was lifting, letting it clank off the others, and turned to look at him with widened eyes and squared mouth, like the face of someone taking a great strain. 'Is there no thing, no thing at all, which *you* would swing for? If it came to it? You know that Alastair split and cut these planks on our own saw-bed. If Flemyng forces us out, then we will have nothing left but our hands.'

'They might get you anyway. Is Alastair not listed?'

'Aye – he is just twenty-one. My little brother!'

'So we had better choke this Act –'

'All right. But that is just the start.' They carried timber together for a while after that, one at each end of the planks, eyeing each other with set little smiles. The mood seemed similar at many places on the site – less whistling and singing than usual, more talking. People who had been out together at Castle Menzies, then on down to the Reel of Ballechin, conversed steadily, opening up their private problems to each other with a freedom well beyond the usual. Two masons who were chiselling at the finials which Flemyng had ordered for the gables would stop their clinking from time to time to confirm something that one or other had said. Both were landless men who depended on being allowed to pasture their milk-cows on the water-meadows down at Ballechin, and as Cameron caught the drift of their intent talk and occasional sardonic laughter, he wondered again how many names had been put to faces during yesterday's hurly-burly.

The shadows had grown long by the time Sandy McGlashan came back from Anderson's howff. 'What do I see?' he exclaimed. 'Work, work, work, like Noah's sons at the Ark. And here was I, thinking you could not be building a roof without nails. Well, well, well …' He put his foot between the two bottom rungs of the ladder and then caught at the upright to save himself from staggering. Carefully he tried again but Cameron took his arm and told him not to hurry unduly, the joists had only been pinned in place and they were still waiting for the long nails from Grandtully. Work slowed to a halt until Donald Stewart clattered up on his cart and began to lift down hefty canvas bags from the tailboard.

'Sorry, Angus,' he was saying, 'my lad from Ballinluig never turned up, I had to get my father to blow the bellows – ouch! some of them are still hot – that bag has charred, spread them out to cool, or keep them for tomorrow. Unless you want to burn down Flemyng's mill before it is up.'

'Aye, why not?' said Iain Logan. 'It would keep us working.'

'What a week!' Donald Stewart was talking and working in a steady frenzy. 'And it is not over yet – you know we have Mary to marry off to Alex McLaggan this Friday coming. Will you be there, Angus? We want you there. And Iain – and Alastair, of course, and your father, if he will come so far.'

'I will come so far,' Sandy McGlashan proclaimed from six rungs up the ladder, 'and I will sing them a song of William Ross's to send them on their way. "I went to woo a young girl",' he trolled out,

'As fair as a swan,
But I turned for home
Like a bald old man.
On a misty Sunday –'

'All right, Sandy, keep it for the wedding. Young Donald – will you bring your Jean? She had better see what is in store for her.'

Donald McCulloch grinned with pleasure and then turned it into a look of complicity for the younger men. James Menzies had locked up his warehouse for the day and come over in time to be included in the lengthening list.

'Mind now, Donald,' he put in, 'or Angus will be telling you to keep it down to forty-nine. A fine thing for a wedding if the laird came in and read the Riot Act.'

Donald pretended to grow grave at this. 'There is a lot in that. Supposing they came down on us with Thomson the constable from Pitnacree – they could arrest us all, and behead the movement!'

'No no, you have it wrong, Donald,' James Menzies objected. 'There are no leaders here – we are all on a level. What do you say, Angus?'

Cameron was taking off his head-band and shaking out his hair. 'I say we are all leaders. Sandy can lead the singing. And Donald can lead the cart. And James can lead the toasts. And even old MacDiarmid can lead a prayer. As for the laird –' he looked round with a quick black glint, 'he can lead us by the nose.'

A rising sound between a crow and a cheer came up from the men. Along at Moness House James Flemyng and his wife looked at each other apprehensively and wondered if it was time to bar the shutters. Next day and the day after that Mr Flemyng rode his horse along the slope south of the town, as though to exercise his dogs, and looked down at the site through an opera-glass, trying to make out whether the workmen were forming a mob. He had no idea that little Willie McGlashan was posted in the trees just below Moness. As soon as the gentleman came round from the stables on his horse, the lad pelted down town and across the building sites to alert the men. By this time they were starting to review the situation steadily, forecasting the Duke of Atholl's likely moves, wording formal requests for warrants to meet in larger groups, arguing furiously over the likelihood of being able to get weapons from the armouries at Atholl or Taymouth Castle. When Willie came running, they at once dispersed around the site. Through his glass James Flemyng observed a fine exhibition of model workmen sawing and hammering industriously at his great new masterwork.

CHAPTER 7

The Wedding

On the night of Thursday Cameron slept badly, for no reason that he knew of. The river dream came to him again, he was wading deep into the current, its coldness gripped him by the crutch, shocking him, he must reach that bluish hovering light on the far bank – trees towering above – a house, a tall bulky building towering above him … He half-woke, and saw the window-square glimmering with the pallor of sunrise … The river again, the far bank was nearer but here was a black smooth stretch, he half knew that he was dreaming, he wanted to stop the dream and he wanted to get across, if only he could raise his mouth and nostrils above the swell of the water … He made himself wake finally and lay under the covers feeling weak and hot, as though he had been spending energy incessantly all night.

Outside the day was fine enough, too clear perhaps; each roughness on the skyline was sharply visible, as though it might rain later. Just now the autumnal coolth was tonic and he breathed it in like drinking draughts of fresh milk, then took dippersful of water from the butt at the side of the house and sluiced his head into activity. In other parts of the house James Menzies and Allan Stewart were stirring with a clumping of boots. In an hour they were all ready and stood in the parlour looking humorously at each other in their best shirts of white linen and clean breeches. James's had a brown mark on the leg the shape of an iron. When Allan grinned knowingly at it, he said, 'Oh aye – this house needs a woman.'

'Maybe we will find a willing girl at the wedding,' Allan suggested.

'Donald's other daughters are like their father – too hefty in the arm. No man will ever cow them.'

'Did I say a Stewart? The Duke will bring a fine tail with him –'

'The McLaggan women – do not mention them, they would eat you alive!'

'You are hard to please, James – I wonder you ever married,' said Cameron, then regretted he had spoken.

'Kirsty was a gem - there is nobody else like that.' James's eyes filled suddenly with tears, he wiped at them and looked disbelievingly at the wet on his fingers. 'Ach, come on, you would think I had been at the whisky already. Let us get on the road.'

They stepped out briskly in the chill of evaporating rime and dew. By the time they came to the sharp bend at Borlick they had caught up with the McCulloch family, old Donald limping and muttering to himself, Donald hand in hand with Jean, Mary and her friend big Mary striding on ahead, their arms pulled down by heavy baskets of pies and eggs.

'Where is old Iain Logan?' said old Donald irritably as they came abreast.

'They will have gone down by the other side,' said Allan Stewart, 'it is their quickest way.'

'Ach – I was sure he would be with you – we could have taken our own time then.'

'Take it now, Father,' said Mary, putting down her baskets and easing her shoulders. 'What is the use of dying on the way to a wedding?'

They all moved off together down the tawny dust of the road, close beside the shingle banks and black deeps of the river. Here it ran between quiet green glades, the remnant of an oak wood which had been stripped to build ships for the navy and then, in a last plundering, to make charcoal for the insatiable furnaces and foundries down at Carron forge. But here a thin frieze of very old trees had been preserved for the delectation of the lairds who looked out from their houses on the slopes – Cluny, Grandtully, Clochfoldich, Pitcastle. At two of the gates on the roads up to the houses dogs had been stationed, chained to posts newly hammered in. The animals barked themselves hoarse as the little party tramped past and they were amused to see men watching them, one from behind a ruined byre, another behind a thick tree-trunk.

'What can the lairds be frightened of?' asked Menzies innocently. He waved and the man dodged further behind the tree.

'Once they are frightened of their own servants, then we will know we are doing well,' said Cameron.

Donald McCulloch was humming to get a tune going. After a little he remembered it and sang out loud,

> 'George of Hanover,
> When you came to London
> You piped a feeble tune
> To charm yourself a kingdom …'

The others took it up, humming or singing, and walked in time to it until old Donald got breathless and they had to saunter for a while. Jean had her arm round Donald's waist now and from time to time she skipped, roused by the fighting spirits of the menfolk. Well before noon, beside a small church whose roof sagged under clumps of grass and willow-herb, they came to the bridge over to Grandtully and looked across at the dense little settlement, lumpish houses made of undressed river boulders with brown smoke streaming through their heather thatch, hovels of branches littered through the trees, a few solid cottages with level roof-trees. It was a place of moss and mud and standing pools, myriads of flies twirled in the sun-rays, and dogs and children ran out to greet the newcomers in a raucous chorus. Behind a one-storey inn the Duke and his tribe of brothers and uncles lived in a cluster of rough stone houses, one built onto the end of the next as the family grew. Their sheep-fanks and cattle-pounds spread away, across land rented from the inn-keeper, in a close mesh of stone dykes. Droves of grey and brown horses grazed on the haugh beyond, milling round the still point of a tall grey monolith which thrust up through the turf like a stone sword.

Little clusters of guests were standing about on the cobblestones between the houses, looking at a loss. Mary McCulloch and big Mary went straight along to the Duke's house with their loads of food and as they went in the Duke came out, dressed in a long plaid of turquoise blue, and had a quick low word with them.

'Now what is going on?' James Menzies asked the others. 'I have seen livelier funerals.'

But the Duke was coming over with his usual smile, broad and toothless, mantled with crazy mirth. He saw their questioning looks and said, 'No bother, no bother at all. Donald came down two hours ago, and would you believe it, Bisset will not come to marry them.'

'He will not marry –'

'He will not marry them, And why? Not because we made a fool of him at the Reel on Monday, no no, not at all. He says that the church is dangerous – "not fit for a man of God to officiate at a most solemn sacrament".' The Duke intoned the words in a hollow boom like a ghost in a graveyard.

James Menzies burst out laughing. 'It is as well he is not a Papist, then, or the Pope would take off his frock.'

'He what?'

'Take off his frock. That is what they do to wicked priests.'

'Is that so, now? At least our ministers wear trousers – though you would wonder, if Bisset is frightened to come here among the desperate sinners of Grandtully.'

'Have you tried at another manse?' asked Cameron.

'It is not worth shoe-leather. After this past week they will all be thinking the same.'

'What will you do, then?'

'That is up to you.' The Duke gave him a squint grin.

'To me?'

The Duke leered more than ever. 'Well – Donald asked me to ask you – would you do the honours?'

'Ach, come on, man, what does he mean?'

'Just that. We need a little ceremony' – he dropped his voice – 'it will keep the women happy. What do you say? The marriage is the man and the woman wedding each other, that is the common law we all believe in. What does the minister do but add the mumbo-jumbo and the bit of paper?'

'That is right, of course it is. But why pick on me? I have no –'

'You have a black coat and a long tongue, Angus – they can hear you from the back of the crowd.'

'I should have stayed at home,' said Cameron.

'Not at all,' said James Menzies. 'Think of it – if Flemyng sacks you, you can get a job as a preacher.'

'Good man, Angus,' said the Duke, clapping Cameron's shoulder. 'Will you go along and tell them, now? And say we are coming in no time at all.'

The families of guests were drifting along the river bank towards Donald Stewart's a quarter of a mile upstream. They looked like the camp followers of an army, with their bundles of food, but they were carrying their best shoes in their hands. One or two looked questioningly at Cameron but he was absorbed in thinking up phrases. What could he say? Declare them man and wife? Not declare – pronounce. The one was as pompous as the other. He would ask young Alex for the ring, and see that it was put well onto Mary's finger, he would wish them to be happy and fruitful and true to one another and that nothing would ever part them. And that was what he said, at one o'clock in the afternoon, in the smithy yard at Ballinluig. The house was much too small; people made a deep ring round the couple and Cameron, standing on the cobbles among piles of bar and rod iron, the children perched on tree-stumps and on the lower branches of the very old yew tree which made a dark thicket with its multiple trunks. Donald's wife Aileen looked upset and redeyed, without a minister the occasion seemed rough and ready, no better than a ceilidh, unlawful even, and her misgivings about the McLaggans had all revived. She glanced repeatedly at her daughter in the long white linen gown which had been her own wedding dress. But Mary was delighting quietly in the atmosphere of freedom. The ordeal she had expected had turned into fun. Her father stood behind her, sweating and beaming, and behind the bridegroom stood the Duke, tall and shaggy, holding a long pine branch covered with fresh green cones. The clusters of needles spread above the young couple's heads like a canopy. Angus Cameron stood up on the oak stump which Donald used as a chopping-block, held out his hand to each part of the crowd as though drawing them into the circuit of the ceremony, and said, at first quietly, then gaining volume as he felt the truth of his words: 'Alexander McLaggan, Mary Stewart – you love each other, and must wed each other, and that is right and good. We all of us feel your happiness and we have come to celebrate it with you, and with your families. Alex – have you the ring?' The young man passed it up, the little circlet of gold glistening between the tips of his thick hard fingers. 'All right, Alex, but that is for you to do, I have only to make sure you do it right,' Laughter rustled quietly through the crowd. 'Now, Mary – will you accept this ring from Alexander McLaggan?' The girl tried to say 'Yes' but her mouth had dried and she had to swallow before the word would come, 'Now Alexander, do you give her the ring.' Alex put it on her finger with a sure movement, took her by both hands, and kissed her closely on the mouth. The Duke held his branch still higher, waving it slowly from side to side, and the piper started a long, echoing note on his drone.

'Now,' said Cameron, letting his voice peal round the yard, 'we wish you happiness and health, Alexander and Mary McLaggan. We wish you will be fruitful, and true to one another. And we wish and trust that no ill will of man or woman, and no act of government, will ever come between you.'

The piper was moving into the ring of people. When everyone expected him to break into a nimble tune, he played a slow air that sounded Irish in the long luxuriant unfolding of each phrase. People listened entranced, laced together by the tendrils of the melody. It finished, he tapped his foot, one two three four, and then he did launch into a jig, springy and violent. Young Donald McCulloch whooped and two of the McLaggan girls whooped with him. Donald Stewart had his arms round his daughter and son-in-law. He squeezed them and kissed them and went off into the house. Bumping noises came and he reappeared carrying a door. His wife was bringing out heavy ashets piled with pies, her daughters brought out clothsful of new loaves, still steaming. Now Donald was bracing himself to take the weight of the heavier outer door and Donald McLaggan was helping him, easing it up off its hinges. The guests were crowding slowly past the wedded couple, kissing them, shaking their hands. Sandy McGlashan had arrived late, his hair plastered down with sweat; he was spluttering over the tale, to whoever would listen, of how he had 'come upon Flemyng and Menzies of Bolfracks, in the street at Aberfeldy, they had their heads together and were plotting something wicked, no doubt about it, if only he could have heard what they were saying'.

Young Donald listened sceptically for a moment. Jean was pulling him by the hand towards the dance. 'Ah well,' he said finally, 'if he tries to get his own back for his son's trouble, we will have to crack his head too,' and he swept off into the dance. Jean's black curly hair flew out as they swung round and her cheeks, always so ripe that they looked as though they would bleed at the touch of a straw, reddened more richly than ever.

At one end of the heavier door, now held up on trestles, Donald had hefted a stone jar of whisky into position and Donald McLaggan was drawing off cupsful and handing them out. People were blowing on their bowls of broth and mingling its savours of onions and mutton with the harsh fire of the whisky. Aileen Stewart had placed an eighteen-inch pie in the very centre of the board; its summit gleamed yellow with a basting of egg. Donald held up their biggest knife, kissed its blade, and cleft the crust. Steam puffed out and people cheered.

'Where is Angus Cameron?' Donald shouted out. 'Come on, Angus, you have earned your meat!' He heaped a plate for him and Cameron took it thankfully. Still caught in a clench of emotion after the effort of the ceremony, he had accepted a spilling cup of whisky from Donald McLaggan and drained it as though it was milk to quench a thirst. Now he felt his brain slowly expanding, the noise and sunshine seemed to have entered his skull, and he badly wanted some food to settle the turbid churning of his feelings.

At the far end of the yard the Duke had planted his branch in the ground and was sitting under it like a potentate. Now he beckoned Cameron over and shook him formally by the hand. 'I heard the bit of politics in your address. And that was good. That was right. We are deep into it now, and there is no avoiding it. Did you hear the news from Atholl?'

'No – nothing for a day or two.'

'The Society teacher at Fincastle – Forbes. A few folk went to his place before sunrise yesterday, just to let him know he had better have no hand in the lists. Well, he fired a pistol and someone went for him with the blade of a scythe.'

'Fincastle? Where is that?' Cameron was trying to concentrate.

'Not two miles from Atholl Castle - across the ford and over the hill. The damned Duke will make the worst of it.'

'Is the man dead?'

'Dead enough. They took him away on a cart, soaked with blood from head to foot.'

'Like a soldier … I know, I know – we want no battles here. But they hate the Act so bitterly, not everybody will hold back their hands forever. Are you trying to stop your people carrying blades of any kind?'

'They will do what they like.' The Duke gave him a quick, keen look. 'What about your folk?'

'They had none at Castle Menzies, as you know. And I saw none at Ballechin. Some women had stockingsful of stones that would have felled a bullock. I would not stop that. We have to show our mettle.'

'Well, I did not expect that from you.' The Duke laughed with pleasure. 'Let us drink to that.' He held up his cup, clinked it on Cameron's, and gave him a deliberate nod. The audience was over. But Cameron could hardly move away – the dancers filled the yard, flying toes and heels banged against the shins of the onlooking elders as the dancers twirled. Donald McLaggan had gone too far with Flora Stewart, swinging so wildly that the girl flung against the smaller table and fell onto it with her hair in the great bowl of broth. For a moment she looked furiously at Donald, her teeth bared like a cat's, then she shook her hair out, spattering Donald with bree and barley, and hauled him back into the dance. Sandy McGlashan had taken out a little yellow fiddle and was adding a frenzied strum of strings to the piper's notes. As the dancers changed partners, set to each other, backed away, then set again and spun with crossed arms, Donald McCulloch became masterful, gripping the girls' hands strongly, spinning so hard that the balls of their feet ached on the cobbles, and passing them on with an almost lordly flourish of his arm. Jean felt belittled; for as long as the dance lasted she seemed no more to him than any girl there, but then he came round to her again and clasped her closely as they stepped it down the aisle between the lines of dancers.

Sandy McGlashan was wild now with the sound of his own music. When the dance ended and everyone was standing in clusters, sweating and smiling and breathing heavily, he sang out in a high voice with a laugh in it –

> 'When I reached her window,
> The watch-dog heard.
> He started barking,
> She never said a word.
>
> There was nothing for it
> But to cower and hide
> Like one who lacked the courage
> To give a girl a ride.
>
> I cannot sleep a wink now,
> Bed I cannot abide
> For my merry member
> Rising by my side.'

There were ooh's and aah's when he finished, and some unbridled laughter. Aileen was looking dubiously at her husband but he was in no mood to disapprove. He winked at the Duke and called across to him, 'What a grand thing, your Honour, to have a wedding without a minister!' The Duke did his stately bow at that and then Donald was calling for another song. Some of the veterans were on the point of giving tongue but young Donald McCulloch was on his feet and moving into the middle of the ring, he was full of himself, sparkling with mischief but with an undertow of ardour.

'Duncan Ban MacIntyre wrote a song for his wife Mary. I do not know if Alex used it to court his Mary – he must have used something–' The joke was unconscious but crowing laughter came from the young men beside the whisky jar. Donald silenced them as he sang the first line, rather solemnly, in a rich baritone:

> 'I went into the thickets
> To cut a wand of love
> And searched among the saplings
> That clustered close above.
> One branch was all blossom,
> I gently curved it down,
> No-one else must cut it,
> I claimed it for my own.'

His tribute was meant for Alex and Mary McLaggan, but as he sang he half turned towards Jean, he could not keep his look away from her, and as the words enveloped her she felt herself choking in a warm cocoon, her cheeks burned unbearably, he should not be doing this, it was too much in front of so many friends and strangers.

> 'My net was in clear water,
> I hauled strongly in
> And landed me a sea-trout
> As lustrous as a swan.
> The share I won has made me
> Content in heart and head –
> Star of my early mornings,
> Dear partner of my bed.'

It was too much but she loved him for it and let him kiss her when he came and stood beside her again.

There were cries of applause and as they died down Donald Stewart turned to Cameron and said, 'Now, Angus, let us hear from you.'

'Och – I have said my say already.' Cameron realized he was having to form his words carefully. He felt a brimful of yearning – of some mixture of emotions that were hardly expressible, that must pour outwards.

'Come on, Angus,' Donald persisted, 'let us hear a song from over the mountains. Come on, now –' He had no need to say more because Cameron had risen to his feet in the greying light and a song was coming from him in a steady flow of sound and a hard gravelly voice that resonated like a pipe:

> 'I grieve for the white bodies
> Scattered over the hills
> Without shroud or coffin
> Or burial in holes.
>
> Those who survived the battle
> Lie in the hulks in chains.
> We are called "rebels"
> And the Whig reigns ...'

'John Roy Stewart,' he said, sitting down heavily. 'Well – if he hated the massacre, he should not have been at the battle.'

Iain Logan had been listening to him as though fascinated by the stress of experience which had lengthened Cameron's face and closed his black brows over his eyes. 'You are right, Angus,' he said excitably. 'Hired murderers – in it for the blood money. Flemyng of Moness is no better, you know, no better at all. You know where his father got his money? Canada – trading rubbish for furs. And why was he there at all? Army quarter-master – selling off the soldiers' rations to the traders in Quebec. And why were the soldiers – the soldiers – why were they ...' He had lost his thread and Cameron's head was too ravelled to think much about it anyway.

In the gloaming the Weem folk made their way home along the dark gorge of the road. Above their heads bats flickered almost invisibly between the treetops. Donald and Jean had disappeared and Mary was in a black mood, striding along and making old Donald gasp. Behind them the nests of little lights at Ballinluig and Grandtully had dimmed to orange sparks in the fine drizzle.

'That was a sad song for a wedding, Angus,' said James Menzies after a time.

'It would be a sad thing,' Angus answered at once, 'if Alex was taken away from his Mary into the army when they were not a year married.'

Or if my Donald was taken, married or not, Mary McCulloch was thinking. But she kept the thought to herself.

For a mile or two nothing more was said. They knew when they were opposite Pitcaple, and then Cluny, by the barking of the dogs and the rattle of their chains.

'They would have our throats out if they could get at us.' Allan Stewart's voice sounded tiredly out of the darkness. Cameron had not the energy to reply, but he was thinking, So would their masters. Dogs would do it to us with their teeth but *they* have laws and guns instead.

They had passed through the blackest part of the valley now and it was a relief to see a light or two at Weem, and across the invisible river at Aberfeldy. The McCullochs turned into their cottage with a brief good-night and Cameron, James, and Allan let themselves into the tall, silent house along the road. It smelled of wine dregs, damp soot, and whitewash. A day's work still to do before the Sabbath and they would have sore heads in the morning. But at least their wits would have cleared again in time for Sunday's meetings and the next milestone in the struggle.

CHAPTER 8

The Speech

If they managed to exact a sworn and written abrogation of the Act from every single proprietor in the strath (and over into Tummel and down past Dunkeld), at least they would have built a paper wall round themselves. More than that? How keep the gentry to it? How reach through and past them to the axis of power? It felt like hauling on a rope that ran half round the world. You strained till the blood came – still no movement at the far end. They would never get the Act repealed. Make it unworkable – yes, do that. How? The Tranent folk had had a notion (but look what happened to them) – say to the government, *'You cannot trust us* if ever you make us fight.' The young men must resolve to be mutinous. How could they stick to it, though, once they were under a sergeant-major, a trained bully, lashed to a gun carriage and flogged to pieces? They must not go at all. They must lie low here, amongst their own folk, where they know the ground, where they can be fed. But. But the government troops are devils in the thoroughness of their searching and destroying – would it be like 'Forty-six again? Houses burnt – gardens and orchards uprooted – herds and flocks driven off wholesale – sparing nobody, even when there was no proof or likelihood that the family was harbouring a wanted man …
No – the government will find it hard to sustain that again, when there has been no army in the field against them – no pitched battles – no weapons, even. Maybe our weakness is our strength, thought Cameron – we are *seen to be democrats*, nothing like the Prince's bands of warriors. But they hate the very word 'democrat'! To Atholl's friends in Edinburgh, the Dundases, the Abercrombies, a 'democrat' is *the* worst thing, a wrecker, a traitor. And our own people here have never heard the word at all … Is that it? To disappear the young men into their own terrain, make use of every cave and wood (and send them over the water if need

be)? Not till after the harvest. People would never put up with it before then. If we can afford to wait that long. To organize it will demand utter secrecy – utter. Anything less and we might as well not do it at all. There must be several hundred quiet, individual meetings with individual families. *If* the broad plan is agreed. How to discuss it secretly? Probably there are government spies amongst us already (but who? which friend at the wedding? which fellow-workman?). We must do two things together (Cameron found his thoughts concentrating to a point at last). We must keep up the pressure on the lairds, the stream of meetings, so that we are all welded together, we feel our accumulated powers, day in day out. And the lairds believe that that is all. Under the cover of the hubbub we must organize the families, until each listed man knows where he will go, and who will feed him, when the platoon comes to march him off.

Cameron's brain reeled slightly under the weight of all these alternatives. He had better try them out on James. They were walking steadily up the strath, past Castle Menzies, looking unreal in its composed beauty under early Sunday sunshine, past the close-built cottages and huts of Dull which looked like scree left by a spate, heapedup boulders, shaggy heather thatch, dykes built recently with field stones and already falling down. Now they could see the broad glitter of Loch Tay, and in the foreground their destination, the gable of Kenmore church perched on its knoll at the loch-end. Down every track and path and road the knots and files of people were converging. If the minister had been looking out from his manse windows, he would have thought that his prophecy had found honour in its own country at last. In fact the service would be nearly over, if Cameron and Menzies had timed it right. They felt they had done well enough already to endure the service at Dull, and that there was no need to martyr themselves yet again (the Reverend William MacIvor's sermons were notoriously long and repetitive).

Cameron looked at Menzies and said, 'James – what will come of today's work?'

'What we said,' James answered, mildly surprised. 'Petitions against the Act from all the villages. Signatures in forty-nines to escape the Riot Act. Undertakings to be won from the lairds binding themselves to undertake nothing punitive against tenants seen at meetings.'

Cameron let him finish. 'Do you think it is enough?'

'Nothing is enough, so long as we have no hand in government.'

'We are putting paper chains on their arms; they can break them with a gesture.'

They stopped and looked at each other and James laughed. 'We are talking ourselves into a fine slough! It must be the Sabbath getting into our bones.'

'It is as well to take a full look at the worst.' Cameron would not let him go. 'You know well enough, James – you must have thought – once the government is resolved, and we have talked ourselves hoarse and there is no ink left in the country – then the dragoons will come in and cart the young men away as though we have done nothing. We might as well be *praying*!'

'The young men should take to the hills.'

Cameron looked at him to make sure he was in earnest. 'I was thinking just that myself.'

'But if they do, we should go with them. If you were Atholl, who would you come for first? Why, Cameron king of the rebels and Menzies his henchman.'

'Leave us aside. I will *never* go to prison. But leave us out of it just now. There is enough to do, if all the listed men are to be visited and spoken to.'

'A few have gone off already. From Killin, and Rannoch of course – they like this kind of thing up there.'

'Oh aye, in this easy weather. But how will they live through the winter?'

By now they were in among thickening crowds of people, nodding to acquaintances and looking out for their own key men from down the valley. There were the Logan brothers from Moness, watchful, keeping to themselves. There was Sandy McGlashan, carrying his fiddle in a bag. There was Donald from the smithy, joking with young McLaggan from Grandtully and two of his own daughters – they had brought parcels of food and bottles of drink and looked ready for a good day's outing. Young McCulloch was on his own – where was Jean? Clusters of dark clothes marked out contingents from up Keltney and beyond. A solid snake of people still wound back along the north shore of the loch. A waft of singing sounded from the church, like a great collective musical groan, with an overtone of keening – the final psalm. People presently came flowing out of the door and spread between the gravestones. A few went home. Most stayed, under the shadowy evergreens, among the tall sycamores and beeches on the bluff above the water.

Cameron waited for the minister to finish his ritual of nodding and handshaking with the congregation. He then passed quickly through the crowd, eyes studiously on the ground, black gown folded round him like a rook's wings. The crowd was still thickening, filling back down the high street, but it looked like time to start. As Cameron opened with his usual explanation of the Act, he did not know that the Reverend William McIvor, a tall whiskery man with coarse orange hair and very pale blue eyes, had stayed outside his manse, in the cover of a thick yew tree, and was listening hard with a hand cupped round his ear.

'This Act will enslave you,' he heard Cameron saying, 'and not only the young men among you but every family with a son who is in his prime. For how are we to bring in the corn harvest with all those strong hands and strong arms gone? You will *manage* – oh yes – although *you* have no servants to feed your animals or cook your meat for you – you will *manage,* although you are a year married with a wee child learning to walk, and no wet-nurse to mind it for you while you milk the beasts – and no young husband to thatch your house above your head. The lords in parliament, and in the courthouse and the castle, they do not know how we live – they know nothing about us, except that we will die for them, to protect their forts in India *and in Scotland*' – his voice sharpened suddenly, his arm swung round and pointed north and a gust of response rose out of the crowd – 'we have always been good at that, their demands can never be satisfied, regiments for the colonies, indentured servants and labourers for the plantations, they have scoured Scotland like a killing wind and the men have been whirled away in the blast of it. When the *Philadelphia* – now remember this name – when the *Philadelphia* put into Stornoway in Lewis, and gleaned young boys from the beach, and stowed them in the hold like trade-goods, what constable or what factor raised his arm or his stick to stop the slavers? When seven slave-ships – now this is true – when seven slave-ships were cruising in the sound between Taransay and Harris, did Lord MacDonald's men protect Lord MacDonald's tenants? Not at all – the *price* was too good – MacDonald's factor was far too busy *agreeing a price* for the young folk that he *sold* to the Carolina merchants. When the pressgang came to Aberdeen last year' (had it been last year? Near enough), 'did the baillies and the constables protect the citizens from the bully-boys with their clubs and handcuffs? Oh no – never – the bribe was far too great to refuse – they *ran a cordon* round the Green and delivered over their own folk to the men-of-war. Where will it end,' he cried out, 'where will it end?' (feeling the helplessness in his own depths, knowing that to the crowd it came as an incitement to great anger). The feeling was soughing through them, every face was turned fully towards him, features naked, eyes widened (they were too expectant, too dependent on the next sally, their wills must be gathered up and channelled towards an irresistible action). 'It *will* never end until we feel our powers, until we see how few and weak they are' (this was the merest wishfulness), 'and how strong they are, for consider what they have now, and in what sort of a country we are living. The forts and barracks have gone up, an iron chain along the Great Glen, an iron ring round the coasts – *you* have built it for them, you have clamped these fetters on your own wrists, and I do not excuse myself – my first work was mending the roof of the arsenal at Fort Augustus in 1784. I should have known better, but we are learning now. We are not free people under this Constitution – not any longer, if we ever were. There is a Bastille in every glen and firth, and this Act is the final fetter' (but it would not be, there would be plenty more). 'Let them put it on you and you are done for at last – food for the cannons, and the swamp-fever, and the hulks. But remember' – he had lifted an arm now and was prodding with his forefinger as though pointing to the furthest corners of the country (he was feeling the attention of the crowd and letting it recharge his energy), 'the people are mightier than a lord.' He paused, letting the crowd dwell on the proverb (hearing the rooks caw above his head). 'The people are mightier than a lord, and if we know that, we – can – not – be – put – down.' Each of the words came out separately with the force of an oak peg hammered into a hole. A roar of arousal sounded out at once and he spoke above it, formal and explanatory now (letting the standard phrases quell his own misgivings).

'It is very clear what we must do. We petition against the Act, a petition to go from every parish. We must all join in this – there is no room for anyone to hang back. We have paper and ink here – make a start now if you have not already. No more than forty-nine names on a paper, or the Deputy-Lieutenants will infer a gathering of illegal size and bring in the soldiers under the Riot Act. *Do not fail*' – he was having to shout now above the stir (was everything clear? or had he only thrown water on a fire?) – 'do not fail to put in a clause calling on the proprietors to undertake nothing punitive against tenants seen at meetings. We are within the Constitution as it stands, nothing illegal is going on and we claim the right to be treated as democratic citizens assembling as we are free to do. We carry no weapons, the guns are all in Taymouth Castle, but if they threaten us or fire on us' (behind the yew the minister listened harder than ever), 'then we will *reply in kind.*

'Now, can everybody see a paper? James – Alastair – Iain – Donald – Angus – hold them up. *There* are our arguments –I believe we can muster sixteen thousand names – they must listen to that. So sign your names, friends, or make a mark if need be. We must have one great voice in this, and it must come from every quarter, up to Rannoch, along the loch to Glen Ogle and Loch Earn. We will meet at Fortingall tomorrow, and let us make it the biggest meeting of all – the Glen Lyon folk will join us there, and once Breadalbane joins with Atholl, then they will know that the whole people is on the move. I know there is hay to cut and turn, but it is the harvest that will suffer if we let the Act stand. So come to Fortingall, to the Green, at noon. Now – can everybody reach a paper?'

In the midst of the crowd a huddle of men and women were using a flat-topped gravestone as a table. The point of the quill broke through the paper where it lay over an incised letter and a woman in the group pushed the man with the pen and crowed out, 'Donal, you great fool – the King will never read that now!' People were flocking round each paper, jostling and craning to see what it said and who had signed so far. The fringes of the crowd loosened and eddied as people slipped away and stragglers arrived. Over at the manse the Reverend William McIvor, in a drab overcoat, let himself out by the back door and rode off to the north-east by a back path through the woods near Taymouth Castle, keeping his grey garron on a tight rein and stepping slowly so that the hoof-beats were nearly soundless. Hemmed in by backs and shoulders, besieged by people wanting to shake his hand, put questions, or merely to remind him of past meetings, Cameron was struggling to respond and make each person feel attended to. He still felt naked and drained after the speech, yet now was the time to be weaving more individuals firmly into the spreading fabric. 'We only have the year's agreement on our place – will the laird turn us out if Kenneth signs the paper?' a nervous yellow-haired woman was asking him. Her face was only a foot from his. 'Who is the owner?' he started to ask. A surge in the crowd behind him jolted him forwards and he saved himself, and the woman, by setting his feet wide and holding onto her shoulders. He smelt smoke in her hair, felt her flesh soft under her shawl, and then a further quake in the crowd parted them. He rose up on tiptoe, looking round for James, Allan, and the rest. The crowd was gradually thinning. The papers, covered with crosses and signatures, were passing back to the organizers.

Within an hour Allan, Donald the smith, and the Logan brothers had set off down the strath to Weem with the petitions in a leather wallet, to add to the already thick bunch in James's strong-box, and Cameron and James had got horses from a sympathizer in the village and rode off towards the narrow glen of Keltney. Among its tortuous water-courses, its hidden back-glens and caves and dark deformed woods choked with fallen trees knee-deep in moss, there might be refuges for a hundred listed men, if the worst happened. And word of the meeting at Fortingall must be spread. The sawyers at the government mill at Kinlochrannoch were good friends of Cameron's, and might try to bring out their neighbours, although they themselves were still felt to be incomers. If the people from the hill farms around the loch foot could be mobilized, they would add a fierce thrust to the movement. If they kept to themselves, the whole northern end of the area might as well be written off.

CHAPTER 9

The Sawmill

An eagle planed over miles of country without a single flapping of its wings, curving and rising on the air currents generated by the warmed mass of Schiehallion. In eleven miles Cameron and Menzies had passed three houses – all the fewer people to betray the refugees, they told each other. The fewer also to provide food. How to balance out these factors? Their eyes followed the bird as its image shrank and lost itself in space. All around them the shoulders of the hills were browned by the fading of the heather, dulled by the weakening sunshine, their expanses turned dusty-blank as though a great grinding had sifted down on them, decades of labour and hardship, and left them blinded. A desert, Menzies thought, a wilderness where you might just manage to survive for forty days and forty nights, especially if there was an angel at hand to minister to you. He thought of trying this fancy on Cameron but his face looked so closed and dark, eyes narrowed and mouth-corners turned right down, that it forbade pleasantry.

Cameron was thinking: Those upland folk who were at Kenmore this morning – they nearly all kept on towards Tummel when we forked north-west for Rannoch. So: up there they are with us, some of them; but here we might as well be among foreigners. Are we stretching our lines too far? The whole campaign dragged on him with a dead weight at this moment. 'The people are mightier than a lord' – it was easily said. But they were so scattered, their power diffused through a thousand little steadings – not concentrated into arsenals and parliaments and prisons. You had to tell yourself, again and again, that there were links between all the little homes, filaments that tensed and hummed with power when the time came. Look how readily the thousand had turned out to besiege the laird at Castle Menzies! Yet all that feeling, all that energy, discharged itself into the void so long as it did not flow down one of the channels that made the great wheels turn – in Edinburgh, in London and Paris. *Our* people should be there. How can a belted knight speak for us? It is in his interest to speak *against* us, to force up rents, not fix them fairly, to give his friends a charter to chop down our forests. *Our* trees, he thought, as the moss-green heads and bronze trunks of the pines round Dunalastair came into sight – our meadows in the low lands round the lochs. How could it have come about, he marvelled afresh, that they had parcelled it out and tied it up with strings of law? He knew full well: by Acts of Parliament, voted by landlords to benefit their like. In France they had loosed the strings. Paine was across there now, it was said, helping to write new laws. If he came back, to spread the word, no doubt they would hang him like a felon. But he had written his book – the people in Glasgow and Paisley knew it by heart, nearly – now it was up to themselves.

They trotted west straight into the broad golden glare of the sun and came among the scattered settlements of the Rannoch people. The houses were huts – branches and small tree-trunks caulked with turf. Plumes of shining pink and amber grass flourished on the thatch of their roofs. As the horses trotted past, kicking up gravel from the rough road, women in dark-brown shawls picked up their babies and shouted at their children to come inside – as though strangers from the east were liable to spell trouble.

'It must have been like this in Arkaig when my father first went there,' Cameron said to Menzies. 'How did he ever settle?' 'Perhaps he was as savage as they,' Menzies replied.

'Och yes, that is true – not like your fine slave-traders and money-lenders down at Perth.' Cameron turned off down a churned, peaty track towards the wooden roofs and palings of the sawmill. Among orange mounds of dust and evil black pools the sawyers squatted, self-reliant Lowlanders who perched here like colonists and were tolerated because the sub-tenants and cottagers on the poorest land could get a few days felling trees when they were desperate.

A man was sitting on the ground outside his house. He looked up at the horses, shading his eyes against a sting of sun from the west. He was tall, sun-reddened, with a big lower jaw and a nose like a wedge. He was smoking a clay pipe and his hair was speckled with sawdust. 'Angus Cameron!' he said and got to his feet. The two shook hands and Cameron introduced Menzies.

'James Menzies – my partner. Kenneth Byers.'

'Is that in business, now, or in politics?' asked Byers.

'Business! What do you take me for?' Cameron pretended to be affronted.

'Ach well – I thought you were all in the money down there.'

'Gunsmiths are doing well,' said Menzies. 'And chainmakers, and bankers.'

'And lawyers and spies,' said Cameron.

Byers regarded them quizzically. 'You should move up here, then. If you want to starve in peace. Come on inside – the midges will devour you if you don't smoke.'

The hut had a muddy wooden floor, patched at the edges where the planks had rotted. A partition of rough studding hung with ragged cloths divided the room into two. In the public end a fire flamed in a stone hearth. Black pots stood steaming on a pair of hobs. On a bench a young woman with red hair had been suckling her baby. Now she tidied herself up, arranged her shawl on her forehead, and soothed the baby, who was still nuzzling for her breast.

'Ella – here is Angus Cameron. And he has brought his partner, Mr Menzies. You're in luck – we found a fowl this morning, and it didn't look too well, so we had to put it out of its misery.'

'No wonder they look darkly at you hereabouts, if you steal their fowls.'

'What? I wouldn't take an egg from the village folk. No no, this fat old bird was round the back of Bunrannoch House, when I took wee Alex for a walk. They've plenty to spare, and they're always in among other folk's corn. The laird robs his tenants and his hens steal the harvest. Sit down – will you take a dram?'

They all, except Ella, took a pull at a stone bottle of fierce whisky. 'How is wee Alex?' asked Cameron. 'Is he five yet?'

'Five past Easter. When were you here last?'

'The end of March, when the drifts cleared from the road past Keltney falls.'

'You came about the timber for the mill at Aberfeldy.'

'I did. We are still at it. But it is not easy to keep working just at present.'

'Does James Flemyng keep you up to the mark?'

'Och, he comes snapping about, with his dogs and his "man". He calls McHarg the factor "his man".'

'I heard you were busy at other things. Ella – where was I hearing the news?'

'Down at Atholl, when you went for the new blades,' his wife answered from beside the fireplace. The baby was lying in a cradle of osiers, crooning to itself like a wood-pigeon.

'It's all a stramash of gossip down there, Angus,' said Byers, giving his visitors a look. 'How your mob have murdered a teacher, and thrashed the Duke's servants nearly to death. Well – I believed the half of it.'

'That might be a bit too much.' Cameron was moved to deny the atrocities – he could see the doubts twingeing across Byers's forehead. But there were other things to find out. 'What else did you hear? Any word of the petitions?'

'Petitions? They said there was a wild night of it somewhere down about Ballinluig. They called you "King Cameron". I thought to myself, that doesn't sound like Angus. But I said nothing.'

Cameron and Menzies were looking seriously at each other. Where to start? How to convey the gist?

'Seventeen lairds have sworn to oppose the Militia Act,' said Menzies flatly. 'And six thousand people have come out to the meetings.'

'I heard there were great crowds about. What's next, then?' Cameron did not want to be asked this. Byers was offering him the bottle. He drank and let the burn of the whisky pass slowly down his gullet.

'We are meeting again tomorrow, at Fortingall. Drawing in the Glenlyon folk, and your neighbours here, we hope. Once all this country is solid against the Act, and all across the Lowlands, then the government must think again.'

'Do governments do that? And anyway – suppose the war hots up, and they're desperate for men – ?'

'Our people are steeling themselves, Kenneth,' James Menzies said at once, talking excitedly. 'They mean business. They will never follow a drum now. March when a laird's son gives an order? They know the lairds are straw men now!'

Cameron watched for the effect of this on the sawyer's face. Byers heard Menzies out, looked over at Cameron as though wondering whether he believed this too, and then stood up and stretched. He knocked his pipe out on the stone above the fire.

'I wonder if they will take orders once they have red coats on,' he said at last. 'I believe the Breadalbane men were up in arms against their commanders down at Glasgow a few years back. But now there's a war on, and everybody's frightened at the French … He let his words trail off. They all went over to the fire for plates of meat and bread. In his mind

Cameron continued the argument throughout the meal. He found in Byers a bracing scepticism like his own. Yet speculation was actually fruitless now. They were no longer debating the rights of man at a Club for Equality and Reform. They had committed themselves to a movement and had no option but to drive it through to its end. What he wanted from Byers above all was an offer – a plausible offer – to bring two hundred people down to Fortingall. And this was what Byers could not make. They sat on arguing for three hours while Ella went into the other end of the house and sang quietly to the baby and wee Alex came home filthy from playing and sat drowsily beside the fire, chewing at the bones of the fowl. The hut was sweltering with smoke and steam and everybody scratched as vermin crept and bit under their clothes. But it was no better outside: midges boiled in clouds out of the sodden peat around the saw-bed and the timber stacks. Byers felt the pressure on him to offer something and was restive under it like a dog on a tether.

'You know my position,' he broke out at last. 'I work here but I don't belong here.' Am I any different, Cameron was wondering to himself, and Byers, sensing the thought, grew more heated. 'Do you know what it's like when people turn away before you've finished speaking? Or refuse you milk or an egg when you have an ailing wean? The government put this here after 'Forty-six because they wanted one spot of safety in a wilderness of hatred, and because they thought they might as well get some good of this country once they'd ruined it. Well – it might have happened yesterday, for the Rannoch folk. They can bear a grudge forever, like a fire in a mine. Don't you know that, Angus? You speak their language, man!' His eyes were wide with stress, his face glared with fire-heat and whisky.

Menzies tried to intervene. 'Surely, then, Kenneth, this great grudge of theirs will bring them out against the enlistment?'

Byers turned on him as Ella came through to ask them to hush their voices. For a moment he looked from Menzies to Cameron and back again, then he nodded his head towards the doorway. Once they were outside, he pointed across the level land towards the loch. 'Look,' he said. Perfectly calm water mirrored a sky which shaded from smoky orange through turquoise to night blue, reflecting nothing but the sheerness of space, unlit by stars. Smoke wisped up from huts invisible among the bunched darkness of trees and spread in faint blue webs. Silhouetted against the gleam of the water human figures moved about.

Cameron and Menzies recognized the swaying shoulders of men leaning as they scythed, the reach and drag of women raking and turning the cut hay.

'Those are the folk you want to walk fifteen miles to your meeting,' Byers said in a low voice. 'In the middle of the hay harvest, With the weather holding.'

'There will be fewer to bring it in next year, when the listed men have gone.' Menzies brought out the familiar argument.

'They will settle for the devil they know. Who doesn't? They get mad here after the last wisp of hay – I've seen old women down on their knees, gleaning it with their fingers.' Byers's voice had tightened with compassion and distaste.

Menzies started to answer but Cameron put his hand on his arm, shook his head slightly, and said to Byers, 'I see the trouble. It is softer down our way and there is hay enough. But, Kenneth — there is a war now – it is between the government and us. They are going to draw the young men out of the country like pith out of a rush. We cannot let that happen – can we?'

'No.' Byers's voice was low, even sulky. 'No – we can't.'

'So we need all help, all resources, everybody, if we are to win, and save ourselves.' Cameron was speaking in a low-pitched, pressing whisper. 'And there is a thing that this wild part is very good for. A refuge, Kenneth – a haven. Will they harbour some listed men here, if it comes to it? Would they do that, do you think?'

'The redcoats will go through the houses like a fire! Remember 'Forty-six –'

'Not in the houses. They must lie up in the caves, if we do send refugees here, and in the pinewoods and the tall juniper – they will do even in the winter. So long as your people will take them food. And so long as they pass them through Rannoch to the west if need be. Are there no families who would do that?'

'The sawyers would do it – that makes fourteen houses, And a good many are obliged to us for the work they get here. Anyway, they would never give a man away to the soldiers …'

Before Cameron and Menzies left they had written down lists of safe houses, sources of milk and meal, and secure points further west. A frail safety-net had started to take shape. They rode east and south under a moonless sky alive with stars, the lustre of the Milky Way making a faint track across the zenith. Their heads seethed with possibilities, worries, further problems. As the deep black shadow in Glen Keltney closed over them, they moved slowly nearer home in a trance of fatigue.

CHAPTER 10

The Hayfields

At two in the morning Cameron and Menzies were still sleepwalking between the ragged dykes of Dull, swaying and nodding in the saddle, letting the horses pick the way. Blenching at the last few miles, shivering as sweat and dew ran down their backs, they turned into Donald Gillies's yard at Camserney sawmill. The house door was locked. They stabled their horses round the back and bedded amongst dry hay with their cloaks wrapped round them. Noises of chopping reached them as they lay there in the morning, feeling stiff and foul. They went indoors to find Donald splitting wood to start the fire. He pretended to be unsurprised.

'We knew you were there. The dog was whining and wanting out at you,'

'But you could not have known it was us.' Cameron enjoyed teasing him.

'That dog has powers,' Gillies insisted. 'One time, a tinker put in a day here, mending pans, and at night off he went, with my best tools hidden in his bundle. Well – at Dunkeld fair that autumn, Roy here bites a man in the calf of his leg – it was the tinker!'

'Would he bite a recruiting sergeant?' asked Menzies. 'Or a teacher, for the matter of that?'

'Is that why you are here?' Gillies turned back to the fire and spoke to them over his shoulder. 'Still drumming up followers for your meetings.'

'We were benighted after a long day's ride to Rannoch, ordering floor timber for the mill.' Cameron covered up without thinking it out. Donald Gillies was a friend. But he had kept well clear of the struggle against the Act – why? 'Will we see you today at Fortingall, Donald?'

'Fortingall? That is a fair step. I am not –' He stopped and looked round, almost in alarm, at a noise outside the door. His wife Aileen came in with pails of milk, scolding at two little girls for clinging onto her skirt and making her spill.

'Early visitors,' she said with a keen look. 'And I have no water boiled yet for the porridge.'

'We must get on the road at once,' said Cameron, still diplomatic, while Menzies longed for a hot drink.

'Take a bite of cheese with you.' Aileen Gillies was all brisk agreement as she wrapped up some food in a cloth and gave it to them while her husband busied himself with laying the fire. He saw them to the door but when they rode past a minute later, it was already shut.

'Well,' said Cameron, after a silent mile, 'he was a friend before. Or anyway he sold me timber.'

'I blame the woman.' Menzies trotted out his hobby-horse right away. 'Keeping her man under her eye and calling it looking after him.'

'The Weem women have not been behind-hand – they would have stormed Castle Menzies on their own.'

'There is a bit more spirit down our way – more spirit and more cash.'

They remembered this two hours later as they stood on the meadow in front of the big house at Fortingall, waiting for a crowd to gather. Heavy mists mantled the forested slopes behind the village, parted silently to show the crests of trees like seaweed under a tide, then closed again. A few dark tracks criss-crossed the grey dew. Black cattle snuffed and chewed. Little knots of people stood about eyeing each other with an air of wondering why they had come at all. When a larger group came tramping in behind a piper, Cameron and Menzies recognized some stalwarts from Foss on Tummel. They went over to greet them and gather details of the events on Sunday when they were said to have ringed the churchyard and exacted an oath against the Act from all the gentlemen in the congregation. But the latest news was discouraging – they had met few supporters on the road down Keltney, a handful from the far side of Tummel, not a soul from Rannoch.

'Wait till they come down from Glen Lyon.' Menzies was determinedly positive. But they waited, and the roads north and west remained quiet. The grey rocks on the hillsides wore shut faces. The barking of two ravens sounded like syllables in a foreign language. A traveller or two, pedlars and shepherds, were persuaded to join the few hundred who were there by the weight of glowering disapproval from dozens of faces when they showed signs of passing by. But no massed contingents from up Glen Lyon and none from along Loch Tay.

'Has Breadalbane cowed you all with his recruiting and his threats?' Menzies asked a grey-haired man who stood bundled up in his plaid, tall and erect as though he was ready to take root.

'Och well, a terrible lot have gone to the colours, that is true. They get the shilling, and a golden promise, and they think they will come back alive one day.'

'Those who do come back should tell the young men what to expect.'

'You can tell a young man nothing. Thirteen went to the wars in Canada from my village, four came back. And they have had little enough to say. I think they are ashamed.'

The mist was shearing from the hillsides like a fleece, the air lightening and warming. A good drying day. People were moving slowly off to east and west. Cameron and Menzies looked at each other, searching for signs of belief that something could still be made of the occasion. The men from Foss were restive. One of them called across, 'Give us a word, then. Tell them what is in the Act, and what to do.'

With a great qualm mining at him inwardly, Cameron got up on a tree stump and said his piece. The scattered crowd drew closer together and listened quietly, but when he gave his warning about the Riot Act, glances were exchanged, a few grinned openly, and a wit called out, 'They must know the law here – that is why they have all stayed at home.'

There was nothing else to be done. The threads of connection binding the people into a fabric seemed to have thinned to invisibility, the little steadings turned in on themselves like snails in a drought. Cameron and Menzies collected a few names for their lists of contacts – the tall old man, who came from Camusvachan in Glen Lyon, the redhaired MacLennan brothers from Foss. They arranged to come that way again next Sunday and then turned their horses eastwards for the long ride home. Each man was struggling to fill the hollow that had opened inside him, to bridge it over with some kind of reasonable structure while saying nothing about it as though afraid it might crumble if it was exposed to the light.

'Maybe we stretched too far beyond our own place,' Menzies hazarded at last.

This was uncomfortably like Cameron's thought of yesterday and he shrank from admitting it. In any case it was much further up to Tummelside. But the Foss men were famously militant, they had been ever since a young minister with lordly tastes and little scholarship had been foisted on them by the laird twelve years before and they had first boycotted him, then run him down the road on a cart. Cameron sensed Menzies waiting for some words — any words. He roused himself to say, 'Maybe. Yet Atholl is as far, and we have good ties with them. There will be many causes, James – let us not be speculating, and frightening ourselves. Everybody in Strathtay is awake now – they *know*. And that is the first thing. Now we have to convert all this commitment into real results and save the listed men. The rest is just froth if we fail in that.' He had reined his horse to a stop and was searching Menzies' eyes for complete agreement – for more, for energy to carry it out. 'James – when we have rested and supped, we will make a start – do you agree? Near home, in our own place. Will you go to Moness and see the Logans and sound them out about hiding? Get them to think of their own best refuge. And I will see the McCullochs.'

'Two families …' Menzies was wilting under the enormity of the work. 'The army will have them all in barracks before we have saved the first ten men!'

'Wait a bit. Some others – the best ones – Donald the smith, and maybe Iain Logan, the real sterling men – they can join in once we have their agreement. Then our net will grow. Your Allan, too, of course.'

'Allan? He talks like a mill-wheel. We had better tell him nothing.'

It was the second cover-up of the day. Cameron felt the dirtiness of conspiracy seeping into his being. 'He will not become sounder by being mistrusted,' he said sharply. 'Ach, James – he is in your household. You must decide.'

They had built up the fabric in their minds again and could even feel some weary well-being as they neared Weem and saw it sheltering between the steep hills and the flood plain of the Tay. The low lands were patched with hayfields at every stage of readiness, from bleached yellow to ferny green, and across the coloured surfaces people moved as though they were stitching and knitting at its texture, arms pulling on rakes, backs stooped under burdens on their way to the steadings. Far up on the left, above the inn and the cottage row, two other figures moved, blue and white, not haymakers – Jean Bruce and young Donald, walking hand in hand amongst the bents of a neglected field at the furthest point of the McCullochs' holding. For years it had not been worked. A grey building with a sagging roof stood inside a stone enclosure with a wind-blown rowan tree beside it. Its berries glistened red under the burnish of the breeze, which came in uneasy gusts from the south and east. Below them the strath spread its pattern like a map.

'I feel like a bird,' said Jean. She held out her arms and spread her fingers gracefully, pleasuring herself in Donald's admiration. As he looked at her, his face closed over with a faintly embarrassed incredulity.

'A bird?' he chaffed her. 'Are you a hen, then? Or a duck?'

'Donald McCulloch! I am a wild-flying pigeon.'

'Yes, you are a pigeon.' He stopped and turned her towards him and tried to kiss her on the mouth. Over his shoulder she was looking at the derelict house. Should she mention it now? She let him kiss her, his tongue on hers, and then she eased him on across the field, her arm curved closely round his waist. 'Who lived here, Don?' she asked him. They parted a way through the tough bracken that choked the enclosure and their feet found the path to the front door.

'Old Donald's uncle Murdo was here for a while. He was never bothered to marry, or to do anything else very much, they say. He just let the place go. And there is enough easier land for us down-by.'

They bent their heads under the lintel and stepped inside. Dusky light came from the two small front windows between the toothed leaves of nettles. A rent in the old thatch let in a piercing beam of sunlight. Jean held up her hand to it and when it made a bright white spot on her palm, she closed her fingers over it and pretended to give it into Donald's hand, like a delicacy. He laughed and turned away to the hearth. An old kettle with a hole burnt in its bottom lay on its side in a drift of twigs and old mortar. The small earthenware cup of an oil lamp stood in a neuk in the wall with the stub of a candle beside it, stuck in a mess of wax.

'You can think of it with a fire going and a light burning,' Jean said. 'It would be cosy enough.'

'There are plenty peats in the hill behind,' Donald answered. 'Father brought me up here on his back in the spring one year, and I sat in the moor while he and old Donald were digging peats. I fell in the brown water and fouled my frock, and the men never heeded, of course, but there was the devil to pay when we got home at night.'

'Would it take much work to make it sound and tight again?' she asked in a carefully ordinary voice.

'This place? The walls are straight enough. But och, who would want to live here, out of it all, and with a weary hill to climb ...'

'Young folk with a bit of spirit.' He turned, beginning to see her meaning. She took him by the hands and said eagerly, 'Don – *we* could live here – it is right for us – would you like that, Don?'

'What?' He laughed incredulously. 'We will live with mother and old Donald – you know that.'

Her whole face drooped and she blushed with chagrin. 'I think you want that, living under their feet, and their scolding and groaning. Why do you not want our own place?'

'Because we have a good house already, with the new beds and windows. There is a year of my work in it.' He looked mulish now, with his hard-eyed expression that she dreaded, that seemed to treat her as nothing.

'It is not ours, Donald. This could be ours. Think of it with the garden cleared and new fruit-trees put in –'

'They would never take up here. Look at the lean of the rowan.'

'Och well, berry bushes will grow well enough behind the wall. And stock will graze down that tough grass and sweeten it again.' She brought out her trump card: 'If we bring this into use, it will raise the value of your holding, and that will please your mother.'

'And if we raise its value, then Robert Menzies will raise our rent.' They looked squarely and intently at each other for a full minute, as blankly as strangers, trying each other for traces of concession or agreement or affection, even. Outside at the back a curlew piped, a lonely single sound, and among the weeds of the garden sparrows cheeped and quarrelled in shrill bursts of noise.

Cameron stepped between the stunted apple-trees and knocked on the McCullochs' new front door. No sound from inside. He stood for a minute, appraising the close-fitted timbers and sleek varnish, then knocked again.

'Who is there?' Mary's voice. It had a frantic note.

'Angus Cameron.'

'Oh –' Her voice seemed to choke. He went in doubtingly. Mary was kneeling with her head and shoulders inside the dark cave of a box-bed. She turned and Cameron saw, under her arm, old Donald's face, eyes staring fixedly, his mouth drooping at one side, a shine of saliva on his chin.

'Mary – what is ado?'

'Father has – Father has – oh, he is very ill, it took him yesterday.' She drew in a great sharp breath which shook her shoulders, then wiped the old man's chin with a cloth.

'Has Donald gone for a doctor?'

'I sent him yesterday. The man from Dunkeld will come today or tomorrow – if he thinks it is worth his trouble.'

'I missed Donald at Fortingall. Is it a fit?'

'A fit of some kind. His right side has gone. Oh Angus – has the trouble turned his brain?'

'No, why? There is nothing desperate going on. It would be worse if the army –' But it was no time to be arguing. Was it right even to burden the family with his plan? To do nothing might be worse – Allan had greeted them at the house with the news (fresh from the great oven of rumour, the widow Duff's at Ballinluig) that a file of English soldiers had ridden out from Perth. 'Mary,' he said carefully, 'you have your own troubles now. I just wanted a wee word with Donald. Is he out at the back?'

'I sent him into the hay. We must bring it in whatever else.' Her voice sounded mechanical as though she were drawing a shutter across her pains and fears. 'Co on through and see him if you must.'

She turned back into the bed as a sound came from old Donald's mouth.

In the narrow field that sloped upwards at the back between scrubby thickets Donald's rake lay with its teeth in a swathe. Most of the field was still quilted with cut hay. It had been so dry that two days under the warm sun had been enough without letting it stand in stooks or draping it on the hedges. Now it could go straight to the byre. Cameron looked round the neighbouring fields, some shorn close and yellow, some still fledged with feathery grass and sparkling with daisies and buttercups. It was close here – midges crawled on his forehead under his fringe – abstractedly he took the handle of the rake and rumpled it lightly across the nearest hay, turning it over. The green of it was bleached through and through, Perhaps he should stay till Donald reappeared, help him clear the field and talk as they worked?

Up at the old house, Donald kicked the kettle in a spasm of impatience and said angrily to Jean, 'Why are you putting me in a vice? You know that I have to work the land down there. The old man will never be good for much now.'

'You could work it and live here, Don – why are you angry?'

'You know why – I am the man of that house since my father … Why should we not live there?'

'Under your mother's eye?' Jean was suddenly shrill with frustration. 'And her thumb. Alex McLaggan and Mary have their own roof at Grandtully, even if it is next door to his father. I want to live with *you*, Donald, not with your old folk. What do *you* want – me or them?'

'That is a trap.' Donald had his brow lowered now like a bullock and his eyes were hot. 'Why am I here at all? I would be better off in Canada, free of all these tethers.' He flung out of the door, crushed through the bracken, and strode down the hill at his fastest pace. She ran after him, calling his name.

Cameron raked on for half an hour, making loose heaps up the middle of the field. Once a dark toad clambered away towards the little burn at the side of the field. It must have been lucky to escape the sickles, he mused, as he watched its clumsy struggling across the cut stalks. Invisible grasshoppers were churring like little birds. When Mary came out, she found him standing still with his back to the sun, looking down the river towards the shady woodlands round Grandtully. He had started out to make a rough count of the houses to be visited and then let his thoughts drift into a reverie of his own old home, the far tropical look of the mountain skyline beyond Loch Arkaig on the rare hot days.

'Where is the boy gone?' her voice broke in sharply.

'His rake was here – no other sign of him.'

'Gone after his girl. Look at that queer sky. If a thunder-plump comes, we will lose this good grass.' He gave her the rake and she went vigorously at the hay while he plaited a grass rope to put round a burden and heft it down to the byre.

'Once the harvest is in, Mary' – he put his question abruptly – 'could you manage here in spite of old Donald's ailment – I mean, if Donald was away?'

'Away? The soldiers will get nobody from here. We will be meeting them with a hail of stones if they show their faces.'

'Stones against guns, Mary? It is all supposition; the gentry may have swung the government against the Act by now. But just suppose – if they do send in dragoons with guns to take the men away – we are helpless, then, you know we are. So let us think of that.' He paused. 'If a deadly beast was coming for you, what would you do? Fight or hide?'

'Hide.' She was looking at him questioningly but he could see she had caught his drift. 'You believe the listed lads should hide?'

'Perhaps we should try it.' Now it was out, it seemed hare-brained. 'Do you think we could feed them if they were in refuges in the woods and the back glens?'

'Of course we could. We know the country, and there is a lot of it.'

'But the redcoats are good hunters. In 'Forty-six they spared nothing.'

'There is a war on now. If we do it right, we can engage more soldiers than they would gain if they caught the lot.'

'Mary – you should have been in the government.'

'Oh aye. And I would not have made the war in the first place.'

Feet sounded on the slope above the field and Donald came into sight, Jean close behind him, her face fiery. Donald grabbed the rake from his mother and began to ply it hard, bouncing its teeth on the parched ground under the stalks. Mary said hullo to Jean and then gave her son a shrewd look. Feeling out of place, Cameron laid his rope on the ground, bundled a mass of hay onto it, and began to make a slip-knot round it. Dry herb smells filled his nostrils. Now the whole family was here, he must broach the scheme and work out the details of at least one refuge. Was young Donald sound enough to be sent to contact other families?

'Donald and Jean,' he said, and waited till he had their attention. 'Here is a secret matter, and it is a mortal secret. We are thinking that the listed men must each have a refuge ready, if this Act is not withdrawn. Where they can lie low. Donald – it is your decision. What do you say?'

'A refuge?' His voice was barbed with irony. 'A cave? A desert island?'

Cameron deflected the jeer. 'A cave can be a trap. But there are other kinds of shelter. Would you lie low, if it came to it?'

'And skulk like a fox? Until I starved? We never reckoned with this when we went and trounced the lairds!'

'We have to think ahead now,' Cameron began, but Donald was staring at him like an enemy. Then he threw his rake down, took two paces across the field, and spoke into his mother's face.

'I suppose you agree with this? To keep me on a string? I will never do it. There is more freedom in Canada and that is where I will go. Jean agrees.'

'I never –' the girl started to say. Mary's fury forestalled her.

'You say that – with your grandfather drooling in his bed! And your friends threatened with the press-gang! And your father –'

'My father? He got out of here, though it was to the colours. Maybe the place is too narrow, that we all want to leave it.'

Jean was clinging onto his arm, as though to stop him inflicting more hurt. As Mary looked at the couple, the fire seemed to die in her. She turned to Cameron in a little movement of appeal.

'They will do what they like,' she said to him. 'The soldiers will come for him and they will be sitting here, dreaming about Ontario.'

CHAPTER 11

The Ride

The thunder broke not long after sunset, as Cameron and Menzies sat with a jug of wine, reckoning up the day's gains and setbacks. Iain and Alastair Logan had agreed at once that Alastair must go into hiding. At first they assumed that he could find a place among the steep woods behind Camserney and be supplied by their good friends Donald and Aileen Gillies at the mill. Menzies squashed this with his news of how cool the Gillieses had been in the morning.

'Sheep and goats now, eh?' said Iain in his tight-lipped way. 'All right, then – Alastair can go up through the Glen of the Birks and use the old byre below Urlar. The Urlar folk will neither help nor hinder – you know how close they are.'

After that Menzies had walked along the hill to Duntaylor and Dunacree (leaving out the lonely man at Dunskiag with his terrifying dogs). Both these families had sons of about twenty, both had been in the crowd that won the signature from Menzies of Bolfracks. They saw the sense of the plan and agreed to find refuges for the boys in the thick forest between Bolfracks and Kenmore.

'It was dry work,' Menzies summed up, 'so I came back then for some refreshment. It must be like this for a minister paying his visits. No wonder they like a dram at every house.'

Outside the thunder grumbled; it sounded pent up, unable to discharge itself. Cameron found himself saddened and frustrated by the episode at the McCullochs' – it brought the dilemma of the movement to a point. The real, mortal urgency of the situation could erode and trickle away like powder under the crush of people's domestic troubles. Which they were used to. Which were always there and would outlast even the war. But so many would not come back from the war. They seemed to realize that always too late – when it had happened. He had a vision of the people of the country, walking and walking in endless droves, like pilgrims, across a battlefield shaken by the explosions of guns; and as the smoke blew into their eyes, the people turned, desperate to see their homes again, but behind them a great dark channel had opened, with torn precipitous sides, and there was no way back … The thunder thumped from some nearer point, the glass vibrated in the window, and Cameron came out of his doze to find Menzies grinning quizzically at him and offering him some more claret.

He shook his head. 'I will sleep without that tonight. Today went on forever. Like yesterday. Will we plan tomorrow's work in the morning?'

'I thought you would have to go to the mill?'

'Aye, but with luck we will do little there. No planks for the flooring yet, and if it is raining we cannot be on the roof. Maybe we can talk quietly to a few of the men – one of the masons from Ballechin has a son who must be twenty.'

Cameron slept instantly, and woke and dreamed and woke and dreamed for hours – the river, the cold shock of the water between his legs, the glimmer of light on the far shore, the current filling his mouth, he swam against it, it helped him, he struck out as smoothly as a seal, skimming effortlessly, he could power onwards forever, the water buoying him, his hand stroking it easily backwards without a splash … I have never swum in my life, he thought, as he lay wakefully at dawn.

Rain dripped outside, drummed heavily, then slackened again. He went over the Tay to Aberfeldy more to keep Flemyng quiet than with any hope of working. The masons were busy with their mallets and chisels inside a makeshift hut on the site and it was easy to talk to them privately. They had worked together for several years and the elder of them readily agreed to help supply the other's son if he went into hiding in the woods above Eastertyre. Both men were dubious about how long someone would be able to endure in the winter; equally they could think of no alternative.

'Do you think,' the elder man wondered, his face as grey as his hair with stone-dust, 'that the generals really want to go into the war with an army of pressed men?'

'It is hard to put yourself in the mind of a general,' Cameron answered. 'But they seem to trust in the power of the nine-tailed whip, and they will continue in that until a regiment breaks out of its barracks and makes its own way home.' The masons smiled at his fancy and went on with their work.

The day passed. Few men turned up for work – no Sandy McGlashan, and no Donald McCulloch of course. Cameron wondered if it would be possible to raise the matter with him again, and bring him into a more realistic frame of mind, before the soldiers came. If they came. During the afternoon, while he sat idly chatting to a few men in the masons' lean-to, James Menzies arrived, his brown horse soaked black. He looked full of himself but Cameron steered him across the street into the privacy of his store before he would let him talk.

'Why bother to be secret?' Menzies asked. 'There is that much talk about hiding and plotting down Grandtully anyway – '

'What! Has that mad Duke been blethering? I said to be chary of the McLaggans – '

'No no, there is no harm really. Only I went to Donald Stewart's smithy and Mary was there, chatting to her mother, so by the time I had fixed things up with Donald and went along to Grandtully to explain the plan to Alex, Mary had already gone back and told him. Ah, young love – she was sitting with her arm round him, crying silently. She looked like Kirsty when I first went off to Bengal – ' Menzies stopped, his own eyes watering, while Cameron let his temper sink back to normal after the gratuitous alarm.

'What does the Duke say, then?'

'Oh, he was not at home. He is off on a stravaig past Atholl, looking for cheap horses. Alex will tell him tonight. No' – he forestalled Cameron's objection – 'you know as well as I do, Angus, the Duke is daft but he is clever, and he has an entry to every house from Atholl to Dunkeld. We cannot do without his cunning, or his tinker friends. And if his own son has to take to the hills – '

'Yes, well – is Alex sound, then?'

'He is, he sees the sense in hiding. But he scarcely thinks it will come to that.'

'He means he wants to stay in bed with Mary.'

'Of course he does, but he knows the score. He and his brother are going to organize the soundest folk among their cousins and get the word to the boys on the other side from Pitnacree up to Cluny. It is good work, this, Angus, it is bringing the thing home to plenty folk who have only been in it for the furore so far, for the chance to squeeze their girls in the crowd and all that kind of thing. Even if they do not have to hide, they will be like lieutenants to us now – '

'So long as we are not like generals to them.' Cameron shuddered inwardly, remembering his vision of the evening before and his exchange with the masons just now.

'Well, sometimes a lead is necessary. Think of these last few days. Who else has been planning anything, or thinking ahead at all? A few at Foss – one or two at Kenmore. We cannot be like Red Indians, sitting in a circle and acting as one man.'

'Do you think we have lost that forever?'

Menzies looked at him in astonishment, then took his flask from his hip pocket and offered him a dram. 'You will be saying next that that is what they are doing in France. Easy on the whisky – there is not much left after the great crack we had at the McLaggans'.'

Typical James, thought Cameron, as he handed back the flask and looked at his friend's flushed face: we are plotting to save our lives and he turns it into a holiday. He looked round the cool gloom of the store, rows of small barrels and big jars clad in wicker, standing on shelves and on the floor, inside thick windowless walls. Like some fantastic prison, where you could drink so deeply and so long that you forgot your bondage. They went home at the end of the afternoon, just as the cloud slid back like a shutter and let clear yellow light stream along the valley from the west. The evening was spent uncomfortably, biting back remarks that might have let the hiding plan slip out prematurely to Allan Stewart.

James Menzies woke abruptly. Still dark. A scratching at the window. Like a claw. A rose-tree branch? Too regular. He got up into the chilly darkness and went to look. A spectre with a shock of wild black hair – the pedlar, John Stewart the pedlar. He had not been seen since Castle Menzies. They had missed his flute at the wedding. He mouthed and gesticulated – what did he mean? Menzies gestured towards the front door and went through to draw the bolt. Stewart came in sweating and gasping, almost too desperate to form words.

'Soldiers – on the road from Tummel – at Keltney, nearly – '
'How many?'
'Eighteen. An officer. And a bigwig, a stranger.'
'Riding?'
'All of them.'
'Who are they?'

'Who? Blue coats – black helmets. I will go and – '

'Wait, John. We must know their weapons and – '

'There are other folk to tell!' Stewart was suddenly violent, he backed away from Menzies, came up against the door, turned, and was gone. A pony's hooves rattled on the road outside.

Twenty mounted men! With swords? How many guns? They *might* turn west along the strath and not … Menzies struggled to stop the racing of his mind and sort out the options coolly. The damp wind blowing in at the open door made him shiver and he went to wake the others. In a minute the three of them were huddled in cloaks, by the light of two candles and the last glow of the embers, trying to think quickly.

'They may be making for Kenmore.' Menzies was staving off their fears.

'Why come that way?' Cameron objected. 'Soldiers from Stirling would have come by Crieff and Amulree, or if it is the Perth lot, then by Dunkeld and the lower strath.'

'To avoid the strath – they must know it is all ours.'

'Then who is the big-wig? Did John Stewart not name him?'

'He ran off before I asked.'

'You should have – Well, he is gone now … Some law agent? James – they are coming for us.'

'I said they would – I said we should find our own refuge!'

'And skimp the other work? Allan – how long do you give them?'

Allan Stewart had been itching to speak. 'How long? Oh – five miles – half an hour if they mean business … Come on, let us load and prime the fowling guns.'

'Why, Allan?' Cameron asked soberly.

'To keep them off – to defend ourselves!' His blue eyes had fired up with excitement.

'Allan!' Cameron was sincerely amused – he found himself weirdly untroubled, as though he was watching a fantasy unfolding in which he was barely implicated. 'They would break in in a trice, while you were putting fresh shot in your fowling gun, and cut us into mincemeat. If we have half an hour, the first thing is to burn the lists. And the petitions.'

'And destroy the work?' Allan Stewart was appalled.

'The work is destroyed already – if they are coming for us.'

'But there is no offence in the petitions.'

'We have committed no offence! But still they are after us! What do the petitions do but name many thousands of folk? The government could pick up anyone they wanted and prosecute at their leisure, if we made them a present of all those names. James – do you agree?'

'Act', burn the lot – burn the house.' Menzies had slumped suddenly. He was looking into vacancy with dull eyes.

'James!' Cameron wanted to bring him round. But there was time now for nothing but actions. Without another word the three of them dressed and then, by the small yellow light of the candles, they opened the strong-box and fed the many leaves of paper one by one into the embers. Flames lit up, for a moment, the soot-flowers trembling in the flue. Black layers curled and then collapsed. Cameron and Menzies looked at each other, their eyes gutted of all expression. Allan Stewart went to the door.

'I will get horses now.' He was looking at them as though they were ill or crazed.

'To run off? Why?'

'Angus!' Stewart strode over and seized Cameron by the front of his cloak. 'You have only minutes now!'

'No. You go if you like – you should go.'

'Come on, Angus!' The man had scarcely heard him. Cameron turned to face Menzies.

'James – I am for staying here – do you agree?'

'Let Allan get the horses.' Menzies' voice was low and automatic.

'James – I say we stay. Flight is guilty. If we stay, we can defend ourselves,'

'With the guns?'

'With arguments.' Cameron felt the frailty of the position as he spoke. 'We could not incriminate the others – well, at least their names are safe now. But we will speak up for ourselves.'

'Och, we are doomed now.'

A thudding outside, which they felt with their feet before they heard it. A flurry of bangs hit the door and before Allan Stewart could shoot back the bolt gun-butts had burst through the timbers, the bolt and its socket tore the jamb away, and soldiers in blue coats and white breeches were stepping in across the wreckage. More bangs from the rear of the house, the door through to the kitchen slammed back against the wall, the room filled with soldiers, and in the wrecked doorway a tall, slim officer was making a small ceremony of ushering in a man with long grey hair and a black coat.

'Sheriff Chalmers,' said the officer in a clear London voice, 'your men, I believe.'

'Angus Cameron?' asked the sheriff. He took a folded document from his pocket and looked at it. 'Is this James Menzies?' He looked at Allan Stewart. 'Or – ?'

Menzies stood up very straight and arranged his clothes. 'I am James Menzies, owner of this place, and I demand to know your business.'

Sheriff Chalmers eyed him sourly. 'I think you know the "business". I am to arrest you, and Mr Cameron, on charges arising from the mobbing and sundry other disturbances in this district. You will be examined in Perth, with a view to preferring formal charges. Captain Colberg – will you proceed with the prisoners, while I search these premises for evidence? I will follow on presently, with Constable Thomson from Pitnacree.'

'I wish you would remain under the protection of my men. But I must be guided by you, sire' His voice changed abruptly. By twos – right about – *march!*'

Cameron and Menzies found themselves moving out of the door in a file of soldiers whose feet were already walking in step. Allan Stewart's mouth was open, his eyes big with accusation. In the darkness horses loomed. A squeak and trundle of wheels – the post-chaise from the inn. Cameron and Menzies felt themselves half-lifted inside by the arms. Then they were rocking past the shut faces of the village houses towards the black thickets down the river.

In the gloaming before sunrise they saw each other's features as pale apparitions. They clasped hands and held them clasped for a time. Tension choked them: they could feel it rising up their throats, threatening to swamp their brains. They wanted to pass it off through words – none would come. Outside, shapes began to materialize – heads, implements – they wanted to recognize friends but they could see nothing but shawls, cloaks, silhouettes. The muzzle of a gun poked up – would they be caught in crossfire? The tines of a fork rattled on the glass of the little window, a face stared in just inches away, they recognized Donald McCulloch before he whisked backwards out of sight. The panel splintered above Cameron's head, the tip of a scytheblade broke through, shone for a moment, disappeared. Nightmare was rising round them. They heard Angus's name shouted out – 'Cameron! Cameron! Fight for Cameron!' Normality flowed into them again, their neighbourhood was out there, friends and fellows, the animals grazing in the fields, the hens roosting in their houses, chimneys and hearths and beds, from all the steadings the people were coming now and would save them.

The glossy black haunch of a horse rubbed against the window. Colberg's voice: 'Cameron! Menzies! You have brought this on your own heads. My troopers may not manage to hold back from firing now. Tell these people to go *home!*'

Cameron and Menzies looked at each other – 'tell these people'! Cameron shot down the little casement of the window and roared out in his own language, with the whole strength of his voice, 'We are here, friends! Stay with us now! Get word to the McLaggans!'

Colberg was still there, fuming. 'Send them *home*! We shall not fire first. But if your men attack we shall mow them down. There are women here, you know.'

Mary McCulloch, Cameron thought, and big Mary and Aileen Stewart and her Mary, and the McLaggan girls – they are all with us. The sun must have cleared the hill beyond Grandtully, its light showed them weapons bristling above a river of faces, small boys with cudgels, women with stockingsful of stones and shards, men with shot-guns and blades set in poles. A horse-rider towered amongst them, forcing against them like a rock in a torrent. Cameron recognized Hope Steuart of Ballechin.

'Captain Colberg!' He was shouting in English. 'A thousand people have blocked Grandtully bridge. They say they will have the prisoners or they'll cut you down.'

'I shall fire if I have to' – the captain's carrying voice.

'Cameron! Menzies!' Hope Steuart's voice. 'You must tell your people – tell them you are going voluntarily – there is bloodshed threatening here.'

'We will not say that!' Cameron's voice shouted back. 'We are arrested for resisting government – our people know – '

'Your people will be cut down…' Steuart's voice diminished as the mass of people blocked his way and the coach forged ahead.

Colberg's voice: 'Load your pistols. No shots until ordered. Coachman – halt. Sergeant Collier – rein in here. Stand with the men. I shall speak to the people at the bridgehead.'

Against the broad yellow light Cameron and Menzies could see the officer in silhouette, walking his horse forwards to meet a crowd in the road where it levelled out after the sharp rise from the bridge across to Grandtully. People flowed round him, shouting. A hush – he was talking

– Cameron and Menzies strained to hear but caught only his tone, several notes lower than his sharp pitch of command. He laughed. He leaned down from the saddle, took off his glove, held out his hand to the spokesman nearest him – Alex McLaggan (where was the Duke?). And Alex was accepting the hand-clasp – Cameron and Menzies were rising from the bench to shout a warning, a plea – the coach jerked under them, flinging them backwards, their heads banged on the panelling, they were pounding down the hill towards the crowd, Colberg's voice yelling 'At them! at them!', people reeling away on both sides, jumping onto the parapet, a woman screaming, a red wound slashed along her brow. The coach tore onwards, lurching and jumping. They were jounced mercilessly on the narrow fitted bench. Brilliant light dazzled in at the left-hand window as they swept past Balnaguard, Balmacneil, Kinnaird. Low thatched houses crouched between hill and riverbank. Their minds reeled, sickness churned as they struggled to save themselves from injury. We should have run for it. We should have run for it. We should have run for it. The words dinned in Cameron's head. They taunted him like a rope dangling just out of reach. We should have run for it. To undo this moment – to force time backwards – to be again at the moment of choice back at the house … Futile. Defeat entered him like a heart attack, stunning the centre of his system. He looked at James, wanting to speak and hear – nothing would come. Menzies was crouching back on the bench, his legs braced, like a cornered hare frozen in a last effort to baffle the enemy. Now they were rattling between the massive oaks of Glenvinean. Across the river the tiled roofs of Dunkeld looked warm and homely, like a picture from another world.

'Steady now' – Colberg's voice. 'We shall bait at Inver inn and I shall cross the ferry for fresh horses. Sergeant Collier – the prisoners may refresh themselves.'

The party was drawing up with a jingle and a grinding of hooves on a cobbled forecourt. Three sides of a square surrounded them with high walls and rows of windows. Cameron and Menzies stepped down, staggered, and were supported into the inn. In a brown-panelled room smelling of tobacco they sat on opposite sides of a cold hearth full of cinders, swallowing hot wine and water under the blue eyes of Sergeant Collier, who was looking at them with intent curiosity like a man staring at a two-headed dog in a freak show.

'If only they had saved us. They should have held solid at the bridge.'

'If they had, the troopers would have had their heads off.'

'But *they* were armed! Donald Stewart owns three guns' – Menzies spoke in a pressing whisper – 'there were spears there, and pikes – '

'Who wins a battle – professionals or enthusiasts?'

'A thousand of us could have swamped them.'

'At a cost.'

'There is always a cost.'

Shouts came in a chorus from outside. Four troopers had them by the arms and were hustling them out into the coach. A horse whinnied and reared; the troop trotted quickly out of the inn yard towards the high road; Colberg rode up as hundreds of people – women, children, men – ran out of the woods along the riverbank upstream. A sharp shout of command – twelve troopers ranged themselves across the road. The people had stopped in their tracks, women were making their children stand behind them. Three men stepped forward to meet Colberg: Donald Stewart, a gun across his arm, Donald McLaggan, holding a shaft with a curved blade at its end, and someone unknown to Cameron and Menzies, also with a gun. Colberg drew his sabre slowly and held it sloped on his shoulder. He looked elegant, as though presenting arms in some courtly ritual.

'Hand over Cameron!' Donald McLaggan was speaking in a loud high voice, for their own benefit, they guessed. 'Hand over Angus Cameron and James Menzies! You have seized them for no crime at all. Or if you keep them, there are four hundred of us here and two thousand on their way, and we will cut you down to a man.'

Again Colberg used his casual voice. 'Come, sir, my charges have only to give bail against their appearance at the Assize Court. They'll be with you again in a day or two, if you don't hold us up. Come now, be reasonable.'

McLaggan shouted louder than before. 'Surrender Cameron and Menzies or the whole country will be fired!'

Donald Stewart was speaking to Colberg: 'What is the charge? You have taken away innocent men. We must know the charge.'

'That's a legal matter, it will all arrange itself presently,' Colberg answered on a light note of reassurance. His voice rose suddenly: 'By twos – to the right about – *march*!' The Grandtully men were looking thunderstruck. Cameron saw Donald half turn to the crowd, then swing back round and raise his gun, The coach wrenched forwards, the spurred boot of the trooper next them stabbed at his horse's side, blood spurted and red drops hit the window. The gables and chimneys of Dunkeld slewed out of sight, a hill bristling with trees reared steeply above them, sunlight glanced from rapids in the river. Then they were plunging into shadow between the woods of Birnam, hauled along like a leaf on a mill-race, and the hedges and trees never ceased to rock backwards past their staring eyes or the horses to gallop onwards with shoulders working and manes streaming until they were in sight of Perth. By then Cameron's mind was rousing itself from shock, there were many things he wanted to say to James, but the moment they stepped down under the massive archway of the prison they were hustled in opposite directions. There was a stench of urine, like a foul byre. The last Menzies saw of him was his head turning, his mouth uttering inaudible words, as a heavy door ground backwards and then slammed shut.

CHAPTER 12

The Prison

The gaoler who usually dealt with Cameron was called Jamie – he called himself Jamie, like a little boy who has not long learned to speak. One of his eyes squinted outwards, he looked massively strong, he always edged in sideways, moving the heavy door with his right shoulder. He seemed friendly: one day he sat down on Cameron's pallet bed, looking sheepish. A choking smell of pig-offal and old sweat came from him. He hugged Cameron and said, 'Mister Campsie, Mister Campsie' – his voice cooed on a high note, not his at all, as though he was possessed by the spirit of a woman who had nursed him once. Slaver ran down from a corner of his mouth. He seemed to fall asleep, leaning heavily onto Cameron. He could hardly ease himself free from the great stinking weight.

The day after, Jamie came in with the wooden dish of porridge, held it out to Cameron, then twitched it away when he reached for it and turned it upside down. The grey mass fell onto the flagstones. Jamie backed away, laughing, and slammed the door shut behind him.

The mess lay there for two days. Luckily the flies had gone by now. At night there was frost. In the morning white rime coated the sill of the barred window-space.

It would be better, it might even be bearable, if only he knew what had become of James. Had they left him in Perth, to keep the two of them well separate? Yet Edinburgh was presumably safer, if the government was still worried about the turbulence of the Strath Tay people. (Was it, though? Perhaps by now they had been totally cowed.)

One morning Jamie conducted him down two flights of stairs and into a long high apartment, like a baronial hall. Shabby men were walking about, in ones and twos. At once Cameron was looking in every face, craving familiar features. There were none. After a time he nerved himself to say to a couple of youngish men, 'Have you heard at all about a man called Menzies? James Menzies?'

They looked derisive. 'Haff you heard at aal apout a maan caald Menzies?' one asked the other in a broad parody of the Gaelic accent.

'Ach, they're all called Menzies in here,' his friend replied.

'Aye, that's it,' said the other. 'A bad lot, the Menzieses.' The men laughed in Cameron's face and they both turned away.

At an early stage he worked out that the cell faced west. Direct light came onto the sill and jambs of the embrasure at about the time when the noises of wheels and voices from the street were at their loudest. As they quietened, the sun-colours on the stone yellowed, oranged, reddened. After dark, drunken shouts, merry and angry, echoed up from the street. Once a man sang with a little laugh in his voice,

> 'She pit aff her petticoat
> An' I pit aff my sark
> An' we sweatit at the yokie
> As we pleughed the muckle park.'

The refrain tailed off down the street:

> 'Hi-dum-do, turn-a-hi dum-day,
> Hi-dum-do ...'

He hated the dirt; he wanted to touch nothing; he lay on his side, trying not to let his ribs come against the inside of his shirt or his hand touch the blanket. He breathed through his mouth to try and not smell the fungus smell from his crutch. Fiery itches tormented him – in his arse, below his armpits and inside his thighs where the fleas had bitten most.

A big-wig came to examine him. 'Cameron – you are required below to give evidence before the Lord Advocate's officers.'

He lay and stared at the wall.

'Cameron! You are to come now.'

He concentrated on positioning his shoulder so that it was in a cave formed by a fold of the stiff, harsh blanket, untouched by it.

'It is an offence, Cameron, to withhold information required in a due process of law.'

He addressed the wall. 'I will speak to you again when I am clean.'

Shoes scuffed the flagstones. The door clunked shut. He focused again on the patterns made by damp and mould on a patch of distempered mortar level with his eyes – piece of coastline seen from a hill, headlands enclosing a bay with a wide curve. As the light failed, it came to look like the mysterious seas on the moon.

He dreamed that he was amongst dark waters, on a mudbank just above the surface. Faces appeared, water streaming from their eye-sockets. He forced them back and down and in, his fingers slipping on their cheeks and brows; they turned into mud, shiny and viscous.

He knew he must have betrayed someone. But what had he done? Or left undone? The petitions and lists – there was the weakness! They had not crushed the ashes in the hearth, the ink would still show up the name, if that sheriff had thought to look! And the strongbox! Could he be sure they had emptied it of its last sheet? He tried to visualize its brown wooden bottom – he could not – there must still have been at least one sheet there. Would he ever know which friends and fellows he had delivered over to the government in that one fatally careless moment?

Jamie began to let him out daily, down three flights of stairs to a yard where buckets of water stood beside a drain. He could sluice himself, shuddering, take off his clothes and scrub them on a stone kerb, then hang them one by one out of the window. They dried slowly.

No doubt this 'concession' was to soften him up for the next examination. Unnerved by his betrayal nightmare, he wanted more desperately than ever to escape and flee. One moment of confusion and he might give someone away, or incriminate himself.

After bringing in the evening meal one night (some ribs of mutton with a jacket potato – they were softening him up), Jamie left the door unlocked. Cameron chewed slowly. His gums were aching. He eyed the door, expecting the handle to turn or a key to rattle in the lock. It was perfectly quiet (no sounds ever reached him from the rest of the Tolbooth; it was hard to believe that it existed, the street below was more real). He put the platter on the floor and got up stiffly. He put on his cloak and padded over to the door. Tried the handle delicately. It turned. He pulled. The door opened. He looked out, The corridor dusky. Empty. He padded past the other cell doors and reached the door at the end of the corridor – massive, clenched together with square-headed nails. He grasped its iron ring-handle and pulled confidently. The door did not budge. He wrenched in a spasm of desperation and tore a fingernail. The door was as rooted in the wall as a pine-tree in the ground. Heartburn rose in his throat, tears in his eyes.

He turned back down the corridor, which was now as dark as a catacomb. Were the other cells unlocked? He tried a door. It gave. The cell inside was empty. So was the next one. And the next. Hollow cubes drained of all life, movement, noise. They might have been like this for three centuries, and could be for three centuries more. Sucking his torn finger-end, he went into the cell next his own and sat on the floor, his back against the wall, looking at the scraps of scratched lettering on the distemper opposite him.

LAT THAIM SAY – what did that mean? ALEX^R FRASER. 1746. JN OGILVY 1694 – he would not write ANGUS CAMERON in his cell, it would be like leaving a vital part of himself here forever. Lower down the wall, an unfinished sentence: PRINCE WAS. Lower still a woman's name, with green mould edging up to cover it: ANNE – BELOVED.

Perhaps his worst betrayal had been nothing to do with unburnt papers, it had been whatever he had conceded, or let slip, or left ambiguous, at the second long examination after arriving in Edinburgh. Three big-wigs; two clerks at one side, scratching continuously with their pens. Yes, he was aware of the provisions of the Riot Act. No, he had never 'flouted' it; on the contrary, he had repeatedly counselled meeting in forty-nines at the most. No, they had not 'intimidated' the proprietors, they had urged them to sign documents pledging themselves to appeal to government to rescind the Act. 'Urged'? Yes, urged. By a show of force? By reasoned arguments concerning the hardship it would bring upon the district if some hundreds of the most able-bodied young men had to go.

'Mr Cameron, are you suggesting that your repeated speeches – and mind, we have abundant eye-witness testimony concerning them – contained no word about the *driving out* of proprietors? Or of ministers and teachers? Or the desirability of a republican form of government?'

'Not at all – I was concerned with one thing only, this Act and the difficulties and sufferings it entails, that kind of thing.'

' "Kind of thing"? Be exact.'

'The numbers of men who might be taken. The likelihood of their serving at home or oversea –

'Were you not aware of the government's express assurance on the latter point?'

'Oh – a crisis, a set-back in the war, could surely force the government to send more men to France or elsewhere.'

'Given the known sympathies of yourself and your associates with the "republic" in France, you would clearly be eager to counsel young men against warring with that country – '

' "Associates"? I have friends – '

'You are fencing. We know very well that during your time in Glasgow you became familiar with the secret and unlawful society styling itself the "United Scotsmen". It would be convenient to know the extent of its following in Perth.' Pause. 'And Mr Cameron – it might be convenient for you as well.'

'If I could tell you…'

'Yes?'

'I would not tell you if I could. I will never name any "associate" – any friend or fellow of mine.'

'We are not asking for names, Mr Cameron. Did I ask for names? General evidence of the activities of that society would be quite sufficient for the time being.' Pause. 'The present charges against you are not immutable. If you are reasonable, we shall be too.'

Had he struck a bargain, or seemed to have? He spent many hours of darkness, sweating lightly in spite of the autumn and early winter cold, wishing some of his replies unsaid, and wishing above all that he had said *anything at all* after the examiner's last remark. His silence must have seemed like complicity. Now they expected information from him. When he turned out to have nothing to give, how would they punish him? As for their hint of a concession, he hated the thought of that loophole being closed. And hated himself for depending on it. The conflicting thoughts gnawed at his mind like wasps at a timber.

In the meantime the meat continued in the evenings.

Who, if anyone, had been the spies? On the very day after his arrival in the Tolbooth, the Lord Advocate's officers already knew the name, the trade, and the movements of several people (the Duke, Iain Logan, young Donald McCulloch). To think of a traitor amongst their own people lacerated him as much as the thought of Iain or Donald lying in some cell. But someone must have been slipping amongst them like a stoat, noting, memorizing, carrying word stealthily to the Duke of Atholl. James had said that John Stewart the pedlar had seemed frantic that night – more so than the emergency warranted? It was true he was footloose, and unmarried. And he had not been seen for some days. But surely, if he had been spying, he would have had to continue coming to all the meetings?

There was no end to such supposings – he shook his head like a dog with a bad ear, trying to rid himself of these crawling thoughts. Sandy McGlashan – why had he been off work that Tuesday? He was notoriously avid for every shilling he could earn. And he had seemed almost to be currying favour when he was tumbling out the story of his family's lost lease, trying to get Cameron to agree that the lairds were done for now. Cameron thought of the wee man's rubbery face, his busy scurrying movements – his compulsive drinking. He must have needed money badly for that ... No – stop – this was a cancer of mistrust, spreading through him, eating him. *They* implant this. *They* keep us poor, till we are desperate for bribes. But why is one man open to a bribe, while another is utterly staunch?

His neck and shoulders gradually became so stiff that he had to turn in one piece from the waist up. When he got up in the morning, his ankles felt rickety. But he made himself walk to and fro a hundred times, slowly at first, then more briskly, to keep up some sense of health.

One morning big dry snowflakes starred the rime on the sill. The sky never seemed to wake up and about the middle of the day it darkened. More flakes sifted down like meal, sifted and sifted, drifting in at the embrasure and lying on the flagstones, unmelting. When Jamie came in with the food at gloaming, Cameron asked him for another blanket.

'Naaa,' Jamie said on a coyly taunting note, 'naaa, I winna.' He went out, slamming the door. Later that night he brought a ragged brown blanket. It smelled of horses.

Time was rolling over him like a huge millstone, a broad grey abrasive surface turning and turning just above him, crushing him smaller, wearing him away. He reached out for something outside his prison and found *The Rights of Man,* he concentrated on passages he knew well and summoned them up word for word, 'Rank talks about its fine blue ribbon like a girl, and ...' What was next? Its garter – 'It shows its garter like a child. It – it – ' It was no good, they were going from him. He sweated coldly, shut his eyes, and forced the words to come: 'It is from the elevated mind of France that the folly of titles has fallen. It has outgrown the baby-clothes of Count and Duke and breeched itself in manhood, it has put down the dwarf and set up the man.' A tune was sounding in his head – something from a magazine a friend had sent from Glasgow. For a' that and 'that ... He focused his mind still more sharply and some lines came out clear:

> For a' that and a' that,
>   His ribband, star, and a' that,
> The man of independent mind
>   He looks and laughs at a' that.
>
> A prince can mak a belted knight,
>   A marquis, duke, and a' that,
> But an honest man's aboon his might,
>   Gude faith he mauna fa' that ...

The lowland poet, Burns. Had he read Paine, then? Cameron laughed aloud. It was a nice thought, the lovers of liberty lighting their beacons there, and there, and there. They burned and burned, driving back the darkness. When would Paine be able to come back? and live again in his own country?

He knew that to face their defeat in Strath Tay (he assumed defeat now) would be too wounding, too dispiriting: it would bring him near despair. If he was still himself, he *should* be able to face it. It began to be a test – the test – of whether he could still live with himself once the months (but probably it would be years) of imprisonment were over.

Why had they failed? He found that his feet had cramped in a clench of anguish. He pulled his toes backwards, hard, to ease the cramp. No, he was not ready yet to face the defeat. Perhaps after the hot food in the evening? Yesterday's meat and vegetables had been high – soft and sweet with badness – he had made himself swallow it and then in the night the shite had poured out of him until he was too weak to stand. He must wait till the poison had all gone. Then he could think back over the rising and understand and admit its weaknesses and set himself to imagine a better future ...This small piece of reasoning was as frail as wormwood – memories welled and streamed in his head, washing away all effort at steady thinking. Colberg galled him most – the officer's gentlemanly aplomb helping him to swim like an eel under and between the weapons of a thousand angry people. Colberg was *confident*. They themselves had not been so. They had at Castle Menzies – at the sunrise of the movement, striding from house to house, irresistible. They should have kept that up – the Castle, Bolfracks, Ballechin, Kenmore, Fortingall… The gentle mists draped over their moment of failure, when impetus ran down, as though they had no goal ahead of them. They had not. To save six thousand men, that was goal enough? But they had merely asked for it – petitioned – begged – like 'humble servants' – if your Grace would graciously grant … How to *exact* this 'favour', that was what had never been thrashed out (except for some loose talk of getting weapons from castle armouries). He and James should have broached it early on, devised sanctions (the withholding of rents; the blocking of highways and sieging of the big houses), called for practical suggestions from among the crowds – all that tradesmen's and farmers' skill and nous and energy, coalesced for a moment into a great ball of force, then left to collapse under its own weight, to crumble again into its thousands of separated grains …We have not the gift of combining, he thought bitterly. The clans are gone and we stray about, waifs in our own homeland, letting government suck us in and swallow us and spew us out on foreign shores. *They* can combine. Behind Colberg, the sheriff. Behind the sheriff, the duke. Behind him the king. What an irony – the republican ideas they had accused him of propagating were exactly what he had left unsaid, and should have said. No good to say that Strathtay was not ready for them. If they had said this about the Paris workmen, Louis would still be on the throne…

Through all the turnings of his thoughts one image dogged him – Colberg's face, so sharple carved, his eyes a wee bit slanting at the corners, his nostrils cut on a long shallow curve, his forehead not rounded but angled above the glossy black hairs at the outside ends of his eyebrows. A professional cavalier, who enjoyed excelling at the game of soldiering, who gave his orders with the perfect authority of a corps whose drills have been tempered by a score of successful wars, a hundred victories, a million unsung deaths.

They prepared Cameron for his appearance in the High Court of Justiciary by one final interview, a dry recapitulation of what had been said before, with the slightest of hints that it would go well for him if he divulged something about the United Scotsmen, who evidently still preyed on their minds. The days had lengthened slightly, measured by the breadth of the pale sunlight on the sill. He was stupefied with cold. When the officer said, 'You will be charged with sedition, over and above the mobbing, but in certain circumstances that might not be pressed,' Cameron distressed himself by making a small, indefinite sound which could well have been taken for agreement.

A quick, bewildering passage through cold air, strange faces turning to look, a flapping of black gowns topped by frosty wigs. Dark corridors smelling of snuff and dead flowers. The court-room, high, with ceiling timbers like branches in a forest. At the far end, a judge in a high-backed chair, looking at him once over little gold-rimmed spectacles, then disregarding him. Charges were read (in a strong Lowland accent) by a tall stooped grey figure, like a heron. Black figures stirred and poked their heads at each other like rooks in a rookery. Sedition, mobbing, rioting (so 'sedition' had not been dropped). A constable had him by the arm and was turning him about – was that all? no arguments? The musty corridors again – dazzle of sunshine. As he was handed back into the Tolbooth, there was a bustle at another door – a man's face, focusing suddenly into familiarity: James, a patch of high colour on each cheekbone, red on white, his hair more grizzled than Cameron remembered, looking ahead of him with wide eyes. No time to shout out – the door clunked behind him. Hot liquid of tears brimmed in his head. He felt as abject as a convalescent child and had to be helped up the three stone flights to his cell. It seemed filled with people – officers, clerks, a constable.

'Mr Cameron' – a bigwig with painfully slow and clear articulation, his back to the window, his features invisible – 'now that the charges have been preferred, you would be well advised to apply for bail.'

He gaped stupidly. (Where was James? In court? Would he come back here tonight?) 'Bail?'

'Your trial will of course commence tomorrow. However, a short stay may well be granted against bail, to enable you to order your affairs, and in particular to find guarantors.'

'I would like to see my friend, James Menzies.'

A pause. No sound of movement in the cell. The clear, harsh voice again: 'There is reason to believe that an application for bail would be allowed.' The cell was emptying. Cameron was staring at the shut door. It felt like the underside of his coffin-lid. Confinement, which had gradually become accustomed and endurable, now chafed like chains. He wanted to roar out James's name, his own name, to scream for help, he tried to pull up on the sill but his fingers scrabbled uselessly and he dropped back. He fell onto his pallet, breathing hard. Slowly the offer of bail was seeping into his understanding. It was a nasty joke. It was a trick. If he was freed tomorrow, they would follow him (to the underground den of the United Scotsmen, no doubt). But no deep thought was needed: he would accept their offer and see what happened. The law-machine was clanking and clattering to its own weird rhythm. Let it carry him along for a bit longer. Where was James? He would ask Jamie in the evening. But Jamie was replaced that night by a tall, white-faced man who said nothing when he handed in the plate of food. When Cameron spoke to him, he pointed to his ears and shook his head.

In the morning Cameron felt exhausted. His dreams had come back after many nights which had seemed as empty as death, dreams of walking between high hedges, it was daylight on the other side of them but gloaming where he was and thick earth rose up to his knees, to his waist, stopping him, he tried to open his mouth but his jaw-bones jammed, he was choking … Again the movement through fresh air and corridors (the smell was not old flowers but cloth and mildew, like church). The judge looked at him as though along an oval tunnel lined with gowns and faces, 'Accordingly,' he was saying, 'I grant bail for the sum of £500 against your appearance in this court tomorrow, when trial will duly commence.' £500! A vile joke – he could as well sprout wings and fly straight up to the sun as find that sum! In the Tolbooth they stayed in a panelled room on the ground floor. The officer with the harsh voice was advising him that the money would be 'charged to the Lord Advocate's account' if he himself could not 'procure the funds'. A quarter of an hour later he stood alone at the edge of the High Street with as little notion of his next steps as a soldier discharged in Madras with the whole of India, Arabia, and Africa lying between him and his homeland.

Interlude

On Wednesday, 17 January 1798, Angus Cameron's case came up in the High Court. His name was called out, three times. The macer then shook his head as a signal to the judge. The prisoner had not reappeared when his bail expired. He was nowhere to be found.

Sheriff Campbell, who had interrogated him in Perth, thought he must have taken refuge in the Highlands. Sheriff Chalmers, who had arrested him in Weem, was ordered to go and get him again but thought it was useless, the man would have run off straightaway to Ireland or America. And there was already a gang of rebel fugitives in Hamburg, who had founded a 'Society of British and Irish Patriots' … In the meantime the court pronounced Cameron an 'outlaw and fugitive from his Majesty's laws'. He was to be 'put to his Highness' horn' and 'all his moveable goods and gear to be escheat and inbought to his Majesty's use'.

In the years between the rising in Strath Tay and the end of the first French war, eight new regiments were raised in the Highlands, in Sutherland, Ross and Cromarty, Argyll, Lochaber, and into their ranks disappeared forever the many Scotsmen who were sentenced to prison, followed by banishment overseas, for their revolt against the Militia Act and who chose military service as the lesser evil.

Twenty-seven years after the rising, on 8 February 1825, a petition arrived, forwarded from an address in Glasgow, in which Angus Cameron pleaded to be declared no longer an outlaw. He claimed that for several years he had not known he was outlawed and that he had believed, from the day he was granted bail, that the Lord Advocate had decided to drop the case against him. He now wished to be a free citizen again and 'in the meantime prays your Lordship to recall the sentence of fugitation and to put him upon his trial'. On 14 February he was granted bail and then the Crown case was dropped.

Part II

Island

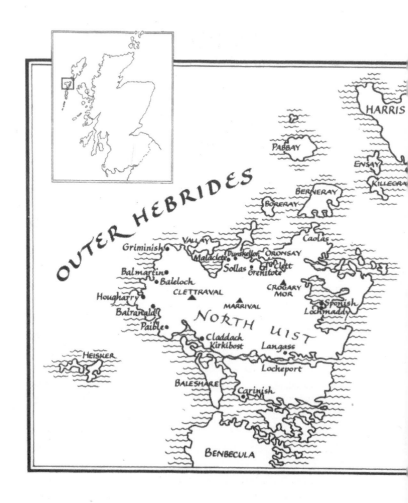

Chapter 1

1825

Mairi MacQueen stood on the small stony rise beside her house, knitting a stocking. She was looking down to the shore, to the smallest of the houses just above the high tide-mark. Her mother called impatiently from inside but she paid no attention. She was waiting for Allan Campbell to come and ask her to marry him. Was he at home? He should be by now. He had come back from the smithy more than an hour ago, and he must have kindled a fire – a small blue haze was gathering above the thatch, in the windless air. Against the white glitter of the sea the house made such a shallow hump that it reminded her of a kelp heap smouldering on the shore. No movement there. And not much in the rest of the township – evening meals were being cooked, her mother would be badgering her to put a fish in the pan, her brother Iain could do that for a change, when he came through from the byre. Allan *must* come today – had he forgotten what she had told him, that Thursday was the trysting day? Maybe he scorned the custom. Maybe she had been a fool to get so close with a man almost thirty years her elder.

Half an hour later a heron beat steadily across the sand-flats between Malaclete and the island and took up its watch in the weedy pools below Allan's house. Mairi sighed, bitter as well as sad, and turned towards her house, then started as a tall man came round the end of it – Allan. As always she noticed first the band of grey, almost white, that streaked his thick black hair. It reminded her of a blackbird with one white feather in each wing.

'I thought you were eating your tea by now,' she said with a sharpness she scarcely meant.

He looked amused. 'I had a bite as soon as I got back with the irons.

111

But I was not hungry, I made a fire because the place seemed – empty. Mairi – let us walk up the hill.'

'Where to?'

'By the peat road. Towards the shieling. Do you not want to?

She glinted at him, suspecting him of teasing. 'I will tell mother I have gone to set up some peats while it is dry. She will not believe me, but och…'

In a minute they set off into the moor behind the township. At the last house big Alasdair Matheson was standing outside his door.

'It is a nice evening for it,' he said to them, nodding towards the hill.

'It is dry and quiet,' Allan agreed. 'It puts you at peace.'

'Are you doing a turn at the peats? I will give you a hand.'

'No, no,' said Mairi decidedly. 'They will still be damp. But we will set up a few.' She was not at all bothered by the transparency of her excuse. Big Alasdair seemed like an uncle who wished her well. She walked on with Allan up the loose stones of the track. In another month they would all be coming this way, with the animals, herding them up to the shieling for the summer, and the young people would stay on there in the huts. Was she herself still a young person? At times she felt seasoned – but stuck – stranded on the edge of things. Her years of relating to Allan had marked her – nobody else would touch her now. What did that matter? Nobody else quickened her thoughts as he did (although she had had great conversations with Peter Morrison about the creatures of the shore and how they lived on one another).

They passed the peat moss with its little dark stacks of drying turfs. The track became green and comfortable. She stopped and took off her shoes and as she stooped Allan put his arms round her from behind, his hands on her breasts, and said, 'Mairi, let us go up to the old trysting place. That is where we should be.'

She leaned back against him. 'Yes, that is the place for us.'

They moved on, hand in hand, through moors that were turning spectral with a drifting white haze. The westering sun suffused it – it looked a world where unheard-of animals and plants might loom forth into being. They were unaware that the sun was throwing huge hovering silhouettes of themselves on to the drifting face of the fog. A little lad (Roderick McPhail's son) who had been guddling for trout in the burn looked up and saw the blurred giants above him in the sky and ran and ran, terrified, falling through the heather towards the safety of his home.

The hill levelled out round the green hollows of the shieling pasture, the litter of collapsing turf walls and roof timbers, like plundered nests, which would have to be built up again in June. Mairi half expected they would stop here – what was the point of trudging still further, to the last cup of grass behind the little crag that bounded the shieling? Still they walked, swimming in their own atmosphere, the world circling into invisibility behind and around them. The heather here was a low jungle and they pulled up it by its woody stems. He cut his finger and when she saw it she put it to her mouth and sucked at the salty blood. He let her, and as she finished he clasped his arms round her, almost smotheringly, and said, 'Mairi – we should be wedded.'

'I would like to wed you, Allan. But is there room in your wee house?' (Why had she said this? Usually she had no time for the customary bargaining.)

'I can build it again. And make a family house.'

'Allan –' She looked full into his eyes, wanting no falsity of rose-coloured hopes to confuse things at this point. 'You are – quite old for that. *I* am quite old for that!'

'You are not thirty. And I feel young enough – when I am near you. Let us wed now.'

'I like you being older. But why now?' A doubt checked her suddenly – an excuse for holding off commitment.

'Och – I feel free now. I am selling as many carts as I can make. Let us wed now.'

'Before the autumn? Can we build the place before winter?'

'*Now*, Mairi – let us wed *now*.'

Lie together, did he mean? She swithered between desire and disappointment, and looked into his face for his meaning, and found it serious, set not towards her but towards his idea.

'We do love, Mairi. It is a real thing. Let us make it a real marriage. A handfast marriage.'

'A handfast – ? Oh Allan!' She started to laugh at his solemnity. Fear stopped her breath. 'And not a real – not in the church – ?'

'The church is not real, Mairi – is it? A cold house, with the Reverend Macrae talking through his nose. Oh Mairi – I will not argue. The Sollas people used to wed up here until the ministers shamed them out of it. You told me that. Well, we are past shame, you and I. Eight years' knowledge of each other – everyone knows we are coupled.'

'My mother hates it. But Iain does not. He knows you are good to me.' Happiness was welling in her, brimming up from her belly into her arms – it was in both of them, heating and rising, bearing them up in circles of joy and relief that spread across the clumped houses below and out across the stream of the tide between Vallay and the shore

She laughed. What do we do? Allan – do you know what to do?'

'We use our own words. We say what must be said.'

'But what do we *do?* We must take hands.' She held hers out to him; they were brown already with the spring sun and the palms were rough; they had always touched him firmly with no flicker or fidget and this was the signal to him that they belonged together.

They both stood, upright, facing each other, hands clasped at the full length of their arms.

'I wed you, Mairi.'

'I wed you, Allan.'

'I will live with you as a bridegroom.'

'I will live with you as a bride.' Mirth was stirring in her, her voice quivered with it and she saw his long pale cheeks lifting as he responded to it.

'And this will hold between us till death parts us.'

'And this *will* hold between us till death parts us!' Her last words came suddenly on a flush of feeling and she moved with a quick step inside his arms. They kissed, smelling the smoke in each other's hair. She drew back, seeing him in a new, impersonal revelation: the quizzical lift of his eyebrows, his long nose curving to his down-turned mouth with a look that could seem sarcy, as though he found little worth believing. This was her husband – this funny thoughtful independent man, who seemed beyond or to one side of domestic ordinary things, yet she knew he was not.

'You are looking at me.' He waited quietly for her response.

'I suddenly thought – you will call this silly – we should not be marrying today – it is not a Friday.'

'It will be Friday before we go down again.'

They looked towards Malaclete. The mist had gathered over again, the shore was a blur, the island invisible.

'Mother and Iain will be wondering –'

'They will assume you are with me. And you will be. What are you doing?'

She was loosening her heavy tweed skirt. Under it he saw the stripes of her second skirt and below that the red flash of her under-skirt, which always excited him because it was like seeing the inside of her body. The cool moisture of the mist deterred him.

'Mairi we came here to wed!'

She looked up at him as she spread her skirts on the turf beside a stone which stood up like the stump of a shaft. 'So let us wed now,' she said and smiled at him in a way that made his heart turn over.

Chapter 2

1826

The MacPhails, who lived on the seaward side of the MacQueens, tired of going hungry as rents rose and the kelping wage remained a pittance, decided to build another fishtrap. The village was half again as populous as it had been when the old one was made on the far side of the burn. And of course old Roderick and young Roderick disagreed, while Allan, Mairi, and Iain enjoyed the comedy.

'No, no – put it here – there will be fish enough in here,' old Roderick insisted.

'Out there is better. Nearer the soft bottom for the flounders.'

'They are slimy eating, and thin. And storms would roll the stones apart. What good is that?'

'Out there you would get more fish, and that is what matters.'

'We will get the shellfish on the stones, whelks and buckies –'

'Ach' – young Roderick spat. 'How can you live on them?'

'Sometimes you have to, when there are no more cockles in the strand.'

'Ach man, build it out there round the corner of the point, and then we can smoke a pipe to keep the midges away, and the women too for the matter of that.' He laughed at his own joke.

'Oh yes – very good, to be sure – and the wee ones will come and pester us and down that slope they will roll, into the water where it is deep. In-by here, at least they will not be drowning.'

'Are we building a fishtrap or a nursery?'

'We had better think of everything or someone will complain.'

'They will anyway.'

The two men were still arguing when Morag, young Roderick's wife, came to the door with a baby in her arms and screamed at them that the meal was ready, such as it was.

'Where is the trap, then?' she asked Iain. She seemed to avoid speaking to Mairi if she could speak to anyone else.

'It is only September,' he answered, 'there is a winter's argument in it before they will be making their minds up.'

'A winter of salt herring and their minds would fairly change.'

'They are made up.' Old Roderick had heard her. 'There is a right way to do it and there is a foolish way, but if he spins out his folly for long enough, we will all be starving before there is one stone shifted.'

'We can be rolling stones down from the old cairn and still be keeping an eye on the flock,' said Morag.

Old Roderick was triumphing now. 'But Morag,' he pretended to be bewildered, 'how can you roll them down the hill and away out to the point?'

'The point? You are never making it out there!' Morag hooted. Young Roderick flung off into the house and threw two peats onto the fire with such force that sparks jumped as far as the bench, charred the foot of the cradle, and made them all cough when the smoke bellied. In the morning he went down early to the shore, with the oak-wood levers and a peat spade, and started to rive at the boulders which the ebb had bared. The spade grated on the barnacles, it gave great friction, and presently he had the first line of stones in position, marking out the wall on the seaward side.

When his father came down, he cursed him for using the spade. 'You will blunt the share, and rust it too. Are the levers not good enough for you?'

'I have finished anyway.' Young Roderick flung the spade up into a clump of bracken, head over heels like a caber. 'Are they not coming down yet?' He always called the women 'they',

'Morag is still milking the sheep, and mother is churning. And the wee ones are helping them.' He looked benevolently amused.

'The men's work is here. I wonder you left them.'

Old Roderick said no more but took a lever, waded in thigh-deep, and started to fashion the next length of wall, curving it out from the shore to meet young Roderick's piece. Under the foot or two of water the boulders glimmered naked and white as they turned over slowly. In the shallows they pulled clear of the sandy ooze with a suck like a calf draining a trough. Sheep bleated, Morag and Iain came down across the turf, Allan and Mairi behind them, the wee ones running on ahead. They moved stones all day, prising them from their sockets in the cairn, exposing the scurrying ants and the ants' eggs like lice in a seam. Mairi kilted up her skirts and went deep into the water to settle the outermost stones, her long fox-brown hair wetting and darkening in the sea-water as she stooped and struggled. Among the lichenous stones wee Roddy saw a lizard, brown, dry, motionless. What was it? Before the others could come and see it, it had flickered away and they would not believe there had been anything there at all. When they were all sweating, brown clouds came brooding over the sun; the midges swarmed and drove the people mad.

'It will thunder,' said young Roderick. Roddy's face puckered but old Roderick said, 'A wet of rain will thicken up the pasture. Can you lift this big one for me?' He pointed at a small boulder and Roddy strained, raised the stone, and staggered proudly with it down to Allan at the sea's edge. The sea breeze got up, the clouds dispersed, the skyline turned sharp out in the Sound of Harris beyond Berneray. The sea glittered pale gold as the tide lifted the water up the low stone walls of the trap, lapping it over them.

Wee Morag cried out, 'It has spoilt our new house!'

'It is not a house,' said Roddy, 'it is a fish trap, to catch our teas.'

In the morning they all came down with an hour of the ebb still to run. They had brought bushes and brackens to thrash the water. As they beat it to a foam, the children started to shout: 'Get in there, fishies! I see one! A big one!' Dark backs were breaking the water, rushing in zigs and zags, dodging the slaps and slashes of the branches, darting for the open sea, turning back as the people closed in. Then they were grazing over the boulders of the trap, the children were stumbling, standing on the walls, jumping across. The stones sparkled as the water left them and the plan of the trap rose clear of the sea. The pool boiled with fish, the water drained and drained, and then the place was all fish, haddock and herring and a few plaice flapping in the shallows. Wee Donny squealed as a snake squirmed under his toes – it was a striped ling, eeling and writhing to escape. Allan told him it was harmless. The men and women were clubbing the fish, throwing them up the grass. Blood darkened the puddles in the trap.

For four hours after that they all sat round, splitting the fish, flinging their guts and heads to the yelping gulls and the soft roes to the dogs, while the flies came whining, settling on their forearms, fizzing in their hair. They kept back a few long haddocks for their tea, and some more to smoke, and packed the rest in the barrels, layers of fish and layers of salt. Allan, Mairi, and Iain nailed on the lids and rolled the barrels up the slope to the barn ends of the houses while the MacPhail women cooked. A breeze had swept the midges inland and they all ate in the open air, even widow MacQueen, who stumped outside on her shiny yellow stick and sat on a stone, accepting pieces of fish and boiled potato and snapping quick fierce glances at Mairi and Allan.

'Well – there will be a bit of taste in the pot this winter, even if the meal runs out,' old Roderick said at last, leaning back on his hands and looking contentedly out to sea.

'If there is no bread or brose, it will be all taste and no substance,' said his son.

'They would like that on St Kilda, on Hirta,' put in Allan, 'Over there they put a puffin in the porridge to taste it up.'

Mairi laughed, Morag's face screwed as though she had bitten on a crab-apple, and Roddy pretended to be sick.

'What is puffin?' clamoured wee Donny. 'What is puffin?'

'Now, were you out there yourself?' asked young Roderick, and Allan felt eyes looking at him, Morag's and the widow's.

'A sailor at Lochmaddy was telling me,' he answered, and this was true.

'There is no salt out there at all, they say,' said old Roderick, 'except what the MacLeod might be giving them.'

'Giving?' Allan queried. 'Bartering for their fleeces and oil, more like.' 'What oil is that?'

'Well, it is too steep out there for seals to come ashore,' Allan answered, while Mairi looked at him, suspecting a tall story, 'but they catch birds and render them down – fulmars and the like.'

'They must be like Eskimos,' said young Roderick, 'living on the chances of the sea.'

'I have lived on worse myself,' said his father. 'Do you remember the bad year of 'Seventy-three, mother MacQueen?'

'Do not be shaming me,' put in old Morag, while Mairi's mother was still mumbling on a crust and trying to separate one bad year from another. ' 'Seventy-three was bad enough and 'Sixty-nine was worse, but we ate barley-bread, when we could, not soft potatoes –'

'Mother,' her husband interrupted her, 'in 'Sixty-nine we were eating limpets, your father died of it, and before the winter had turned there were folk bleeding their cattle to make little black cakes for the wee ones.'

'And it will come again,' said young Roderick, 'the preacher was saying that, it is in Scripture, "the hay is withered away, the grass fails, there is no green thing", and "they shall be broken in their purposes, all who make sluices, and ponds for fish".'

'That settles it,' said Allan, giving Mairi a look. 'If God has damned the fishtrap, only a miracle can save us.'

CHAPTER 3

1827

By late autumn the price of kelp had fallen to below £3 a ton, a third of its value at the end of the French wars, and a great deal of the crop still lay unsold at Liverpool. During the summer the estate had not employed all hands at the cutting and burning: families who made the usual move to the kelp shores were told to go back home. The summer was weirdly uneventful and by September people were waiting idly for the oats to ripen, while their horses grazed on the edges of the moors with nothing to do.

Mairi and Allan lifted and brought home a fine crop of potatoes from the plot which Alasdair Matheson let them work on his croft. But there was not a penny to replace ageing tools and their rent was a term in arrears. As the days darkened and grew short, they often lay late in bed as much because there was little work to do as for the pleasure of being near each other. In the boxed-in bed he had built along the wall at the back, Allan separated himself a little from Mairi's body, which always lay as closely as possible along his thigh and hip, moulding him, making him feel secure,

'Mairi.' He spoke quietly but above a whisper. 'What are we to do?'

He had not looked to see if she was awake but she answered at once, 'Yes, what are we to do?'

'No order for a cart – no timber to make one if I had – no money to pay the debt at the smithy.' He recited the hackneyed tale of their troubles.

'I have been thinking about it all night.'

He put his hand onto her brow and then her hair. She put hers on his to keep it there. 'And did you think of anything?' he asked, with an irony that implied she would be a genius if she had.

'I thought you should apply to the estate for abatement of the rent. Or at least some work in lieu – draining, or fencing. And I thought you would not like to do that.'

He tensed his hand slightly to ease her face towards his and looked into her sea-coloured eyes under her thatch of crinkly brown hair. 'Do you think I am a proud fool?' he asked.

'Och yes. And I am another. But why should we delve like moles when you have a good skill? And I could be selling stockings if people were still buying anything new. But what is to be done?'

'I thought I could make spinning wheels, if only I had money for a lathe to turn the spokes…'

'We could try prayer.'

'Ask the good Lord for something on my account.'

They lay for some minutes, their eyes on the gloom above their heads. She felt his restlessness and presently he said, 'I thought of one thing: I thought I should walk over to Kyles Berneray and see if there was any work to be had in the boat-yard.'

In the silence that followed this they could hear the wind soughing in the thatch above their heads.

'Would you like to work there?'

'Like? It is a matter of livelihood.'

'But you would like to be near Katrine McLeod – to see what she has become.'

'She is Katrine Cameron now – I have not set eyes on her for eleven years.'

'You know the date exactly.'

'Och – Mairi – do you not remember your own old flames?'

'There was only one, and he was lost at sea. But your girl is well-to-do, and pretty, they say … Ach, go along there if that is what you want.' She turned into the shadows of the bed space and when he put his head in to say goodbye before setting off, she did not move or speak.

Cloud like a dirty fleece trailed low on the moor behind the township. The track east twisted past Alasdair Matheson's croft. As usual big Alasdair came out to speak and when Allan said he was going to the boatyard, he raised his brows and said, 'You might not get much there.'

'Why not?'

'Ach well …Everybody is on the tramp for a job.'

Allan strode out after that and within two hours he was on the soft plain of Trumisgarry machair. Shallow ponds spread over it after the downpours of October and November. He would have liked to see the blunt horn of Crogary Mor as a landmark inland but the cloud was still funereal, it draped his mind, weighting it, adding to his feeling that the burdens trailing from his shoulders would drag him back forever. They had all slaved at the kelp – now their rewards from it were being annulled like straw in a furnace by the government's letting in foreign chemicals. But they could all have been comfortable by now if they could have kept what they had made! The landlord took all except the poor wage – he gave nothing. They had even had to bring their own pokers to stir the burning ash! The ware came out of the sea, where nobody had sown it, the sun in the sky made it blossom on the rocks. They had filed notches in their own sickles to chop it off the skerries, they had hauled it out of the shallows by the straining of their own shoulders. And then they had sold it to the laird's agent, at the laird's price. They should have sold it themselves; sent samples to Liverpool; guaranteed a cargo of so much weight at such and such a time and hired a boat to send it. But Lord Macdonald had stolen the march on them long ago and made Uist into his little Peru. The weed of the sea! And yet by old law any soul could gather and eat the fruit of the foreshore, and bide there if he lacked a home… Why did I not get the solidest men, Iain and big Alasdair and old Roderick and Finlay the smith, to make a group (before the War finished) and challenge the laird's factor on the head of who owned the sea-ware? No, no, people would have said, he has always traded the kelp and paid the wage – take him on and his friends in Edinburgh will find for him. And that was right – well, it was true. The quiet mass of folk see how things are settled and bow to that. And the next stage: give the fixity of things a name, 'God'. And bow to that.

He came to himself as he walked on, his wet shoes plashing, and his eyes focused on the narrow lochs where the highest tides forced in through neuks in the rocks and made the inland water brackish. The edges of it were black with iodine; no water-lilies would grow there; under the low cloud the flat pools glistened like lagoons in hell. The sea had drawn back out of sight in a blear of small rain. He could see nothing ahead, nothing behind, but pigmy vegetation, salt-seared heather and the narrow blades of the bents with rain-drops running down them. Colour was leaching out of the world, his horizon cramping down to a few featureless feet. He shuddered through to his spine and drove on at a trot across the machair, aching to reach Caolas and the activity of the boat-yard.

Above its inlet the McLeods' house was a shell – a steep-sided gable, black charred roof-timbers slanting towards nothing. The timber-yard was a few stacks of lengths, weathered and drenched, and one whole oak split into planks. No keels lay in the stocks, which were leaning helplessly in the water. The thatch on the roofs of the small houses was drab, soaked, and their doors gaped.

Allan stood for minutes, staring at the stricken place where he had worked for nine years until a rumour of a privateer sending its pressgang into Lochmaddy had driven him further west. The McLeods' house – he slated it in his mind's eye, glazed its windows and lit lamps behind them. He imagined Katrine coming to the door to feed her geese, her waist slim below her small breasts, her eyes blue under dark lashes and her hair incongruously yellow, flicking the feed from her fingertips with a delicate gesture. Compared with Mairi she was fragile, finicky ... but she had been so eager and mobile in his arms ... she had stood back, her head on one side in a fetching pose, wanting him to admire her new straw bonnet from Glasgow ... He should not be thinking so much about her. (Why not? He felt wholly rooted with Mairi, clasped to her; Katrine was a memory, perfectly clear, like a plant under the surface of a still pond.)

He looked round once more – nobody even to ask about the ruin. He turned away and went back along his steps, his head down against the sifting of the rain. He felt as marooned as Alexander Selkirk on his island – Mairi was with him on it – the two of them with the desolate water streaming past, eating away their last foothold. Ever since he had come here, years and years ago, he had accepted, without any chagrin of false pride, the status of a cottar. He had not expected a croft or tried to get one. The Malaclete folk had finally accepted him for his skill at making carts and wheels and sledges, and occasionally boats, and the estate would let any number of people (all too many) settle near the shore to work at the kelp. He had no real stake in the land. Now his skills were unwanted, and would rust.

The ground shook. Hooves sounded in the mist ahead. A horseman came abreast, a scarf masking the lower half of his face, and Allan recognized the large-pupilled eyes and flushed cheeks of the factor, Captain Cameron – riding home to Sponish, no doubt, after a visit to his friends at the farms of Balranald or Baleloch in the west. Allan called out his name, the horse galloped past, clods and pebbles spattered him. But some yards past the rider reined in and then waited until Allan came back within speaking distance. Their looks met, each appraising the other.

'Allan Campbell, isn't it?'

'Yes.'

'Cottar at Malaclete these days?'

'I have a house there, I have been building carts, but now the trade has failed.'

'Well, it has been rather a thin season – yes. At least you are well placed to get weed and shellfish … Just my joke.'

'I believe I could live if I had a croft.' He had had no intention of saying that – the outcome of his earlier thoughts had jumped on to his tongue without his will.

'Oh, now, Campbell, the district is desperately congested. One township runs into the next. You aren't a family man?'

'No family.' His little spark of hope died out suddenly. 'I wedded Mairi MacQueen. But we have no family.'

'So that is in your favour. Because quite candidly, Campbell, the estate cannot encourage the settling of the fertile young, who may become a drain on our resources. Had you a plot in mind?'

Allan gaped, then tried to swallow back his feelings, to think of nothing but what might be won from this powerful man.

'There is some old land,' he answered slowly, 'to the side of the shieling track. Behind the township. On a bright day, when the sun is low, you can see the striping of the lazy-beds. It must have raised corn and potatoes. In an easier time.'

Cameron smiled. 'In a harsher time, Campbell. Come to the house in Sponish at next term day and we will see what can be done.' He looked down keenly from the saddle, as though to imprint something (the image of his own generosity? Campbell's features?), then rode off along the track.

Allan went quickly homewards in a fury of thought. He had found them a foothold on the future. They would survive. He had dropped a yoke onto their necks. Start a croft with nothing (no stock, no seed), when they knew nobody who could afford their rent, and he himself had nothing like the bursting energy of youth (had he twenty years of life left?): Mairi would scald him for it. She would accept it (it was her life).

Alasdair Matheson was carrying peats in from his stack, two creels, one in each hand, swinging them as though they were handfuls of grass. Allan called out to him in a cheery, rallying voice: 'Why did you not tell me the yard at Kyles Berneray was ruined, Alasdair?'

'I had heard something … Och, Allan, you know what you are like, you believe nothing unless you have seen it with your own eyes. And not always in that case.'

'Am I as bad as that? Well, I saw it was ruined, so now I am sure it was. But I may have found something else.'

He went on down towards the house, surprised at the lack of smoke. But blue appeared above the smoke-hole before he reached the shore.

New peats were flaming on a bed of white ash.

'I let it go out,' said Mairi. 'You were a long time, so I went to bed. But it was cold in there without you.' She went to fetch two curved, encrusted fish from the barrel at the other end. He put his hand lightly on her shoulder, chary of touching her in her prickly mood.

'I met factor Cameron between Clett and Trumisgarry.'

'You will hardly have had much to say to him, or he to you.'

'I found myself asking – if we could work the old place up by big Alasdair's. He said we might – to try him again on term day.'

'You want to be beholden to Katrine's husband.'

'I never thought about that. It is true – I never did.'

'So you never went near the McLeods' – are you telling me that?'

He stared at her back, stooped over the steaming pot. He was talking about their livelihood and she could only harp and suspect. He said, 'They have had a fire, seemingly. It is all a ruin – the house, the yard – '

'Would you have taken work there if you could?'

'Mairi – they are all gone. Empty. Windows out, no roof. The yard is a swamp full of rotten timber. Ach, you are not listening. You are mad.'

'I am jealous because I love you. If you do not know that, you know nothing.' She turned to look at him, impersonally, not fondly, then looked back again into the seething white steam. 'Can we plough the land next spring?'

'I think so. He did not say no.'

'And if it is some plan of Katrine's to keep you dangling –'

'How could she know about it? I did not know myself till it was on my tongue!'

'They are hounding people off the land, not taking them on. Why are we different?'

'Well – he knows we are only two.'

'So we can go on living here so long as we have no children.' She turned to face him, the light of the flames making her hair an aureole, her face no longer sharp and challenging but sad.

'Well – nothing has happened yet.' He could not keep his eyes from her waist.

'That it should come to this – hoping that I will be barren.'

'Not *hoping*.' But he did dread another mouth to feed, and it harrowed him terribly to realize that he could never express his, and that if he did, it would seem like a ban on her womanhood.

CHAPTER 4

1828

The people were leaving the islands in their hundreds, swarming towards Lochmaddy where the boats lay waiting to carry them to Canada, the boats with the glamorous names, the *Dove* and the *Ceres,* the bird of peace and the cornfield; they were rotting, the berths collapsing with the wood-rot that breeds in coalmines; typhus brewed in the bilges, people crawled or were carried ashore on the far side skeletal with fever; porpoises heard the splash of the bodies of the emigrants dropping into the Cabot Strait ...

> The brave folk of Scotland,
> their souls were broken,
> driven out of the kingdom
> across to Nova Scotia.
> Black ship for their lodging
> and the brine to drink
> more fitting for the Spaniards
> who tan their skins like leather ...

The families went, despairing of paying their arrears between then and doomsday; rents had been trebled during the Wars, in the heyday of the kelp; now they clung to the congested coastal fringes like seagulls on a lighthouse, nerving themselves to take to the waters, selling their small stock to pay their passages: a good cow paid for three square feet on shipboard, or twenty black-faced ewes; there might be five in the family; there was meal and salt beef to pay for on the six-week voyage (nearer two months if they were butting into withering headwinds), plus the weeks huddled in stuffy lodgings waiting for the ship to fill.

And now the parasites were at them, emigration agents, shipowners, factors' men, dosshouse keepers in ports, chandlers dealing in wormy victuals, blowflies clustering round the open sores, bluebottles laying their eggs in the dying meat of Scotland…

> They came to us, crafty and cunning,
>> to wheedle us out of our homes,
>>> singing the praises of cold Manitoba
>>> which has no coal or peat.
>> I need not bother to tell you –
>> when you arrive you will see it –
>>> short summer, quiet autumn,
>>>> then the long harsh winter.
>> If only I had two suits
>>> and a pair of shoes
>>>> and the fare in my pocket,
>>>>> I would sail for Uist …

Every discouragement to stay, every trick to move them out. The tacksmen on the larger farms (Macdonald of Balranald, his crony at Baleloch) said they were going too and sent their gear in bales to the quay at Lochmaddy but when the ships weighed anchor the farmers were still on the quay; they had filled their bales with peats; the crofters crossed the ocean alone, leaving the clever men to acquire their land and stock it with the great sheep, the Cheviot from the Lowlands.

Finlay MacRury the smith was leaving, caught between his creditors on the mainland and his debtors in Malaclete; he could not bring himself to hold off the one or squeeze the others. Peter Morrison the harness-maker was leaving; he knew the small tunnelling life of the sands and had written it down in a book; his trade had collapsed, folk were mending their gear with plaited bents or selling off their horses for a song to the rapid-tongued dealers from Dunvegan. Big Alasdair Matheson swore he would leave, three children in four years, they were living on thin brochan without butter, but Flora cried in a great volley of tears, between rage and sorrow, Did he want his baby of two months to freeze to the ground in Manitoba, or wee Flora and wee Alasdair to choke to death in the hold of a hulk? The big man shrugged and went outside to look at his potato fields; the pink flowers were thick, a heavy crop might last till March. Iain MacQueen was leaving; their mother had died in the winter; he might find a wife on the other side; the arrears of rent had brought him down so low he had lacked the will to plough and then the sight of the dead ground was unbearable, and the looks from the other men; he would write every month from Nova Scotia. A letter came at Christmas: he had worked at riving out tree stumps till the snow came down; they never heard again (he died of a heart attack on Cape Breton Island).

Everybody who left carried with them a handful of earth from Malaclete to pour into their graves, wherever they might be.

Many of the liveliest folk were going, the strong and confident who could afford passages and expenses; the government and the estate had refused to help. Before the end of the year, four hundred and forty had gone from Rhum, six hundred from North Uist, seven hundred from South Uist and Benbecula, seven hundred from Harris, over a thousand from Skye and the same from Ross...

> Oh God how sad I am
>   In the clearing with the cattle,
>   I am tired and heartsick
>   In this foreign country.
>   It was not like this
>   Before I left the Brae of Rannoch.
>   Sister and brother beside me,
>   I dallied with my sweetheart,
>   Happiness in the bothy
>   With its door of birch branches,
>   Our bed was made of rushes
>   And our pillow of bog-cotton...

CHAPTER 5

1829

When they approached factor Cameron, he stared as though the previous conversation had never happened. But he conceded that Mairi had some *moral* title (he emphasized the word) to the croft she had been born on and lived on for thirty-three years, and which her brother had now vacated, while making it sound like a personal favour that he would re-let the place at all.

'On your own head be it, Mistress MacQueen,' he said, 'or Campbell. But understand – we will no longer countenance arrears.'

Allan let out a breath of relief at the thought that they would not have to open up the old ground beside the shieling track – he had feared that it would break their backs. He expected Mairi to want to move back into her old home, but not at all.

'We have made this place ourselves, and I like that best. Anyway, we had no windows there. It will do for a byre and a barn.'

Yet she was wistful to the point of tears as they were clearing out the old place one evening soon after the spring equinox. The light was fading over the ridge beside Griminish – the sun had not been seen for seven chilly days but now its fire came through in broad rents and mouths, orange turning to vermilion and then scarlet, as though the world's energy was still renewing itself in some other land, on the far side of the ocean. Their minds must have followed the same track; for Allan it was like hearing his own thoughts voiced when Mairi said, 'Do you think he went to Canada to make it easier for us?'

'He never said so.'

'He never said anything. He was as close as our father, and like him too, a red face and bristly black hair. I wish father had been buried at Dunskellor and not in some Dutch graveyard. We are so scattered – do you think *we* will mend the family, Allan?'

He looked into himself for the optimism she wanted and found a kind of resignation – he had begun, inwardly, to take on each dilemma (shortage, setback, forced choice) as it came, rather than try to look beyond the horizon, and it was making him feel old.

'We are still here, dear,' he said, putting his arm round her waist to make up for the sparseness of his words. She then looked up at him, saying nothing for so long that he kissed her on the forehead and said, 'Mairi?'

'I tried to tell you this morning … I think there is a baby in me.'

'Why?'

She drew away from him a little. 'I know it. I feel it.' She wanted him to take her hand, and he did.

'Maybe you are right,' he said. He squeezed her hand. 'We will soon know.'

He was not rejoicing, but at least he was not louring – in a moment of black fantasy that morning she had thought that if he refused to welcome their child, she would move back here to her old home and stay on her own for good. But it was all right, and ten days later she said to him quite evenly, 'I have not been bleeding – there is a child there.'

The door was open, and as he clasped her and looked above her hair at the slow dark lift of the hill towards the skyline, he was thinking, Another burden – money debt – the croft – a child … Why am I here? I should be lonely, like that buzzard. But it was as tied to the world as any person, by the blood-need to circle down again to its ramshackle heap of sticks and feathers, to rove out all day and every day to find its stomachful of nourishment somewhere among these shores … He was letting too long go by without words; he wanted her to feel not one tremor of his fears (he must turn his fears into energy to drive on the work for their subsistence). He said, 'You wondered if we would mend the family. We will now.'

She hugged him, firmly but not for long, almost as though acknowledging that he had offered his due of support rather than completely joined her in the act of bringing the new child into the world. Their lives drew subtly apart after that. She still worked with him at the less heavy labour of the croft, she sowed the barley and oats and dropped the seed-potatoes into the lazy-beds which he had dug and fertilized with the old thatch and soot from the roof; and when they went up with the MacPhails and the Mathesons to the peat moss on the level moor beside the shieling road, she helped Morag, Roddy, and Flora Matheson to set up the peats in fours while the men stripped off the uppermost layer of heath and cut the peats out of the wet black iron-smelling ground. But once the summer was well into its lull and the men were planning desultorily to fish or catch lobsters by way of substitute for the lost kelp work, Mairi concentrated more and more on spinning the wool she had carded from the last fleeces Iain had shorn and knitting it up into blankets and shawls for the baby. It would be coming well on in December, near the darkest day of the year, though not the coldest.

As April slowly warmed and lightened, Allan had gone at the croft in a creative burst, wanting to put his mark on it (and wanting to prove to himself that he could manage it). He carried creels of bladderwrack from the shore to fertilize the ground, which had been underused for two years. But a pain snapped across his back; he had to leave the loads down near the water's edge at the very end of the croft; he spread it there and presently dug it in with the foot-plough. When a thin crop of oats came through, he was delighted with the green stems fledging the ground next to the rippled surface of the shallows. When mist drifted over in the early autumn, the dry yellow of the corn blended with the grey-green water above the white shell-sand to make a zone of enchanted peace. He made Mairi come and walk there, handing her carefully over eroded gullies at the edge of the land until she said, 'Allan Campbell, do you think I am made of glass!'

They were girding themselves against the winter now. He had renewed the thatch on their own house; the bents had been so heavily harvested these last few years that he had to use rushes and iris leaves for the first layer and then the heather above that. They brought home creel after creel of fine dry potatoes, relieved at the ease of carrying them a short way along the shore instead of the haul down from the plot on big Alasdair's croft. The gales soon after the autumn equinox frightened them, the corn harvest was shivering under the blasts, and once the ground was saturated the sky remained overcast and the ears of the oats on some of the wetter crofts began to look grey and speckled. But October was benign; the blond tracts of the township, Middlequarter and Sollas along the shore and Vallay across the sea-channel, were populous with families harvesting, some with sickles, the most prudent (Allan and Mairi among them) pulling the corn up by the roots to make long straw for the cattle. At night he looked at his bleeding hands – they had opened in chaps around his old carpenter's calluses – and he was grimly satisfied. All that could be got from the croft was being got. They had clothes enough and would be able to sell next year's fleeces. Their shoes were not worn out. The meal (two kinds) and potatoes would see them well into the next season. He had a crop of curly kail standing in the plot behind the house which he had dunged from the midden. They had eaten fish and eggs and cheese enough for Mairi not to fear that she would be unable to nourish the baby. In a very good year they could live, the two of them (or even three?). If they did not have to buy anything. Or pay a doctor … He had better not terrify himself, or turn broody until Mairi thought he was against the child and she tightened inwardly, blighting it (they had both had such fears).

November, being windless, bred fog – bluish-grey days when the sun seemed not to rise. Allan brought Iain's old loom from the other house and began to replace warped and cracked parts while Mairi knitted a stocking, the long leg of it piling down the round of her belly, or let the needles droop in her hands while she looked into the heart of the fire and let her tongue follow the tune of a dandling song:

> 'An old man won't get Mairi,
> An old man won't get Mairi,
> An old man won't get Mairi
> As he got her mother.
>
> No old man will get my darling
> But one thats strong and healthy …'

'Oh, it will be a girl, will it?' Allan roused himself to answer her teasing. 'You know that, do you, Mairi?'

'Yes, I know that – why should it be a boy?'

'Have you been to the spae-wife, then?'

'The only one here who used to tell fortunes was Morag MacVicar, before she married Roderick MacPhail, but when she turned so churchy, she gave it up.'

'Macrae is broad-minded – he would have let it go.'

'Is he broad enough to christen our wee one – supposing we asked him?'

'Aye, supposing. Will we take him up to the wellspring of the burn, Mairi, and give him his name ourselves?'

' "Him"? I tell you, a girl is coming. An old man won't get Mairi but one who's strong and healthy…'

The baby was past its time. Mairi's spine ached and her mind felt strained and dulled now from so long fixing on something that had already happened a million times in her imagination. Margaret Morrison the harness-maker's wife had always helped the women in their labour but now that she had gone to America the only person with much of a reputation in that way was Murdoch Cameron's wife on Vallay – they were the minister's neighbours and Rachel Cameron had given Allan a queer look and a doubtful 'Yes' when he had asked her if she would be able to come over when Mairi's pains started.

Three nights before Christmas, when the embers were shedding their last glow and Mairi and Allan were wrapped in the shadows of the bed, she turned rigid from head to toe beside him and said, 'The waters have broken.' The phrase seemed Biblical – it weighted him with dread. He put his hand on the straw mattress under them – soaking – and her shift, soaking. He clutched her hand.

'Kindle up the fire, Allan. Put water on.'

He was out of bed, building broken peats above the embers, pulling on a jersey and a cloak. He went to the door to look into the fog towards Vallay and saw a shimmer of water not five yards away – the spring tide was full, nobody would reach Vallay or come from it for three hours at least. Behind him Mairi caught her breath with a hiss. He turned.

'A pain?'

'The first.' She rolled heavily sideways and he put a fresh straw mattress under her, then swung the big pot into position above the climbing yellow flames. They waited silently in the flickering light until she hissed with pain again. He took her hand in both of his and said carefully, 'Mairi – the tide is full – very full – there is no going across for Rachel Cameron, not before half-tide.'

'Stay here, Allan. I will tell you what to do.'

'How will you know?'

'I know.'

Two hours went by as the pains sharpened and seemed to hurry through her. The pot had boiled, and a kettle, and Allan had put all their clean linen cloths at the foot of the bed. Outside the door the water had vanished outwards into the dark nothingness of the bay.

'Allan' Mairi's voice was stretched into a shrill shout. She slid down the bed, her head pressed onto the mattress as she arched upwards. As she felt the strain between her legs growing too great, to the point of tearing, she relaxed and opened her legs and a moan utterly unlike her voice came out of her mouth. Panic shattered him, he craved not to be there, she was dying, he wanted to stop this thing, to shove it back. Her voice reached him: 'Allan – help the head – ease out the head –' The head? Between the tops of her thighs, among the hair and bloated flesh at the base of her belly, a dark bubble formed, it distended, it was bluish-grey – lighter than that – transparent. Under the skin of it a face came into focus, tight-shut sleeping eyes, a nose pressed down into a closed mouth, an ear moulded against a thin-haired skull, a person was forming under his eyes, and as Mairi raised her head and looked she said in a steady voice, as though reciting a familiar recipe, 'Break the caul.' His hand lifted (he was automatic now, beyond fear), his fingers pulled on the slippery membrane, the baby's shoulders were out now, the cord shiny with blood and fluid was visible between it and its mother. The baby shuddered, its legs flopped onto the mattress, bunched pink feelers, and a small desperate cry came from its mouth – another – shrill pumping cries. Mairi's fingers reached towards it. Water was brimming from her eyes, making their blue shine and glisten. Allan looked at the baby, between its legs – no genitals, only a wee fold. Mairi whispered as he bent to hear. 'Little potato nose,' she was saying, 'little ugly rabbit. Let me touch him.'

'It is your *girl,* Mairi,' he told her, and suddenly he cried in a flood himself; inside he felt the quick of his being boil and gush in a greater bursting and whelming than he had ever known could happen to him. She smiled at him, laughed at him almost, and he laid his face next to hers, content to mingle with the hot life of birth and pain and happiness and relief. Then he did what he was told, cut the cord and seared it, knotted it, and washed the baby and Mairi. A few hours later, while light grew coldly in the sky, he carried out the sodden mattress and the afterbirth to bury them beside the midden.

The other houses were hidden in the fog. Allan was content to stoke the fire and sit by it in a trance of exhaustion while waking dreams blurred in his head (dreams of skimming in a boat across lustrous water). Mairi and the baby were sleeping in a cocoon of clean linen; he would have been content to stay in this spell indefinitely. But presently people were knocking at the door, as sure of the birth as though he had put up a notice about it, bringing presents (a cake, a shawl, an embroidered linen bonnet) … The MacPhails came and said a prayer while Donny lifted wee Eileen up to see the baby; she fell forwards out of his arms and nearly crushed it so that Mairi had to turn wincingly and protect her with one arm while not making Eileen feel she had been bad…The people they most wanted to see, the Mathesons, came in the afternoon, bringing a dish of fresh fish stewed in milk and a pot of laver soup. Savoury smells filled the house. Big Alasdair carried in a cradle made of willow canes and said apologetically, 'You are the carpenter, Allan. But I thought this might be needed.'

'You never made that in a day!'

'I made it four weeks ago, just to be sure.'

'I should have made one – what kind of a father am I?'

'A canny one if you delivered a baby with no harm,' said Flora. 'Did you not like to go over for Rachel Cameron?'

'How could he have gone without a miracle?' her husband scoffed. 'It was all water from here to Vallay. But the minister might have arranged for a miracle, if only Allan had been a shining light among his flock.'

Wee Flora was reaching up to touch the baby's hair with delicate strokes; it had dried to a dark silky brown. The little girl laughed and called her brother over to see when the baby started to suck, stuffing her fist into her mouth, her face crumpling and the shrill cries pumping out. Now Mairi must try to feed her, the Mathesons left as their own baby stirred in the shawl behind Flora's back and began to whimper. Darkness pressed in as the new family settled into its new routine. Once the baby was fed and deeply asleep again, Allan sat on the edge of the bed and said, 'She needs her name – we should have one ready.'

'What name would you like?'

'I would like to call her Flora. Because we planted her in the spring.'

Mairi looked at him with a glint of humour but he was perfectly solemn and she loved him for his fancy. She tried it out: 'Flora Campbell. Or Flora MacQueen?' She looked at him with a bold question

'Or anything else at all,' he said, returning her look. 'She is Flora. That is her own, true name.'

Chapter 6

1830–1835

How could the eight MacPhails live off their little croft, or the five Mathesons off theirs? When the children were babes, the mother was too tired and taken up to help her man with the field work. As they grew up, they ate more and more and the parents snapped at them for reaching a hand out for another potato or wanting butter in their brochan. As they became men and women, they were able to put in a full stint of labour, but where could they work? All the spare land was being sucked in by the farmers, who could afford horses and iron ploughs to grow long spreads of corn on the machair land between the old crofts and the dunes. Who could the crofters appeal to for an abatement of rent, or more land for the old rent? Nobody: the factor was always a farmer, and why should he help his rivals?

The new man in Sponish (since Captain Cameron took a stroke and retired to Lochaber) was Duncan Shaw, a lean bald man with level hazel eyes, a good listener, a clear talker, a mind as detached as a lawyer's. Letters from the laird's fabulous new castle at Armadale in Sleat were answered the same day and their orders enforced on the next. Lord Macdonald's bankers were displeased that Lord Macdonald's assets were dispersed through so many of Lord Macdonald's petty tenants; it was past time for the land to be managed in a more rational and paying way. The more it was improved (and the more directly the improvement went into Lord Macdonald's bank account, which was nearly £100,000 overdrawn), the less likely he was to have to clear the people and bring in the sheep.

So Duncan Shaw rode out and back along the coast from Caolas to Griminish, and round the headland to Houghgarry and down the machair meadows by Kirkibost and Carinish, always talking from horseback like an overseer in the Carolinas, keeping the men at it: carting stones to lay straight roads from the croft track to the shore, digging black wet drains, leading loads of shell-sand up into the peaty edges of the moors, the grazing must be improved – hardly for the crofters' sake, they could not afford a head more stock to take advantage of it since they never handled the wages for their work; these were credited against rent arrears, and for that reason they could not refuse the work. In the winter it was bearable, if they were robust enough to swing a spade when their plaids were sodden, but in the halcyon season from May to September, when they wanted to be shearing their own sheep and mowing their own hay, they had to do it by moonlight or the glimmer of the afterglow; they moved through the island stupefied with labour; between the strand and the moor they were like sleepwalkers. Towards the close of one long sunset Roderick McCuish from the second-last croft in the east end of Malaclete met big Alasdair, who was leaning on a post, and he spoke to him, wishing him goodnight, The big man said nothing; his eyes were on the waning of the yellow lustre in the north beyond the rising and falling of Vallay's crest. When Roderick came closer, he saw from the unblinking mask of Alasdair's face that he was sleeping on his feet.

Alasdair was the strongest man in the whole of Sollas; nobody dared to wrestle with him, though he never fought foul. Near the shore at the north end of the township a wedge of grey stone stood in the heather; a strong man could budge it in its socket; only Alasdair could lift it, digging his fingers into the moss beneath it, setting his feet astride, straightening slowly from the hips while the young lads cheered. It was Big Alasdair's Burden.

'When one of my own sons can lift the Burden,' he said one day, 'I will know that time is passing. And when I cannot lift it, I will know that I am passing.'

If a man with that strength was stunned by the toil of the times, how could the rest survive?

CHAPTER 7

1831–1836

The grizzled strand in Allan's hair was so broad now that his head was more white than black. People smirked or smiled, according to their natures, to see him teaching his Flora to walk – he looked like her grandfather, not her father. But he was unaware of their looks, and Mairi disregarded them. Allan was as active as any father, and when the two of them swung Flora along between them, over pools on the shore, plumping her down onto a rock, and she demanded more, and more, and more, there seemed to be enough spirit and love amongst them to last forever.

There were days when his back hurt so much that he could not even play with his daughter. But she had found a 'brother' in Roddy. There were plenty of Roddies in this and the neighbouring townships but plain Roddy always meant Roddy MacPhail. He was a byword for the queer, laughable twist he gave to phrases and for his daft doings. Not long after they built the new fishtrap, he became fascinated with the shore. When he found you could split the bladders on the bladderwrack by stamping on them on a rock, he called them 'popbangs', and this spread and became people's name for them. He wanted to know how everything worked, he took nothing for granted, not even the tide. When it flowed, it seemed to carry things in with it, but he had noticed a surface layer of very fine sand swimming out to sea as the under-water moved in. One day, to try this out, he took one of his new sealskin shoes to the sea's edge and launched it as the water came rimming in. Sure enough, the shoe floated out, bobbing like a little yellow boat, further and further away, out of sight in the troughs, sailing across the channel towards Vallay. His mother found him there, 'playing the fool as usual', and when she saw the loss of the shoe she shrieked with anger and dismay, it had been their only skin that year, she herded him back to the house, whipping his calves with a willow switch, and for months after, as the winter reached its coldest depth, Roddy had to go bare foot. He sat next to the ashes of the fire; deep chaps were opening between his toes; he picked the scabs off when they itched, staring at his mother with his big hazel eyes under his almost furry brown brows, so self-contained, so set against repentance, that she hit him again for 'defying her'.

So long as his grandfather was alive and active, he could get between Roddy and his parents' heavy hands; he never sided with him in words or spoke behind the parents' backs; he silently supplied comradeship, taught Roddy and Donny to scrape out mussels and bait a line when their father and mother had gone to a prayer meeting, and entertained the boys endlessly with stories of the old days fishing for herring with the Lochmaddy fleet.

As old Roderick's eyes became too dim and uncertain to follow the boys along the foreshore, Roddy took to wandering towards the Campbells'. He would turn up as though he had come out of the sea, take Flora's hand, and walk her down to the rock-pools, where they sailed limpets, calling it a race as the breeze puffed them along, and he told her the names of things, hundreds of names, pop-bangs, razor shells, anemones, sand-hoppers, cuttlefish eggs, while she pointed at one thing after another in her silent, curious way and listened, absorbed, to his explanation of how the lugworms sucked in the ooze at one end and leaked it out at the other; if you dug quickly between a little pool you could seize the limp worm as it lay helplessly among the dirt.

When she was nearly six and he was fourteen, he was whispering to her one October evening in the shadow beyond the firelight. Mairi wondered what could be the secret but she had no fears, the two were grand companions, and Allan was asleep. To save firing and seal oil, they went early to bed while Roddy slipped off into the darkness. An hour later he was back; he made a curlew call and Flora tip-toed out at once. They ran through the darkness to where the boats were moored between two boulder dykes. Roddy had brought oars from home. He pushed off over the invisible water as silently as a heron, and when their eyes could see into the night and they knew they were opposite Big Alasdair's Burden, he lowered a stone on a rope to hold them there and they began to fish. Flora impaled lugworms on the barbs; they let down the pairs of hooks on stiff sticks weighted with old iron until they felt bottom, then raised them a little and waited. A full moon came wheeling up the sky and the long beaches glimmered under a mist of spume from the breakers.

'Roddy?' She was pointing as fluorescent drops ran down her line.

'It is fossforious,' he told her. 'Fossforious that lives in the sea.'

Her thin brown arm tensed as she felt the line thrill; it wanted to get away from her hand; then it went slack.

'Roddy?'

'Go on, Flo! Haul it in!'

She pulled and pulled while he patiently retrieved the slack from the bottom of the boat and wound it onto the frame. She leaned out, tilting the boat, and saw pale bodies eeling in the water. In a flurry of green sparks fish were coming over the side, jumping and twitching, a haddock and a flounder, wet and muscular against her legs. She did not flinch but watched as Roddy gripped the haddock hard, forcing the hook out of its mouth, and thumped its head against the thwart. She imitated him, doing the same with the flounder, and then she could not bait and fish fast enough. A fish or two, then a small horde, until their hands and ankles were coated with slime. Roddy wanted to stop, there would be too many to dispose of, but Flora was avid now, they must fish on till the bait was finished. For half an hour nothing more happened and then the line wrenched away from her and Roddy trapped the frame under his foot before they lost it overboard. The fish was still in play, tugging, arrowing sideways; at first it resisted when she tried to haul it in but then it yielded reluctantly. Over the gunwale came a slim grey shape, convulsed, flailing and scraping; it flayed the palm of her hand before Roddy could shout 'Dog-fish! Watch out!' She jerked back, shoving her hand into her armpit and squeezing it, while Roddy banged at the fish with a short hardwood club until it fell exhausted among their catch, its slit eyes fixed like a snake's.

'No more fish tonight,' he said, 'and just as well. Bring up the anchor stone.'

On the shore he showed her how to thread a line through the fishes' gills and then they trotted silently off to their homes. For his night's work, a meal for the whole family, Roddy was thrashed. At the Campbells', Allan and Mairi woke up soon after sunrise to find Flora asleep at the foot of the box-bed, her hand red with abrasions, her legs filthy with mud and the ooze from the fishes' vents. Her catch was laid out on the table in a straight row, tapering from the largest to the smallest, five fish worth eating and six she should have thrown back. When the girl woke, she seemed to have no sense at all of either adventure or misdemeanour.

'Can we have one each for breakfast now?' she asked, while Allan ran water over her palm and bound it in a linen rag. Before they went along to the croft to rake and turn some hay, Mairi showed her how to head and tail a fish, strip out its guts, and cut it down the backbone so that it would lie flat in the pan.

Roddy rarely came next year and Flora would sit on a stone near the shore, gazing along towards his house, her little brown face turning pale with expectancy. For years the herring shoals had been ebbing away from the sea lochs and now the other kinds too were growing scarce. A few men would sit in their boats for hours, their lines trailing limp, above the banks where the fish had used to feed. The summer was sultry; glassy lanes stretched sinuously across the water; Vallay hovered like a mirage. Last year's potatoes had long since run out and women desperate to put something on the table were creeping along the shore at low tide, bent double, probing in the sand for cockles with their potato-lifting hooks, pushing aside every clump of weed on the rocks in the hope of finding a clutch of buckies that had escaped the dozens of other searching hands.

Roddy and his friend Archie Maclean (the youngest brother of big Alasdair's Flora) ranged further and further along the strand, making the food-gathering an excuse for an escape from home, and for a chance to chat with the girls from Grenetote, Belle and Jean, the plump one and the slim one. As the lads paddled along the shallows, feeling for sand-eels with their toes, they knew they were getting near the girls, and the girls knew it too, eyeing each other, saying nothing, fizzing into giggles.

'What have you got?' Archie asked Belle abruptly, trying to look into her grass bag.

'Keep your hands off!' She swung it away from him. 'I have got – one big flounder – mmm, we will have it with butter. And one long sand eel,' she was speaking in a teasing sing-song, 'and one big crab – ooh, ooh, I feel it nipping me – ooh, ooh!' She swung round, the bag flying out at the end of her arm, and set off at a mad rush into the sea, which was pale green and too calm to raise a single wave. The two girls ran in bursts of sparkling water, the boys chased after them, deeper and deeper into the expanse of water between Uist and Vallay. Breathless, they stopped and looked back. Their own shore was already far off, a still picture of white dunes and the scatter of croft houses among the fields. Hardly a person moved there. The moor behind was blank blue-grey under a white sky. The four looked at each other, flushed and sweating. Roddy suddenly stooped and dashed water over the girls; they shrieked and came at him; he turned and waded, unable to hurry. The water was cold, gripping his bones; he knew he had reached the flow of the main stream which drained the bay seawards. He struck out with frog-like strokes towards Vallay; now he was down amongst the water, the flowery turf of the island looked unattainable. Feeling no bottom he almost panicked, then steadied and went with the current, letting it urge him at a slant across the channel and against the sheaves of tangle on the boulders of the island. He looked round. The others had followed. As Jean gasped and struggled in the shallow water, he reached her a hand. As soon as she was ashore she shook her hair out, spraying him, and then walked on up the slope.

'If the tide turns, how will we get back?' Belle looked excited and afraid, her chubby cheeks duck-egg blue with cold.

'Two hours to go,' said Roddy confidently. 'No harm – we can go on over to the far side, out of sight.'

'Why?' asked Jean innocently. 'What can we do there?'

'Whatever we like.' The boys ran, the girls followed. As they came over a crest fledged with blue marram grass the ground was all brown movement; rabbits were fleeing in hundreds. In a wild burst of energy Roddy scudded after them, running one down; it zigged and zagged, its white scut bobbing; he had it by the neck, it twisted desperately to bite him, scored his wrist with its claws, and then he chopped onto its neck with the edge of his hand; it convulsed, and sagged.

Jean was staring at the flopping body, at the red grooves on his inner arm. 'What was that for?'

Was she put off? or angry with him? 'It is meat,' he said, looking from one face to the other. 'Better than salt herrings.'

Jean took his hand and touched the wounds; He made himself not wince. 'Come and wash that, in the sea.' She looked at her friend, her pupils large, her face straight. Belle was looking up at Archie, who was a foot taller than her. He put his hand on her shoulder while Jean and Roddy turned away and walked across the little cups of grass between the dunes. Eyebrights and tormentils textured the ground with colour; a layer of warmed air caressed their feet; as soon as they were out of sight they closed together, feeling each other's limbs move under wet cloth. Instead of mounting the next slope they let themselves sink into the grass and lie there, kissing each other on the face and neck, touching, then stroking, experimentally, not sure what to do, feeling their quickening pulses inciting them to something more. He felt his stomach contract – would he be sick? – but it was pleasurable, it was too much, he could not tell the sensations, the two of them were in a whirlpool of heat, sinking, spinning, he wanted their skins to cling and mingle so closely that they fused. They lay side by side, frightened, together, wanting the afternoon to shine on and on and never stop.

To avoid the dangerous swim back across the channel the four of them ran along Vallay, past the big house like a fortress, with its roof made of thin flat stones, to a point where the stream spread out across the sands. Once ashore, the girls ran off eastwards towards Grenetote, trying to keep in the cover of the dunes. At the MacPhails', Roderick and Morag watched, then turned into the house as Roddy came up the slope. When he went into the house he smelt whisky and knew that his father had been across at Carinish, drinking with sailors from the Isle of Man who brought in smuggled spirits.

'What have you got? Where is your bag?' His mother caught him by the wrist and saw the rabbit-scratches. 'You were in a fight? You are a rogue and a ruffian and – '

He brought out the dead rabbit from behind his back and threw it onto the table. 'I got this,' he said to her face with his unblinking look and then his head jerked back as she slapped him and came at him.

'Ruffian! Rascal! Dabbling in filth, is it, with the wee whores from Grenetote? You are dirty through and through, you are dirtying this house and I will make you suffer so – '

She was slashing at him with both hands. He tried to shield his face, and then his temper broke, he seized her round the waist and rushed her back against the meal-kist at the end of the room and held her there, his hands flattened against her chest, while she kicked at his shins and screamed to her husband, 'Roderick! Punish him! Tell him what he is! Punish him!'

Donny had rushed out of the house. Eileen was sobbing and crying, 'No no no …' Roderick stood for a moment, his face red and sweating, and then he came at Roddy with a piece of heather rope in his hand. 'You wee sinner,' he was growling. He lurched against a bench. Roddy suddenly released his mother, turned and darted under the swing of the heather rope, and ran madly out and away, making a bee-line through thistles and dung-pats for the Campbells'.

A fly or two whined and buzzed in the dusky interior of the house. Flora looked up from a picture she was stitching with an old whalebone needle and some ends of wool and stared at him. 'Hullo, Roddy,' she said. 'I wanted to go fishing, but you never came.'

'Fish have all gone, Flo,' he told her. He slumped down on the floor, his head against a barrel, and let out a deep, shaky breath. 'I will not live there,' he blurted out. He was nearly squinting with weird, fierce concentration, his thick eyebrows meeting over his nose. 'I will not be their son.'

Mairi and Allan came in a minute later. Their backs were brown with peat dust.

'Hullo, Roddy?' Mairi looked at the lad gravely and waited for him to speak. He sobbed and she put her hand on his hair, then hugged him to her and looked questioningly at Allan.

'Roddy, have you been in the wars?'

He shook his head, hiding his face, letting Mairi comfort him. 'Roddy, we are going to eat soon. Did you come over for a cup of meal, or what?'

The lad looked up, the anger of the fight curdling again across his face and making him glare. 'We only went to Vallay – with the girls – and swam – and ran about – and then my mother – I will not be her son!'

The door banged open. Morag MacPhail came in and looked at each of them, eyes hot with accusation, triumphant almost.

'Aye – this is where he goes. It is fit for him, no doubt.' She was looking at Mairi, scorning her.

'What do you want, Morag?'

'I want that dirty child you are hiding.'

'Och, Morag – he is upset. Come on now, Roddy – '

The gentleness of her voice worked on Morag like a sting. 'Oh aye – cosset him, then, go on, learn him some more of your ways.'

'What are our ways, Morag?'

'He has been led in the paths of righteousness,' the other woman screamed, 'by parents who were wedded in the church, and now he is dallying with all the dirt of the neighbourhood!' She wrenched at the boy's shoulder.

Allan spoke up, 'Roddy – go home now, and we will all be meeting when we drive the herds up to the shieling. Go home now, Roddy.'

Morag was standing by the door, glowering, her arms folded. Roddy was looking wretchedly at Flora.

'Goodnight, Roddy,' she said, 'come and fish soon, Roddy,'

'He will not be doing that again –' Morag was furious but Mairi broke in, speaking directly to the lad through the black cloud of his mother's antagonism.

'Roddy – it is all right, Roddy – we know you, and you know us, and it will be all right.'

CHAPTER 8

1836–1837

White, weeping days came on with the end of the summer; people woke feeling their clothes damp, the milk turned sour before its time in the mild, close air. Somebody said that when the last of the old potatoes were lifted from the pit at the farm of Balranald, they were black as muck, impossible to eat. Now the people longed for the new, firm crop, and the Reverend Finlay Macrae prayed formally in the church for the blessing of an abundant harvest.

Late in September a rumour crept along the coast from Caolas that a field of potatoes had rotted in the ground, followed by another rumour that on the whole the crop was sound and large. It was cold now, winter seemed to stare from the eyes of autumn and the northern sky was a dead grey like a fish-skin; wet pellets of sleet came out of it amongst the hordes of the rain. The local meal was finished, nothing but white dust in the corners of the kists; last year's crop had been scanty, the fields had blenched, unripened, in the long wet autumn; the cattle had grown lean on the sapless straw, their skin stretched over the gawky knobs of their hip-bones, their ribs showing like the carcase of an abandoned boat. Now the men put meal bags over their shoulders against the incessant drench and walked round the edges of the fields, eyeing the potato shaws, willing them to yellow evenly, hotching to delve into the earth with their foot-ploughs, their hooks, their fingers even, and ease out the bunches of round, brown food.

In the middle of October whole fields turned black as though flames had scorched across them; if the sun warmed them for an hour they began to stink; the folk who had come to lift them retched and put their skirts or caps across their mouths to fend off the stunner of it. On every acre of the townships the families delved and scrabbled, wild to find that their crop was wholesome; the children cheered when sound potatoes came out of the soil; in a day they had turned as soft as midden-dirt. When the pocks of the mould appeared on the skins, the whole family scrubbed at them, trying to rasp the blight away; it did no good, the white flesh stained grey as they looked at it; if they put them into the salted water, they collapsed in smush.

Now the families were eating limpets and whelks; the rocks were scoured bare; each low tide the strands were raked as rough as a ploughed field in the search for the last cockle. There was hardly a weed left in the ground; nettles and bramble shoots made a green broth which left the little ones mewling with hunger but at least it stopped the gripe which racked them and left them grey-faced and exhausted. In December the Mathesons's fourth child died; they had called him Iain, after Mairi's brother, but he bore it for less than a year; as soon as he came off his mother's milk he turned listless; he never learned to crawl; the porridge or the gruel came back up as soon as he swallowed it; his eyes followed the family as they moved about the room; he seemed to sleep for a whole day and then they found he was cold; in his father's arms he felt weightless.

They survived the winter on their own meal, such as it was, and a dole of meal from the estate; factor Shaw sent it in on carts; every recipient was required to sign a paper undertaking a day's work fencing or roadmaking for each stone of meal received. The men and women looked at each other silently in the queue: here was slavery, now they had pledged away their time – had they enough years left to barter for their food? (Somebody said that Shaw would meet them at the Gate of Heaven and demand a year's digging before he let them in among the angels.)

If the next season was no better, they might as well go and die in Nova Scotia; better end your days as a free person than as a draught-animal shackled to Shaw. But he did one good thing (somebody said it must have been a mistake): he sent for seed potatoes from Argyll and Sutherland; the blight had vanished back into its unknown sources; the sun warmed steadily, the cattle plumped out as the pastures greened, the sky was set fair above the fields in autumn with a drying wind from the east. The Reverend Finlay Macrae gave thanks to the Lord 'who in His wisdom had vouchsafed an abundance, who had stretched down His hand and filled their basket and their store'. (Somebody asked, which lord did he mean, God or Macdonald?)

CHAPTER 9

1837–1839

The more charity, the more hatred. People complained bitterly about the coarse ways of the factor's men, who had shouted at them like drovers as they queued for the meal, and they blamed neglected fields or patchy sowing on the time they had to spend labouring for the estate. There was always something to blame. If Allan called at a house to mend a loom or a boat, the grievances poured out and some people harrowed their brains over what was to be done; they spoke as though an 'answer' lurked somewhere, waiting to be found, as though there was a book which held the key. His own little library, mildewed, with the initials 'A.C.' on each flyleaf, passed from hand to hand – *The Wealth of Nations* (nobody got through that); Arthur Young's *Annals of Agriculture,* which promised great things if each man had two cows and an acre; Robert Owen's *Report to the County of Lanark,* which seemed like a bulletin from another planet, but they liked its recommending of the spade above the plough (only the factor and his friends could afford ploughs); a tattered copy of *The Rights of Man,* which big Alasdair and Roderick McCuish read aloud to each other, laughing and cheering at the more satirical parts.

Allan had never thought that Roderick would become a friend. He was a cousin of Morag MacPhail's on her mother's side. He had a straight nose, a pursed contemptuous mouth, Irish colouring with black hair low on his forehead and blue eyes under handsome level brows. He looked as though he would respect nobody. The feud between the MacPhails and the Campbells left him untouched, he would not take sides, and now that he was working away on Berneray, on a ferry boat that plied between there and Harris, he came back from time to time, to Allan and Mairi's or big Alasdair's, with news of the struggle at Borve, on the west side of Harris, where the new owner, Lord Dunmore, was trying to clear the crofts.

Roddy spent most evenings at the Campbells', lying on the sanded floor with his head towards the fire, looking from one speaker to another, greedy for any word that promised action. Big Alasdair's Alasdair came with his father; he was his image, growing massively, his hands already like joints of meat sticking out from sleeves that were always too short. His brother Murdo was quite different, solemn and contemplative, with his mother's light hair; he liked to sit next to Flo; he shared his bannock with her and studied her face as it reacted to the emotional temperature in the room. Roddy's friend Archie would come in and sit impatiently; he was eighteen and already notorious for proposing marriage to every girl he went with; they laughed at him, but he kept at them, and his great grievance was the decision of the estate to evict anyone who married unless he rented land already from the laird.

'Why do they not geld us and have done with it?' he demanded furiously one night at the Campbells'.

Murdo Matheson looked anxiously at Flo to see if she knew what the word meant.

'You are a wild man, Archie,' said big Alasdair. 'A wild man, and no mistake.'

'You cannot be a man in this place – a slave or a stirk, that is all they want.' Archie angrily toed a peat nearer the heart of the blaze and embers spilled across the floor.

'It is true,' said Allan, as Mairi tidied up the ashes and rebuilt the fire. 'If they could, they would have nothing here but animals – one shepherd, maybe, living with the laird and completely his creature – a few labourers in a bothy to reap the harvest and lift the potatoes and go back to the mainland in the winter to starve as best they could. It is not people they want but gold in the bank.'

'His castle in Skye has gold pieces in the grates and gold dishes on the table,' put in Roddy, and then looked sheepish and doubtful.

'Now, where did you hear that?' asked big Alasdair, but Roddy would not be drawn.

'Dunmore in Harris is no better,' Roderick McCuish spoke up.

'Does he stop his people marrying before they have a croft?' The inevitable question from Archie Maclean.

'Oh, he is wicked enough for that,' said Roderick, eyeing him as if he were a giraffe or a dancing bear. 'He is adding the townships on to the farms, and driving the families over to the other side –'

151

Archie would not be deflected. 'Have we to wait for our fathers' deaths before we marry?' he demanded. 'And how will we get young brides, then, when we are grey…' He let the words tail off, sensing that this was not quite what to say in the house of Allan and Mairi.

'Och, marry if you have found a girl, Archie,' Mairi said to him, as though daring him, 'and see whether Shaw tries to move you out. The minister will surely never thole it if marrying his flock is to be the surest way of turning them out!'

'And do you think' – Allan paused to make sure they were all hearing him – 'do you think Macrae would say one word against Shaw when his own farm and his own glebe are leased from the estate?'

The room was quiet. Palpably, in the air, there was a new realization of how complete a network was arrayed against them. Roddy came out with a thought that had been perplexing him since Archie's last remark.

'If you had always had to have a place before you married, we would none of us be here. My own grandfather is still alive, let alone my father.'

'They would *like* none of us here,' said Allan, pleased at the lad's perception. 'They will empty the islands into the Americas and leave nothing but a few farmers and a great crowd of sheep.' Old phrases came to his tongue. 'They will make a wilderness and call it peace.'

The good harvest and the gentle winter helped people to pretend to themselves that they could manage. But in the spring three of Shaw's own ewes, from a flock he had taken to pasturing on newly enclosed land beyond Grenetote, were found with their throats cut. They had been laid on three flat stones, like a sacrifice. Remembering words of Roddy's Archie Maclean was appalled and said to him, 'That was an awful thing.'

'What was awful?'

'The factor's sheep? Found butchered past Grenetote?'

Roddy hummed a tune and said, 'It is a great day for a stravaig across the moor…'

'Are you not sorry about the sheep?'

Roddy looked at him hard, his eyes black. 'I am sorrier for the folk who have no meat in their pots.'

Mairi had no doubt who had killed the animals but she would not defend him; why should she when the killer had clearly acted in a gesture of resistance, and not for greed (the mutton was probably on Shaw's own table by now). Allan looked at her as she spoke. The run of hungry years had sharpened her face, making a beak of her nose. Her mouth was set in a straight line, as though she was tensed continuously to bear a strain, and her eyes, which he thought of as sea-blue, were more like a sea reflecting an overcast sky.

'Do you want him tame?' she demanded, seeing his unhappy look.

'Not tame, no' – he paused, thinking – 'and not savage either.'

'Roddy is not a savage.' Flo's voice came from beside the spinningwheel, where she was working. 'He is lovely. He is like a deer.'

She looked happy and Mairi smiled to her, hoping that her hero would not come to grief. She and Allan had spent many hours of the night talking about Roddy; he was nearly as much their son now as he was Roderick's and Morag's, as often as not he slept under their roof and was there in the morning when his father, red-eyed from the drink, came shouting for him to herd the animals or carry oats to the mill. Mairi and Allan knew that the MacPhails would never forgive the 'wiling away' of their son. Equally they themselves would not leave Roddy to turn into an embittered victim of that unhappy house, where the mother made the family pray lengthily three times a day and the father alternated between bouts of drinking and sick repentance.

That night Roderick McCuish came in after his week on the Harris boat and sat for a while saying nothing, staring coldly at the fire. The others waited quietly for his news; most of them had been carrying peats all day and the labour of it, on thinly filled stomachs, had so wasted them that they wanted only to lie about, feeling the evening's brose warm faintly through their innards, hoping that the wellbeing of it would last until sleep.

'Dunmore's factor will murder someone yet,' said Roderick at last. 'His men have been firing the roofs at Borve, smoking the folk out like wasps.'

'The roofs? He does not own the roofs' – a judicious point from big Alasdair. 'Why could he not let folk carry away their own timbering to their new place?'

'It is a war, Alasdair,' Allan told him. 'War on the people. The man is a Napoleon.'

'A war it is,' Roderick agreed, looking across at Allan as though at last the reality could be discussed. 'I saw it. Brown smoke streaming from the rooftrees. The animals maddening off into the moor. The men and the wee ones trying to catch them.'

'What were the women doing?' Mairi asked.

'Stoning the factor's toughs, some of them.'

'What did they do?'

'Hit back with their clubs. One woman, it was Mairi the poet, was left for dead, with her scalp opened. They say she revived on the track to the east. They will be perching like gulls now on the black rocks of the Bays.' He looked accusingly round the ring of faces. 'Have you seen it there?' Nobody said a word. 'It is like nothing. Gutters of peat moss between ribs of rock. No strand. No shingle. No green pasture or machair meadow.'

'It must be like that in hell,' said big Alasdair solemnly.

'Never mind hell. It is like that in Harris.'

'How is it a war, Allan?' Roddy asked a moment later. 'It is not a war if we have no army, is it?'

'No – well – it is like a one-sided war. But I call it a war if they come invading in – and Lord Dunmore is virtually a foreigner – and then, if the folk will not abandon their homes and the fields that they have made, weapons are used on them and blood shed. What do you call that?'

'Aye, but it is a hard word – war,' big Alasdair said, distressed, while Murdo looked doubtfully at him and then at Flo, wanting to know her feelings. But she was watching Roddy, who was fidgeting by the fire, working his feet up and down, tearing fibres from a peat and flinging them at the flames.

'If there is ever a war in Sollas,' he burst out, glaring at people as though they were the enemy, 'we will win it!'

'Oh aye?' said Roderick McCuish. 'Now, how is that?'

'There are more of us. And it is our ground – we know the paths – we could lure them somewhere, into an ambush, and then hammer them to pieces.'

'Aye aye, Roddy, they could have done with you in Harris, to be sure,' big Alasdair chaffed him. (But Harris must have had its own heroines and heroes. Next spring, when the estate made its final moves to herd the people out of the sweet pastures of Husinish, the women hailed stones from behind barricades of old boats and roofing timbers bolstered with turfs. They could not be moved until a frigate anchored in the bay with platoons of troops from Glasgow, their muskets loaded.)

'What happened then?' they asked Roderick.

'They went, of course. Like cattle to the shambles. Bayonets and bullets – what could you do?'

'But would the troops have used their guns?' Allan put the question to Roderick and big Alasdair, and to Roddy and Archie as well; they counted as men now; they were full-grown and the low room seemed filled with tall bodies.

'Who can tell?' said Archie.

'Nobody, because it has not been tried. We never use our powers. They wave their guns and flags, and they shout out their crisp orders, and we die for them, or we shoot down the poor of another country, as though we were happy to be allowed to work for them.'

'Are you blaming us? For being gullible?' Roderick McCuish felt nettled, as though the argument had caught him unfairly from the rear.

'Who is blaming anybody? I suppose we are trying to understand. None of us had a grudge against the French. Yet islesmen went to die there by the thousand, and mainlanders as well, from Breadalbane and Lochaber – they say it is empty there now ...' He paused and his face seemed to droop, a beaten look hung for a moment under his fell of white hair. 'We are many, but we might as well be few, if we never join our powers...'

He had not meant to reason his way out onto the limb of a lost cause, but his sadness was private, his words reached Roderick (and Roddy and Archie, and even big mild Alasdair) as an incitement to make a stand. But where? and on what occasion?

'What should we do then, Allan?' Roddy was demanding, So it had come – what Allan most dreaded, what he knew was bound one day to draw him in again, the demand to go where his insights led him and enter the struggle. He quailed, feeling old, seeing the odds rise against them like a sea.

'We should plan it,' he answered, taking his time. 'We should not wait to be smoked out whenever they choose. We should put our demands, and not be always at bay, always defending ourselves against this rent-rise and that eviction order – '

'Our demands – what are they?' Roderick was not irritable now, he was alert, testing each notion as it came.

'You know best yourself – what *do* you lack – what *do* you demand?'

'A long lease – as long as the farmers.'

'Something in place of the kelp work' (big Alasdair).

'A long loan, to work the land better and do new things' (Roderick again).

155

'What things?'

'A better breed of bull for the township, to improve the stock.'

'The right to marry when we like, without fear of being put out' (Archie Maclean of course, and everybody cheered at that).

'And all this is no more than prayers, like words going up the chimney, so long as there is a tyrant in the castle and "his man" wielding the club.'

'There must be another way.' Mairi hated it when she felt the tenor of Allan's talk curve down again, down into the cleft of the age-old dilemma.

'Plenty of other ways, dear. We could manage the land together, for the good of everybody – it said in a paper they were trying it in Ireland – '

'Well, we are not in Ireland,' Roderick McCuish broke in brusquely, 'we are on Macdonald's land, more is the pity, and Shaw sets the rents, and if he came next term day and said, This is the finish; Balranald wants your land for another farm and I would fine like a piece of it myself while we are at it – how many would resist? They would be calling it the will of God, and Macrae would say no different. They would all troop off like ducks in a thunderstorm.'

'He is right, you know,' said big Alasdair sadly. 'When will we ever learn?'

'The only way to learn resistance is by doing it,' said Roderick, and Roddy's face brightened, scenting action; but it was late, the fire was low, people were letting themselves sink towards sleep. So the talk went round, month after month, while the estate's indebtedness rose towards a quarter of a million pounds and plans were laid to force the 'redundant population' out and send them off to Canada.

Chapter 10

1840–1844

On the longest day, when the families moved up to the shieling with their herds and flocks, they felt their hearts lift as they rose up the hill. Worry lurked in the houses and enmity on the track east towards Sponish and the factor, but up here where the sunlight glistened on the fair hair of the bog-cotton and bumble bees clambered on the flowers of the bell-heather, their hind-legs laden with orange pollen, it was a time of milk and cheese in plenty, short warm nights, and an easy mingling of the young folk which their mothers watched but did not interfere with.

The few sheep led the cavalcade of animals, the calves followed them, the cows ambled behind, their udders nicely swollen with the lush summer feeding. Young lads dashed through the clumps and tussocks bordering the track, feeling useful, heading the herds off from imaginary pitfalls, shouting to excite the dogs. The women and girls carried the churns and the distaffs; the men brought spades and timbers – the strakes of an old boat or good fresh planks from a lucky wreck – to patch the weathered roofing.

The glen of the burn opened out above a stony fall. Here was the green trough of the first shieling, a smaller one beyond it, and where the path climbed between boulders big Alasdair had his important moment, checking the numbers of the families' animals to see that they had kept to their souming. They knew that he was fair, and mild as buttermilk; if you had sneaked in an extra cow he put his hand on your arm (it felt like an anchor) and you said nothing but drove the beast down again that night.

Before the menfolk left, after the settling in, the unloading of the pots and the ropes and the bedding, Morag MacPhail would make her family say a prayer; Donny and Eileen would close their eyes dutifully, mumbling steadily through the worn words; Roddy sat on a stone and shot wicked

157

looks at Archie Maclean, between scorn and irritation, and it did not end there, she never let her husband go back down without a psalm: 'The Lord is my shepherd; I shall not want. He maketh me to lie down in green pastures: he leadeth me beside the still waters,' and Roderick put up with it all, the easy weeks were coming, no wife to keep him on his knees in prayer, evenings free to drink drams with his cronies. They might pay a boatman one of these years to fetch them a copper still from Campbelltown; they would make their own drink and damn the licence; as he thought of it his spirits rose like a skylark and he sang the fifth verse in a ringing voice: 'Thou preparest a table before me in the presence of my enemies: thou anointest my head with oil; my cup runneth over.'

Now the young folk felt the heather stems under their shoulderblades as they lay and kissed among the dry moors. Nobody minded so long as the black cattle were not allowed to stray (the cows and calves kept to the soft feeding among the irises and foxgloves) and so long as their mothers knew where they were at night. Donny and Eileen had a thin time; their mother kept them at it, bleaching a new web or plunging at the churn; they lay on the heather mattress at night staring up at the hole in the peak of the roof and dreaming of excitement. Eileen told herself that if the big brown star that twinkled on its own was still there in the hole when she next woke, it meant she would find a sweetheart that summer. When her eyes opened again the space was blank but she moved her head a little: there was the star again, she hoped it would count.

When Archie, the champion proposer, sensed the yearning in her, it made him look again at her plump chest and rounded bottom; she was only fifteen but womanly already; he tried to speak to her on the other side of the hut but she was as anxious as a foal, edging towards the corner, looking to see where her mother was. He never got to cuddling her even, let alone luring her up to the trysting place to put the question.

> My brownhaired dairy maid
> Who moves so smoothly,
> You hardly bend the grass,
> Your legs are so shapely.
> Your skin is as white
> As a seagull at sunrise.
> Why do we love when
> We cannot be at peace?

Piqued, he thought of making up to her elder sister Morag; some of the lads said her mouth was nice, for all she prayed and scolded as hard as her mother; but she had eyes only for young Alasdair Matheson; his strength and his silence made her feel secure; after another summer at the shieling the families expected them to marry.

Coupling was in the air; the mothers were jumpy, like foxes with a litter in the den, but they wanted it for the young folk, they could not get used to the new discouragements, they were thinking already of more pairs of hands for the digging and the harrowing, the spinning and the waulking. Allan and Mairi watched them in dismayed fascination, like spectators at a tragi-comedy – they were vulnerable enough themselves with just the one child to think of, not a child but a growing lass. Murdo Matheson loved Flo now that she was taller and her breasts were showing; he looked permanently wonderstruck at the burgeoning of the woman in the small companion he had been protecting; but when he followed her about, offering to carry turfs to patch the cheese-house, to hold the cow's head while she was milking or tempt it with titbits to keep it from fidgeting, she gave him a cool look and brought the load herself.

Mairi delighted in her self-sufficiency. It will temper her against disappointment,' she remarked to Allan, but he was rueful for the lad's sake, remembering his own backwardness, his years without a woman; had he passed on to his daughter some weird strain of independence that might keep her lonely, and making a virtue of it? More than ever he thanked his fate for Mairi; her back was still straight. Once she raced with Flo; they belted their skirts up and hurtled down the burnside and Mairi was only a few steps behind when Flo reached the waterfall. Watching them, Allan wanted to live forever between their familiar presences; the less time he had left, the more he felt it; he would not go back down to the wintertown that year; he had renewed the thatch already during the dazzling days of May.

So the families drew ever closer, in themselves and between themselves, weaving the web that would never finish although people tore at it, landlords and governors, trying to wrench it off the loom of the islands.

CHAPTER 11

1843–1845

The scouring of the shore and the land and the sea had stripped them to their limits; there was not even spare weed in the sea to enrich the ground and fatten up the potatoes. The Mathesons and the Campbells took it into their heads to roll some big stones next to the skerries where the weed was naturally thickest, to encourage more to grow. They laboured for hours, Murdo trying to work next to Flo, Alasdair and his father making the stones turn over in the water as lightly as clay alleys. Allan was trying to spare his back; he felt that if he stooped too deeply he might never straighten again, but his wife and his daughter heaved on the levers with him; he knew he was only laying his hand on the rubbed grain of the wood, not getting weight on it, but it saved his self-respect; he was happy to be amongst the others, beyond the reach of the flies. As the families waded slowly ashore out of the glittering water, feeling their hunger and knowing there was nothing to quench it but the last of the salt herring, big Alasdair's brother-in-law, Duncan McLean from Sollas, stopped to speak to them. He was agog with news.

'Oh aye,' he started, as though they knew the score already and he was just confirming it, 'they are going to help us with the flitting, you know. We will easily manage now.'

'What will you manage, Duncan?' Big Alasdair had a habit (nearly everybody had it) of pitying and patronizing Duncan for his agitated ways.

'The passage, man! Oh aye! If we flit to Canada at the term, the estate will find £2 for each passage. Factor Shaw told me himself. Think of that, now – money for old rope! What have you been doing in the water? Hunting more fish?'

They would have told him but the splutter and importance of his great news disabled him from listening and he scurried on towards Sollas.

His sister's face was streaming with tears as they carried the levers wearily up the slope. It had come at last – the family was tearing apart – Duncan (silly Duncan, but he was kind) was going over the sea with his Agnes and their three children (cousins to her own ones; if ever they met again they might as well be strangers). Once she had dug her own feet in, in the ruinous year of '28; now it was on them again, the agony of partings.

She hurried along that evening to see her father and mother – surely Duncan could not be taking them oversea on a crowded boat? Yet how could they be left? The two of them sat rooted, one on either side of the fire, while Agnes stirred about in the room, looking sharply over at Flora, ready for trouble.

'Oh aye, we are surely going,' old Archibald said contentedly, looking in surprise at his pipe (which had been cold for an hour). 'It is the best thing, you know, Flora. There is plenty room on the other side, firing by the ton, and the rivers full of salmon.'

'Who told you that?'

'They are all saying it – why do you think so many are going?'

'My neighbour Mairi's Iain was never heard of again – '

'Ach well, the MacQueens were always a bit shiftless – his father never came back from the war – was he a piper, now?'

The old man was confused; his wife sat on the other side of the hearth following his words with movements of her lips and coming in on the last word or two of his sentences in a frail show of understanding. Flora walked home in a dwam of grief, anger boiling up under it. The coldness of Canada would finish them in a winter – eight of the family going – more than would be left – she wanted to back away down into the depths of some cairn, to the very end of the tunnel, with her own ones touching her, and bite the hands off whatever enemies came to drag her out. Where had Archie been? Had he had nothing to say against the factor's bribes? She found him at the house, helping big Alasdair to twist heather ropes.

'I will never go,' he told his sister before she could accuse him. 'Let them break their backs in Nova Scotia. Alasdair thinks there will be room for me here.'

'Here! What is happening to father's croft?'

'Oh, the estate is taking in all the cleared places. Grenetote is to be a single farm. Our place will join it on the lease.'

On a blowy day, with the rushes bending and shining after the rain, Archie and Roddy lay half-sheltered under the dripping black lip of a peat hagg on the moor, watching the Grenetote families file along the road into the bleared distance towards Lochmaddy. No animals went with them – the factor had bought in the entire stock of the township in payment for the balance of the passages. Belle and Jean walked beside their families; Belle was no longer plump, her father had driven her mercilessly; she was never seen without a loaded creel of peats or seaware. She had slimmed into a gaunt woman, but Jean had gone the other way; the young men appraised her and had little doubt that she was pregnant.

'Did you keep at her, Archie?' Roddy asked his friend. 'Were you well in there?'

'If she has a child in her, it is no more mine than it is some other man's. You know what she was like.'

The two of them were turning into wolves, foragers without mates, skulking round the fringes of the settlement. Roddy was letting his brother Donny take up the burdens of the croft when their father was too fuddled to help a cow in labour or go up on the roof to lay some thatch. One day Roddy surprised them all by making a new head for the plunge-churn, carving a pretty clover leaf on each of its quarters. He had done nothing for the house in years, and when his mother found the work lying on a bench, she could only stare at it, then at Roddy, then back at the carving. Next day he was nowhere about the house; they assumed he was at the Campbells'; when evening came she walked over there angrily, only to be told that they had not seen him for three days. Morag went home and sat for hours looking at the fine sharp edges of the holes, touching them with her fingers. Then she prayed, Donny and Eileen beside her (young Morag was up at the Mathesons'), for the son who was lost and found again. Some weeks later Roderick McCuish mentioned that there had been a Manx boat in the sound of Harris and Roderick MacPhail went over to Lochmaddy to hang about the inn, asking seamen if they had seen his lad and drowning his sorrows when they had not.

Not long after, the Campbells sat on the big stones at the end of their house looking over the bay. The sea was turning as hard and blue as mussel-shells; there was a chill of wet forces massing in the north and east, but the sunlight streamed through at last as the cloud parted, the skyline in the west was fringed with orange, all along the coast the clumps and hillocks in the moors stood out like embers and the houses of the townships showed miniature and clear. The three of them sat on silently until the light failed, seeing the whole of their world displayed.

'The townships are being harried to the quick,' Allan said at last. Roddy's going had dragged at them all for days, like a bereavement. 'Ploughed up and harrowed over.'

'The estate must have enough by now,' Flo suggested. 'And our people will have enough, too, now that so many have gone.'

Allan and Mairi exchanged looks over the girl's head, but they would not belittle her: if she hoped for more than they dared to, she might get it in the end.

'Maybe – maybe,' Allan answered slowly. 'Only we had better know what we are up against. Shaw, and that military man before him – over this past twenty years they have shorn like blades from Kyles Berneray to here. Why should they let any families stay when they can lease it all as farms and bring in men of business from anywhere at all?'

He and Mairi looked bodingly eastwards, as though a marauding force would come from there, eating through the homesteads of Grenetote, leaving them roofless, swarming between the clustered houses of Sollas… But the next thrust came from the other side. Duncan Shaw left the factorship before term day, he went off to the mainland to invest his means in a new distillery in Glasgow, and the families braced themselves when they heard that the new man was James Macdonald, the farmer from Balranald on the broad lands of the western side; they thought of him as a stranger and he behaved like one when he came to Malaclete at Whitsun to make the reckoning.

He trotted into the township, a meaty man with his legs sticking out on either side of his horse, and took up his stance outside the house of Alasdair Matheson, to whom he kept referring as 'your officer'. He called for a table, a chair for himself, and another for 'my man' who carried the leather bag for the money. As the people came flocking up with their bits of cash and the tickets showing the estate work done during the season, Macdonald made each one say his name out loud and then repeat it, looking at him closely and waiting for a moment as though suspecting him of perjury and giving him a chance to confess, Allan would have none of it, he said his name once, in an ordinary voice, and added 'Mr Macdonald', and from that moment the men were more upstanding and had a good look at Macdonald to see what they were up against. They saw a stocky man with a bald forehead which he lowered, looking out from under it, as though he would butt through difficulties. His eyeballs were unusually exposed, like white and black pebbles set between his lids, and his lower jaw thrust out further than his upper. When he shut his mouth on a firm statement, he looked like a pike clamping on a frog. As the reckoning wore on, the young folk along the house wall, who had come for the show, stopped their whispering and giggling and presently found themselves standing in a line, like recruits. The women drew their shawls closer and closer round their faces, as though cold rain was dropping on them; they could not fault the man's figures but his manner froze them out, no jokes or remarking on how the crops were coming on; he only worked the land like themselves, where had he learned to make them jump like a drill sergeant? In the end Macdonald stood up on a stone, pulled his waistcoat down over his stomach while his clerk locked up the money-bag, and made a little speech.

'We understand each other now – we have done some business and that gives a solid footing. These are difficult times, not all the old ways will serve. You have all worked at the kelp – well, put it out of your minds, we are all *farmers* again and what we can find a market for is wool. And the store cattle. They will always do, but wool is at a premium and the estate must act accordingly. Whatever land stands in the rent-roll as grazings must be let as grazings – we cannot allow any number of black cattle to rove about the moor wherever it now appertains to a farm. If any man wants to get the good of such ground, he had better hire as a herd with the farmer, and by this means we will all be satisfied. Better regular work than a poor, scratching kind of life under an unproductive system – what do you say?'

Nobody said a word. James Macdonald rode off on his horse, his man five paces behind him on a pony. His words went round and round for months, repeated, distorted, parodied, interpreted in the most dismaying lights; it even sounded as though the shieling pastures might be threatened; nobody paid rent for them; supposing they brought the new big sheep in to Grenetote and let them come mowing right across the moor? Locusts would not be in it, there would be nothing left for the township herds…Whichever way you looked at them Macdonald's words stank of hard bargaining; he was reputed to work his people at Balranald like cotton pickers; the unmarried men (according to Roderick MacPhail) lived in an old cow-house with green water standing on the floor. When Macdonald rode through Sollas to Lochmaddy, going to pick up packages from Skye, people had a good look at him (from behind) to see if he had horns, or a barbed tail under his coat, but all he had was coarse hairs sprouting out of his nose. His horse was a tall bay, groomed and sleek, and nobody was surprised next summer when an expensive-looking girl accompanied him on a dappled garron, wearing a dark-blue riding habit and a sea-blue bonnet perched on her curled hair. They had heard about Macdonald's daughter Jessie, who got her clothes in Glasgow and danced at the balls at Dunvegan and Armadale. After she had passed, Flo trotted behind her, miming a horse's canter with her hands, then patting and preening her hair into place with voluptuous gestures; people started laughing; Miss Jessie Macdonald looked round, wondering, and Flo dodged behind a house. Inwardly she had been admiring the young woman's style, her easy seat on the horse, her look of enjoying her own appearance. It was a pity you had to have a father who was cock of the midden before you could look the world in the eye or sail along as handsomely as a swan… She went and looked at herself in a pool, opened her blue-green eyes a little wider than normal, leaned her head back and looked below her upper lashes, drew in her cheeks to make her face more oval – how easy it was to act the gracious part! For a minute or two she sauntered along the sand which the tide had smoothed, pointing her toes outwards and inclining her head gracefully from side to side, then she gave a high skriech like a dancer and ran as fast as she could towards her home.

Chapter 12

1846

Flo loitered along the path between the fields, letting the damp air cool on her face and the veiled light transport her to some other country, seen in a dream or a picture. She loitered because there was nothing to hurry for and because she was hungry. Her head felt too light, as though an airy space inside it was gently expanding and would spread right through her, like sleep. But her stomach ached, it wanted thick hot porridge, it wanted well-cooked kail with yellow butter, fresh fish in pure-white flakes. The morning's gruel, the remains of last year's oatmeal boiled in water, had gone off into her like snowflakes in the sea, making no difference.

Mairi had said she had a stitch and sent Flo along to see if there were any potatoes ready for lifting, but the shaws had scarcely yellowed. A few leaves were brown at the edges, black even, but there would be nothing in the ground yet worth eating. So her feet found their own way over the silvered grass; around her the world melted off into grey gloom, nothing to focus on; blurs appeared in it, large and shapeless; as you reached them they shrank into familiar shapes, the MacPhails' peat stacks, the three stones above high-water mark that were shaped like seals; you passed on into the next layers of the dimness, looking for things to recognize, seeing only the bluish nothingness, hearing the crisping of water amongst bladder-wrack and tangle, one repeated note from a shore bird; it flitted into sight past a rock shaped like a seated man, past the grey-green fringe of the cornfield nearest the sea, then sheered off sharply as it saw Flo looming through the fog. A lonely, lonely cry it had given – she thought of Roddy, tried to think of him, but where could he be? Out there on the sea? If he was working on a boat somewhere, he could have sunk in the storms last January and no news would ever come. He could have sent a message, not to her (why should he?) or to his parents (he had hated them so much) – to whom then? To Archie his friend? But the young lads never did that, they took off on their search for work in a spirit of brave independence and turned into men in some other country… The humped shape sitting in the fog really was a man; it was Archie Maclean perched on a boulder, looking as listless as herself. He looked up, apparently as indifferent as if she had been a stranger, but he moved along the rock to make room for her. She sat down beside him, saying nothing.

'Slack water,' he remarked.

'No – it has turned – listen.' They listened and heard the water ticking and rustling as it ebbed through the seaweed.

'I might dig for lugworms in an hour or two. But there is a lot of work in it, these days, for a few small fish.'

'A lot of work in everything for not very much.'

'Is your father still bothering with his kail and cabbage?'

'Mother and I dug the plot this year – his back is too stiff.'

'Aye. I thought that. Is it a job, living with a man his age? It must be terribly quiet in the house.'

Flo felt the heat coming from his body at that moment, from his leg and side next to hers. Was he making one of his proposals? His getting at her father fired her with scorn and she looked sideways at him, seeing a man in his twenties with the gawky features of a youth, his long heron-legs, his high-bridged beaky nose that could look cruel, or silly when it was reddened by cold and wet. He felt her look, half-turned, and put his hand on her skirt. She took it and felt his fingers with a firm touch.

'Soft hands, Archie McLean – is there nothing to do at the Mathesons'? You need a place of your own to keep you working.'

'And who can get that!' He withdrew his hand in a flare of resentment. 'There is my sister's Alasdair married off to Morag MacPhail, he is not twenty, I think there is a child coming, and the two of them have nowhere to sleep but a corner of big Alasdair's house!'

'Did they not think of that before they married?'

'Ach, you get fed up of being on your own, and the old folk treating you like a laddie. What do you say, Flo?'

But she would give him no encouragement. She looked straight out to sea, where the fog had thinned to show the brown sandy mud still glistening. He looked for some moments at her profile, liking its clear lines, her father's nose, long but not fleshy, her nostrils finely curved, her mother's sea-green eyes and light-brown brows. She was too haughty – if only she would banter like the other girls, or laugh at his banter anyway. Frustration spurted in him again: 'Damn it all to hell, why am I blethering on about weddings and croft houses? There is nothing left for the likes of me – not a stone of a house or a rig of ground. Have you seen Grenetote? The new man there is ploughing with horses, it is all corn between the moor and the sea, and he has his own bull too. He will be lucky one day not to wake up and find his cattle hamstrung, or his stackyard fired!'

His anger was like whisky – it fired straight into your head, exciting your thoughts, leaving you sickened. She shivered and got up. They walked slowly westwards through Malaclete. Before they separated towards their own houses, three horse-riders, two men with a woman between them, overtook them and they had to stand aside to let them past: Jessie Macdonald, dressed in green, flanked by a handsome young man, blond and tanned, and a formidable-looking older man, swarthy, with intense dark eyes and a full black beard bristling on his pale face.

'Oh Patrick!' Jessie Macdonald's voice reached them clearly. 'Why do you always make us race?' The riders whisked past and blurred off into the fog.

'Ooh Patrick!' Flo mimicked, 'Who is that? I have never seen him hereabouts,'

'He is called Cooper – a lawyer from the mainland. He seems to be well in with the factor. And with the daughter.'

'Ach – how could she like such a villain! And was that Donald Macdonald of Baleloch?'

'Oh aye, her pretty young neighbour. She has men enough on her string, or so they say. I wonder, does she keep them all dangling?'

He turned off towards the Mathesons' and she went in to tell her parents that the potatoes were hardly ready yet; a few were looking seared on their edges but that was all.

'Seared?' Allan looked up at her from beside the fire. Mairi put down her knitting.

'Black and withered but not right withered…' The girl faltered as she realized at last what she had been seeing in the field. Without eating, the three of them hurried along through the gloaming to the potato fields. More leaves had turned, shrivelling and hanging off their stems, which had gone spindly. Mairi picked one and crushed it in her hand, then put her nose to it, and gagged. It smelled like a toadstool. Allan took the whole plant in his hands and pulled. It came out of the earth easily. In place of full tubers, clots of black rot were clinging to the roots. They fell off when he shook the plant. With Mairi and Flo he worked along the lazybed, then moved on to the next one. The same everywhere. The blight had come again, the crop was smitten in the ground, their food destroyed.

Darkness thickened round them as they stood on the little plateau which held the field and looked at each other helplessly. It was as though they had wakened in the morning to find the roof and the walls gone. Saving possibilities edged into their minds – maybe other fields would be sound? They dismissed them without uttering them. 'Thirty-six was still an evil memory and this time they knew their strength was low already after the poor years when the over-grazed ground had given too little nourishment to the cows and the milk had been thin and scanty even in the summer. They looked round into the gloaming – a window glowed faintly orange here and there – it was hard to believe that the air, the ground, were full of plague. They made their way slowly along to the Mathesons', wanting the relief of company, some escape from the faintly putrid darkness where already they could hear the low wind rustling across the desiccated leaves.

Murdo let them in, saying nothing, looking mournfully at Flo so that she wanted to shake him. Big Alasdair looked up as they came in. He was gaunt now with a deep line trenched down each cheek.

'Allan – Mairi – you have been looking at the fields… Well … I am sending Murdo to Lochmaddy without more ado, we may hear of supplies coming across from Argyll. And Archie will go over to Balranald to let the man know – '

'We should all go there and take what we need!' Archie's voice shook.

'And if we had all his store to divide,' said big Alasdair helplessly, 'would it go round two hundred?'

In the half-dark shortly after sunrise the townships were all afoot; the families went to the potato fields with their creels, the four-year-olds carrying them between them, the babies shawled to their mothers' backs. Neighbours were calling to each other, 'We have a sound bed here! The shaws have rotted but the potatoes are firm!' The men thrust in the footploughs, the women delved with their hooks, the children lifted clods and potatoes in loose handfuls together, shook the earth off, and proudly held up big ones for other folk to see. As the dew spattered off diseased shaws onto healthy potatoes, the invisible spores fell with it and the blight spread. One field in three looked fair and wholesome, the crop was carried happily home, it lay in heaps, reassuring the families that they would survive, and as the autumn loured into a scathing winter, with showers of sleet and then wet snow whipping over the sea in black squalls, the potato hoards sank in on themselves as the blight ate through them and reduced them to a pulp. The houses stank. The families could not believe that even the remnant of the supply was being snatched from their mouths; as hunger sharpened, they boiled the soft grey potatoes and forced their throats to swallow them; dysentery followed; the last strength was running out of them, and now for weeks on end few people were seen outside, on the waterlogged plains of the machair or between the blackened oblongs of the fields, as the people saved their energies and thought despairingly of the coming spring with nothing fit to plant.

CHAPTER 13

1847

F lo stepped out of the house into an enveloping grey silence. The sky seemed filled with a dark bruise. No clear sign of wind or rainfall brewing up. The sea like old ice, gripping Vallay and the shore in one spreading zone of cold. She would see if the ebb left any whelks or cockles, even small ones – they were the one supply of food which did not change much with the seasons. Mairi had got up to go out with her but then bent over, pressing her side – her 'stitch' again. She said no word, just looked at Flo, white-faced. And Allan felt good for nothing, his upper body had to move all in one piece, like a burden lodged in him.

We should hibernate like bears,' he said, attempting a joke. 'But they usually have a good feed first.' This had been the first Christmas since Flo was born that they had not put out special sheaves of corn for the cattle and another for the wild birds. Since Hogmanay they had not gone more than a few feet past the doorstep, only for water to the burn pool and once or twice to the Mathesons'.

Now Flo felt herself amidst such a stupor of quietness that she could have believed Greenland was like this. The houses looked to have slumped into heaps of thatch and old stones, littered amongst the bleached, dun grass. A few brown cattle stood at the byre ends, leaning together. In the hush she became painfully alert, on edge for the least noise or movement. She looked along to the MacPhails' – no smoke – past there to the McLeods', the MacAskills', the Macaulays', and the last croft, the Boyds'. A small blue plume stood above Archie Boyd's house. Beyond that, at the edge of Sollas, a small dark figure came into sight over the brow, seemed to wave, then disappeared again, Flo walked down to the shore and as she passed the MacPhails' door she heard a murmur and called to them, but tentatively – the strain between the families made it impossible to be sure what sort of a welcome you would get there. No answer, She hesitated, and went on down to the strand. When she came back three hours later with a small grass bag of shellfish, the door was half open and a smell of dirt coming from it made her catch her breath. A voice called weakly, 'Please … Please …' Holding her breath she stepped onto the threshold – had that been Eileen's voice? She looked in – Roderick and Morag were lying on the floor under a ragged blanket, their faces smeared black – pieces of furniture smouldered in the hearth, giving out a faint heat – in the closet off the room she could just see Donny, lying on a litter of straw, his face clay-coloured, his eyes big and dull in hollowed sockets. Eileen was holding onto the table, her hands and face sooty, her eyes white against the dirt. She pointed at a bowl of meal and water, pointed at the fire, and staggered. 'Brochan – make the brochan – make the …' The words came out hoarsely in a guttural parody of her voice. As Flo stood appalled, speechless, she heard a light clicking from the floor and realized that the parents' teeth were chattering in a fever, they were shaking all over. She wanted to flee out at the door but Eileen's eyes were fixed on her in appeal. Shuddering, she built up the fire, boiled a pot of water, and made gruel with some musty meal and a little salt. When she left, Eileen was creeping from one member of her family to another, feeding them from a spoon. At her own house she burst into tears, then dried her eyes and told Mairi and Allan exactly what she had seen.

'Typhus?' Allan looked at Mairi. 'It was rife on Benbecula in '36. We have none of us the strength to fight the illnesses when they come. Well – the MacPhails' have not, the way they let their dairy cattle go down, and their vegetables.'

'Is that a judgement on them?' Mairi asked.

'No judgement – just a fact. Anyway – six of them living off the same land as the three of us. It is as well Roddy went away. Did you see the old folk?'

Flo had forgotten about them, Where could they have been? In the closet beyond Donny? And what was happening in the other houses? By nightfall the Campbells and the Mathesons had been round the township. Only four families were free of the fever. There were corpses in three houses where the men were still too weak to make coffins for them. At the Mathesons' Alasdair and Morag's baby Allan, two months old, seemed to have caught dysentery from his mother and was dying as they watched, a scrap of clammy life in a nest of old shawls.

'What is to be done?' said Archie. He looked thinner than ever, like an accusing ghost, sitting in a crouch and looking from one to the other with hard staring eyes.

'Bury the dead,' said Allan. He laboured for several days, splitting old boat hulks, planing the timbers to some level of smooth and decent appearance, and nailing them together: they were rough and rickety but they were better than nothing. With Archie and big Alasdair, Murdo and Archie Boyd, he carried them to the houses and left them at the doors. But he nearly had to fight with Archie to make him leave them there.

'Go in and catch the fever and it will get us all,' he said urgently as Archie knocked at the MacPhails'.

Archie swung round and glared at him, his face inches away. 'You are a cold one – leaving the dying to coffin their own dead.'

'Do you want more to die?' But he would never forget the scraping sounds from beyond the door as Eileen dragged three members of her family across the floor to bring them to their coffins. Old Roderick had died (but his wife, tough old Morag, had not); Donny had died and so had his mother; Roderick MacPhail lay in the wreck of his home while his father, his wife, and his younger son were carried away to the graveyard mound on the bleak plain at Dunskellor.

The families felt utterly beleaguered now. Allan had a vision of the island, an uncanny clod cut off from other life, marooned on the ocean, shunned and forgotten. Was it the same all up and down the Long Island from Lewis to Mingulay? Were they letting it happen on the mainland, under the eyes of the gentry and the government, and the newspapers? He kept his vision to himself as he went through the township with the fit people, burning old litters and pallets, lighting bunches of bog myrtle almost as a rite against the stench of death, serving out to the convalescent a small dole of porridge cooked by Mairi and big Alasdair's Flora. Archie lusted for action, and he got it by an unbelievable windfall; a small coasting schooner foundered off Boreray, the crew were taken off to Lochmaddy, and before the sea broke up the ship dozens of able-bodied men had sculled across the sound and looted it to the last ounce of provender. They brought away bags of flour and sacks of seed potatoes, the half of it too mixed with sand and salt water to be useful, but there was a smell of baking again in several houses and a flush of hopefulness for the coming spring.

At this time the Reverend Finlay Macrae chose to preach a sermon on texts from Isaiah which pointed uncannily at the present troubles:

And the firstborn of the poor shall feed, and the needy shall lie down in safety: and I will kill thy root with famine, and he shall slay thy remnant …

For the waters of Nimrim shall be desolate: for the hay is withered away, the grass faileth, there is no green thing.

Therefore the abundance they have gotten, and that which they have laid up, shall they carry away to the brook of the willows.

When news of his words reached Malaclete, opinion divided hotly on what he had meant: famine was plain enough, but what did he mean about the hay and the grass – was he making a nasty bargain with the Lord to punish them with a bad year for taking away an 'abundance' from the wreck and laying it up in their kists? Small abundance! It was nearly gone already. It would have been more to the point to thank the Lord for wrecking the schooner on Boreray and not, say, on Harris, where seemingly there was nobody left to get the good of it

As the days lengthened and the tops of the new green weeds began to poke through the earth beside the middens, the families began to feel that they might win through. Their gums ached with scurvy – two of Allan's teeth dropped out as he chewed painfully at a dish of cockles stewed in milk – but Mairi's pain had slackened and the three of them were able to cut the turf on the lazybeds at Easter and drop in seed potatoes brought from the wreck: with luck they might be free of blight, they had come from Caithness, which was rumoured to have escaped the disease (but every kind of wishful rumour was flowering with the sunlight).

As they worked they saw a figure, a man, coming along the track from the east with a bag in his hand and another over his shoulder. A stranger? But his loping walk was familiar. Flo called out 'Roddy!' and started out to forestall him; he must not walk in on the remnant of his family unprepared. From close to he looked weathered compared with her image of him – his skin had less of a smooth brown glow, it looked hardened, and his lips were cracked. He took her hand and said, 'Flo – you look thin. But you look well.'

'We are all right, Roddy.'

'Half the folk between here and Lochmaddy look like spectres. Well – they are worse on the other side.'

'Where is that?'

'All round Ireland – they are eating grass. Ach – it is not to be thought of – you would drown in a sea of misery. I suppose I had better go in and say hullo.'

'Roddy' – what could she say? 'They are not all here.'

'Has Donny gone?'

'Gone? He was ill, Roddy. And the old folk. And your parents. They were all ill…'

He knew her meaning now – a quietness fell leadenly over them. He came on to Allan and Mairi, embraced them both, and went on slowly towards his home.

In the nights that followed, the Mathesons' and the Campbells' seethed with talk. Roderick McCuish was home again – his parents and a young sister had to be nursed, and the Harris ferry had failed for want of traffic. He came over bringing his neighbour Archie Boyd, a quiet man with short black hair bristling on a knobby skull – he reminded Mairi of her brother. Roddy had had to stay with his family at first; they were still apathetic and had to be goaded into the simplest work of the house, let alone the croft. But once he had some potatoes planted, the ditches dug out and oats sown, he came each night to Mairi and Allan's; his sister Morag was there too, quiet and close-knit after the dying of wee Allan; she looked from Archie McLean to Roddy to big Alasdair, hungry for their words, charged with the slow-burning zeal to do something for the township which was spreading through them all.

'We are near starving but there is not an absolute dearth,' Allan put it to the group one evening.

'You mean there is meat on the hoof,' said Archie McLean, 'and corn stored.'

'In the big barn at Balranald,' broke in Roddy. 'Put names to the places and then we will all know what we mean. Corn at Balranald, and at Baleloch, beef cattle grazing along at Grenetote, and sheep on all these places.'

'Macdonald still has flesh on him,' said Archie with a laugh. 'And a high colour – he needs some help to get less fat'

Flo looked at his face, his eyes glittering with devilish amusement. He made her feel uncomfortable – just as well Roddy was there to put some reason into their talk.

'Roddy' – Allan was struggling with difficult thoughts – 'I know what you are saying, you are saying "Get food from them that have it and divide it out" I am not against it, but let us think a bit – how do we justify the theft?'

'Theft?' Roddy looked incredulous. 'How did they get their land?'

'Oh, they bought it, or anyway they leased it.'

'From the estate. And the estate – the factor – thieved it from the folk they forced out.'

'You may say that – '

'Allan' – Roddy's voice sounded patiently reasoning, as though tempering his argument to an old man's understanding – 'if we held this place in common we would not be rich, or even comfortable, but we would have more. Do the farmers work to feed their own families? Do they? They work to make a surplus and trade it for the cash.'

Flo spoke up. 'Two seasons ago, when we ate all we harvested and still went hungry, they were sending away potatoes by the hundredweight to sell in Oban. There would be people alive here now if they had had that food to fill them.'

Allan and Mairi looked at each other and at big Alasdair. It was all true, but where would this logic lead? Were they to live like reivers on an ancient border, driving stolen cattle into the hills and camping there like outlaws? Two weeks later, when a late frost had made the bogs firm, Roddy and Archie got two horses from Archie Boyd, muffled their hooves with bags plaited from bent-grass, and slipped through by Glen Drolla to the factor's farm at Balranald in the middle of the night. They cut the throats of two store cattle with their sickles, and two sheep, threw the cattle over the horses' pack-saddles, and carried the sheep on their own shoulders into the hills, across the track from Malaclete to the mill at Dusary, and round the flank of Marrival to the lochan just above the shielings. By the light of the sunrise they dismembered the carcases and cut them into joints and sides. They broke the ice on the loch, washed the meat, packed it with ice, and stored it in little caves under the east side of the mountain. When James Macdonald and Patrick Cooper came riding through the townships two days later, their faces stony, Flo and Morag Matheson were watching from the heather near Big Alasdair's Burden and ran across the sands to warn the others. Cooper and Macdonald were greeted politely in Malaclete and accepted a bowl of sowens from Mairi Campbell; they supped it standing up and you could see their nostrils trembling for the smell of meat. But the families were digging and spreading weed with quiet diligence in the fields.

The spring was a fair one; May was cold and bright week after week; they went up early to the shieling, the depleted families with fewer old folk or babies to care for, and built up their strength with some fine meals of tender beef and mutton. They drank the factor's health in burn water and Archie said a short grace: For what we are about to receive, we have only ourselves to thank: so let it be.'

CHAPTER 14

1847–1848

The blight destroyed the fields again in September, on the heels of rainstorms which blew for days, laying the corn and piling ridges of sea-wrack within yards of the Campbells' doorstep. The crop would have been small enough; the families had not planted a quarter of the usual fields; many of them were so demoralized that they seemed to have stopped believing in the future, even when it was only months away. At times Allan and Mairi felt ashamed to have benefitted from the cattle-stealing adventure, yet shame was an abject emotion; they would need all their pith of sense and pride of worth merely to hold on to life.

Rumours of an emergency supply of foodstuffs had been going round for months; many families seemed to want only to wait for this manna to descend, and now the news became firm that a shipload had reached Lochmaddy, paid for (some said) by the Church, and the turn of Sollas was coming soon.

The Campbells had a short, wry discussion as to whether they would accept a dole and had to decide that they would: hardly a crumb of solid food could be got from their ground before October, and their kists were empty.

Late in September Allan found himself in a silent queue in the middle of the township. Everybody knew each other but they all kept their faces to the front and nobody said a word. Quantities of oatmeal and peasemeal were being weighed out from the tail of a cart. The Reverend Finlay Macrae was standing nearby with a slight smile on his face that seemed to dispense good will in small amounts in all directions. His stiff red hair and pale blue eyes reminded Allan for a blink of someone long ago and then he was noticing, behind the minister, Patrick Cooper, the busy lawyer who seemed to be everywhere these days, with his black holes of eyes that took in everything and gave nothing out.

'Mr Macrae,' said Allan above the mumble of the suppliant at the head of the queue. 'Mr Macrae?' Heads were turning and he raised his voice. 'Are we being fed by the Church? or by the estate?'

'Eh – ah – by neither, in point of fact. The Central Fund for the Relief of the Destitute has been so good as to send supplies from Glasgow.'

'And you are here to see fair play.'

'That is so – that is so.'

'And Mr Cooper?'

The minister was looking impatient. 'I suppose the estate would wish to oversee the wellbeing of its tenants,' he replied, in his weightiest nasal tone. Allan realized why Cooper was there when he reached the head of the queue and presented his bag for his ration.

'Three in the family, with two females? 3 lbs. for the day – I will issue a stone to last between now and Friday, Nothing to pay, but the dole must be worked off on the roads or the drains at a penny-halfpenny for yourself for eight hours daily and a penny for the wife. Next?'

'Of course we cannot do it,' Allan said to the others in the evening. They are trying to kill us.'

'Maybe they want only the fittest to survive,' said Mairi.

'Or is it a religious thing with them? They want the Elect to prove their state of grace by toiling so hard that they get to heaven early?'

'You can see what they really want,' said Roderick McCuish, 'contract labour for their access roads and their ditching. *What* is the wage to be?'

'One and sixpence a week if we all work. This fine young woman here' – Allan pointed at Flo – 'counts as a child.'

'And one man could make six shillings for a week's work on the ferry, when it was running, or at the harbour.'

'There is no need to fret.' Big Alasdair broke into their argument. 'You are going to be all right' – he paused solemnly – 'now you have a committee looking after the matter.'

'Come on, Alasdair,' Roddy said after a bemused pause, 'you have us all in the palm of your hand now.'

'The minister's committee?' Alasdair asked them innocently. 'Och well, you will know about it soon.'

'Alasdair!' Archie McLean threatened him with a potato hook.

'It is nothing at all, only the Reverend Macrae said he was wanting the services of a committee to see that the meal dole works out fairly and the folk put in the hours to earn it – all that kind of thing.'

'Who else is on it?' Allan's face was alight with possibilities.

'Well, he asked me to name a sound man so I said Roderick here – he has been away on the boats so there is nothing against him. And I said he probably had his own list but why not think about Archie Boyd, his father was an elder and he is a good worker himself –'

Jeers and applause were drowning out his words and Archie Boyd blushed deeply while hands hit him on the back and others shook Alasdair's.

'Very fine, big Alasdair – oh, we have Macrae now!' Roddy crowed. 'He never knew how we lived, or pretended not to, but we will tell him *now* – we will tell him!'

'But we could have done with Allan,' big Alasdair said regretfully as the excitement simmered down. 'You should have held your tongue in the meal queue, Allan. We must be cunning now, you know.'

'You heard about that?' Allan replied. 'Och, it is of no account, Macrae would never countenance sinners like us' – he looked across at Mairi. 'There will be cunning enough in the committee with yourself and Roderick and Archie Boyd all mining away.' He looked round the faces. 'We tell them everything – do you agree? Every fact about the forced work, about the wage, so-called, about the price of meal on the open market and what we pay for it in kind according to their *charity*!' The last word jagged like a barb. 'We fight them on every figure and we see to it that the estate does not skin us for its profit.'

The committee needed all its wits during that winter. The families were growing bowed and grey-faced as they trudged up the slopes on the west flank of Marrival, heads down against the drifting rain, straightening out the line of the track over to Dusary with spades and sledge-hammers, shovelling gravel which was hauled up in carts hired to the Fund by Macdonald of Balranald (at his own price). The white stones gleamed raw amongst the black of freshly torn peat; the water coursed unceasingly down the new ditches; the line of people (grey-haired mixed with youngsters) twisted for miles up the hill like a long tether woven out of limbs and bodies, tying them to the rack. Factor Macdonald and smart young Donald Macdonald of Baleloch were organizing the folk of Paible and Kirkibost to drive the other end of the road up from the far side and it was rumoured that the two gangs might be meeting at the top for Christmas.

'Suppose we miss,' asked a wag, 'and drive on past each other into the fog?'

'Nobody would ever know,' answered a friend, 'except the factor and the minister, and they would be pleased to see the backs of us.'

The Campbells tried a week on the road but Allan was past it – the base of his spine seemed to split when he lifted a laden shovel and Mairi's pain came back, doubling her up. Only Flo was left to work and the committee duly decided that she should get the householder's rate – ninepence a week. (Macrae looked dubious but he was outvoted.) There was no more joking now about the rates; it was like being given a licence to die slowly. A new scheme had started to let the women earn: a mill had been opened over in Portree, funded by the government and run by a businessman from Aberdeenshire; it gave out spun wool in hanks and the women found that if they knitted continuously as they walked about the crofts, they could earn one penny on a good day. There was a crackle of bitter reaction in the Mathesons' at night when Roderick McCuish reported that the man getting the profit from the mill was called George Cooper – the father of the law agent.

'Oh aye,' said Murdo Matheson (even sleepy Murdo was being roused by the way things were shaping), 'they have it to a fine art now – a few big men have all the strings in their fingers and we have to twitch and jump whenever they like.' He looked at Flo for her approval and she smiled gently at him.

'I will jump for nobody!' Archie McLean was stung. 'Has your committee gone to sleep, Alasdair? Or what is it doing about these rates?'

'Never mind the rates, we should be selling the work ourselves,' Roddy objected. 'Are we slaves in the Coopers' galley or can we live for ourselves?'

There was nothing to be done about the knitting money – the minister was apprehensive in case the great benefits of the scheme were lost altogether.

'Mr Cooper does not have to be doing this, you know,' he assured the committee when they met in his house over on Vallay. 'He is a very busy man with extensive interests in the Lowlands. I consider that you – that *we* would be ill-advised at this juncture to raise objections to the, er, arrangements. As it is the Fund have asked me to express their dissatisfaction with the operation of the scheme – they find that recipients of the wage in kind are defaulting on the work, on the ground of illness and, er, weakness, yet they are still in receipt of the meal and corn. Is this true?'

Alasdair, Roderick, and Archie Boyd returned his look without glancing at each other. Of course it was true – were they to withhold food from their neighbours when they were too ill to work, or sheerly too fatigued?

'I hope it is not true,' Mr Macrae continued, 'since I am – since we are instructed by the Fund to reduce the daily allowance to one pound weight in any case where idleness is proven.'

The three men left the house shortly after that and picked their way across the ford to Malaclete with little talk between them. They had taken over the actual weighing out of the foodstuffs several weeks before and they were completely resolved, without needing to discuss it, that they would continue to put the staff of life into the hands of their people until they were stopped by force.

The MacPhails were suffering severely now. Roderick seemed to be past working – at fifty he looked aged, his skin hung loose and his hands shook. Eileen knitted away quietly and prayed morning and night – but silently, for fear of Roddy's caustic tongue – and Roddy went daily for a week or two to break stones on the committee road. But the croft was being neglected, cattle broke into the cornfields and ate up or crushed a quarter of what the rains had left. And now he was trapped: if he worked the croft instead of labouring for the committee, he would be refused even meal on credit against a promise that he would work later when he had brought the harvest in.

Big Alasdair stood speechless with embarrassment at the meal cart as Roddy argued the point, his voice rising and rising as people came out of their houses to enjoy the quarrel.

'Is it making you feel still bigger, Alasdair – standing here like a banker? *You* are all right, with a pack of sons and daughters and hangers-on to keep your place going. But if I try to make my own oats instead of coming for them cap in hand, you treat me like a convict!'

'It is the regulation, Roddy – do you not see how it ties our hands? If we break the regulation, they will stop the supplies.'

'Ach, the regulation – that is a fine long word and it feels well in your mouth but I will not let it stupefy me. I will enter myself as destitute before I knuckle under to your *regulation!*'

But he knew he was only going to this length of defiance for the sake of the crowd of people listening. Before he could qualify as 'destitute', he would have to prove that he had neither stock nor store of any value left on his croft – he would have to sell his seed-corn and his cows, and then the staff of life would be snapped for good; the ground under his feet might as well be the rock of the seabed; he would have stopped it from bearing and next year's season would be closed against him.

He walked home past the black pulpy mass of his potato fields, staring into this gulf which sucked at him with its promise of relief from effort – why try any longer? Widow McLeod was destitute. The MacInneses in Sollas were thinking of admitting themselves destitute. In exchange for the word 'destitute' he and Eileen could get for themselves the small ease of a bowl of porridge every day with no more back-breaking in the fields, no more nightmares of worry at the failing of the potatoes, no more humiliation of praying that the weather would relent and spare the corn… He felt lightheaded and sat down on a stone overlooking the sea, letting his eyes close and relief steal into him. But something else was happening in him, he was looking into the depths of his fortitude – below that even – into his resistance, the final core of himself. How much is left of me? he thought. Am I empty in there? If I could let go – now – release my fingers from the edge and let myself slip and go off, forever, into the void, would I do that? Have I the ounce of grip and smeddum still to rise up out of the welter and keep myself breathing? He waited for the stir of an answer inside himself, and got it: he was still angry. Angry at the clouds for their cold torrents. Angry at the owners of carts and meal and money who could sit in judgement on their hunger. He heard his blood quicken and knew that he had resolved to work himself to death before he let his home be scattered.

CHAPTER 15

1848–1849

'If they come for us, we should not sit here, we should make a human chain …'

Flo looked at Allan's back as he stood in the doorway, his shoulder against the jamb, his tall body and rounded shoulders silhouetted against the glare from the sea. Since last winter he had got into the way of raising a topic as though everybody had been talking about it for a while already.

'How long could we hold our ground?' she started to say, but he had gone outside, beyond earshot. She knew where he would go, along the shore to a natural furrow that gave shelter from the sea-cooled north-easterly. It had been blowing across the Sound of Harris for a week, licking the waves into white bursts like gannets plunging, disappearing the further islands into a blue haze that made everywhere outside their own place seem unreal.

Among the yellow irises and the nettles Allan lay down and wrapped himself in his grey woollen cloak. There are various ways of resisting, he was thinking: you could form a massive squad of people, dozens deep, and sit immoveably against any charge. Or if that was too hard to organize, fusing hundreds of minds into a single purpose, you could form a single chain, defy them to hit and break your hands, but if they broke through, there must be another chain in readiness behind. As hard to organize as the squad? Fighting without weapons was bound to be hard … Hard hard hard. It was hard to keep living. But Flo was there, the spirit of the house, quick, quiet, alert, as much a fibre now in the strong net of the township as any of the men. When the Fund had put an end to the committee early last spring, she had been as forceful as anybody in working out the new way. Roderick McCuish had come in one evening, his eyes glinting frostily as they did when the latest bad news had sparked his sense of the sheer wickedness of things.

'We are out of a job,' he said, 'no more cosy ceilidhs with the minister. They say we can as well buy our own meal now from the depot at Portree.'

'Villains –' Archie McLean started to swear but Flo said simply, 'What can you expect? The estate has got all its works done for it so now we are useless.'

Roddy took his cue from her unbothered answer. 'If we clubbed together, we might afford a cargo – do you agree?' He looked round the faces and saw no dissent. 'We can go across before the March gales.'

'And before the price rises,' Flo put in.

'Angus Macaulay's boat is lying idle at Caolas,' said Roderick McCuish. 'He might let me have it.'

So Allan went round the houses, coaxing pieces of money from the families; nobody wanted to part with their savings but they could think of nothing else to do, and the committee turned itself into a crew, Roddy came in as helmsman, and Flo went in place of big Alasdair, whose head reeled at the thought of the crossing, let alone the lift of actual waves under him.

When they had come back safely, and the meal-kists were full for a time, and well-being warmed them, disinclining them to look beyond to the next shortage, Allan found himself telling Mairi and Flo about his own last and only voyage.

'When we got to the middle of the Minch,' Flo was saying, 'you would have thought there was no world left, only a cloud of grey ahead and behind, and we felt so small – I felt so small – but Roddy was singing.'

'I believe I felt smaller than that when I first came here,' Allan told them. 'Skye had fallen away behind and then we saw the islands, one behind another, like grey heads, and I remember thinking, they are like the generations, one behind the other, each dimmer than the last. They looked as old as legends. But as we neared, and saw the fields and houses, well, then I knew that there might still be a place for me to live in.'

The three of them looked at each other, smiling a little; they would have taken hands but the moment passed. Now he wished they had, he wanted that memory of firm touch, he wanted it wanted it wanted it – he rolled over on to his side and groaned aloud, opening his eyes to escape from the past, seeing green grass-blades and small yellow petals in a dense fabric; a grasshopper fell silent as he watched and then leaped out of sight...

In July when the last of the cargo had been eaten and before they could expect any food from the croft except milk and cheese, Flo had been across at Roddy's and Allan was outside at the peatstack. In the house Mairi cried out and then there came a grunt, an animal sound. He went in quickly; she was vomiting, choking and vomiting again, helplessly, as though she would crack with the effort. She looked up with a staring appeal; he went to hold her head; she pushed him away and was sick again; he got a bowl and cloths, sand to throw on the floor, a spade to carry it outside. She lay for a time on the bed, shining with sweat, and seemed not to notice when Flo came in. Towards the middle of the night she tried to sit up; he went and lit a candle and saw a flood of red pour from her mouth. He went and held her, Flo was up and getting cloths and water, Mairi's fingers were clenching into her side and when he put his hand against her belly, desperate to soothe it, it was as rigid as a board. She collapsed then and lay breathing limply, her face perfectly white. They washed her and changed her, feeling her limbs as light and limp as drying hay. If only the supple tension would come back into her body … Her face had gone expressionless, the eyelids bluish; in the grey light from the window her hair was like a colourless shadow on the pillow … She was too cold; they put on another blanket but she cooled and cooled, passing beyond their reach.

Now his brain seemed to split; half of him reeled away backwards and went from him irrecoverably. It was like being buried alive. Footsteps sounded overhead; there might be people doing the usual things somewhere above; he wanted only to black out, for good, to extinguish this unbearable agony of remembering. He made himself see her in his mind's eye (her forehead pale under the aureole of her fine brown hair) as he stood beside the lip of the sandy trench on the mound at Dunskellor, watching the coffin he had made for her drop out of sight into the sand and the old browned sea-shells, while big Alasdair read aloud a passage which he and Flo could believe in (he had wanted to read it out himself but he knew his voice would break):

'For everything there is a season, and a time for every purpose under the skies:

A time to be born, and a time to die; a time to plant, and a time to pluck up what we planted;

A time to kill, and a time to heal; a time to break down, and a time to build up;

A time to weep, and a time to laugh; a time to mourn, and a time to dance;

A time to cast away stones, and a time to gather them together; a time to embrace, and a time to refrain from embracing;

A time to get, and a time to lose; a time to keep, and a time to throw away;

A time to rend, and a time to sew; a time to keep silence, and a time to speak;

A time to love, and a time to hate; a time of war, and a time of peace.

What profit do we who work get from our labours?

All go to the one place; all come from dust and all turn to dust again.

Who can plumb the spirit in us that leads us upwards, or the spirit of the beasts that leads downwards into the earth?

And so I perceive that there is nothing better than to rejoice in our achievements, for they are our lot, and which of us can see what will come after us?'

The Reverend Finlay Macrae might have conducted a more elaborate service, but they did not ask him. It was not his graveyard…

It was easier with only two to feed. How can the fathers and mothers welcome their babies into the world? he asked himself. 'They want to stop us bearing,' he said one day out of the blue.

Flo looked across at him, considering. 'Alasdair and Flora are expecting a baby,' she said very quietly.

'Alasdair and Morag, do you mean?'

'No, no – big Alasdair and his Flora.'

'When?'

'In the spring.'

'I hope it does not kill her.'

They lived quietly into the winter, working automatically at the harvest; the blight was less virulent and they brought home a fair weight of potatoes but they did not trust them to stay sound in store; they spread them out to keep them as dry as possible and peered at them anxiously when they scrubbed them, looking for the least stain of mould. Roddy, Archie McLean, and the younger Mathesons went across the water to shear corn in the Lowlands and bought another cargo of meal and Indian corn with their money; they had to wait till the gales had passed before they dared to cross. Every time of peace and quiet now seemed to be a lull between crises.

'Old Roderick MacPhail said it was called the Stream of the Blue Men,' Allan remarked on a winter night as the wind whoomed in the chimney.

'You mean the sea?'

'The Minch. There was a woman, a poet, over on Heisker, she was more than six feet tall, Rachel, the wife of John Macdonald, and she made a big song when he was drowned at the fishing ...' He sang in a low voice, trying to find the tune:

> The shade of your memory keeps you alive for me,
> Death can never freeze the warmth of your kiss,
> Our love was still fragrant...

He had lost it, he let the words tail off, unaware that Flo was waiting to catch the drift. He had been thinking, as the wind shuddered outside, that the two of them might as well be on a raft. They could go under at any time. The little hoard of money was spent; he was far from sure that he could manage to plough in the spring (but Flo could maybe plough and he could sow?); their last supply of food had been got by the hands of others ... A cross-current of emotion took him and he felt suddenly unafraid; he did not care enough about himself to fear for the future; since Mairi's death he had felt weightless at times, invulnerable (except when a fearful pain of regret turned slowly inside him like an illness). If Flo and Roddy married, there would be the two crofts to support three young people; himself and old Morag and even Roderick could be written off; they ate little, and for his own part he was willing to stand on the edge of things and witness what went on. ...

As spring trailed gradually over the island, with its few small signs that the easy half of the year was coming (green buds on the willow scrub, an egg or two more in the turf hen-house), it was hard to keep to the onlooker's place. Hunger gave rise to short-winded bouts of anger, like a recurring fever. When people from the factor's clique rode past, people stared at them, unspeaking, as though they had been officers from a conquering army. The public comedy of the three-sided affair between Jessie the factor's daughter, young Macdonald of Baleloch, and Mr Cooper the brusque estate commissioner was watched like a cock-fight. One Sunday afternoon Jessie galloped through the township uncomfortably fast, hens flustered away from the horse's hooves, young Macdonald was laughing as he kept pace beside her, and then as they disappeared over the moor beside Big Alasdair's Burden, who should come foaming along but Patrick Cooper, his eyes smouldering. The young folk gave him a cheer and he raised his whip at them but then he thought better of it and hurried onwards like a maniac, standing in the stirrups.

It was as good as a fair; the men were putting wagers on who would get the girl; Cooper was favourite, he was as savage as a boar but he had the resources of the estate behind him; everybody knew that the gentry married for money, not for love, and young Macdonald was only the third son of a mortgaged house at Monkstadt in Skye. But the odds were stood on their heads soon after the planting of the potatoes. Roddy had been over at Balelone on the west side to bargain for a few sacks of seed and nobody would believe him at first but the old man had resigned from the factorship and young Macdonald had been given the job!

'A fine setback for Cooper,' Roddy crowed as he told the news. 'He will never play second fiddle to his pretty young rival. I tell you, he will be off to where he came from, to grind down some other bodies.'

'Never mind that – why do you think James Macdonald has made way for the younger man?' Allan had had to rouse himself to take an interest, but now a new train of possibilities was coming into sight and he felt disquieted.

'He has enough to do farming his own place.'

'He can never have enough to do, he is like a tribe of apes. If he has let go, it is because he means to make the lad his cat's-paw.'

'What to do?'

'Whatever he means to do. We will see soon enough.'

June failed them for once; heavy showers raked across the sea and the runnels between the lazybeds could scarcely cope with the running off of the water. As Archie Boyd walked over a sodden stretch of machair between his croft and the dunes, two horsemen appeared out of the driving grey and nearly ran him down – Cooper, in a long black cloak, and a stranger in a broad-brimmed hat and a leather bag slung over his shoulder.

'Mind the ground there!' Archie shouted out. 'Can you not see where there is corn coming up?'

'I can see that the ground is waterlogged,' Cooper said shortly. 'Note that, Fairbairn.'

They cantered off westwards, leaving Archie fuming; at night nobody else was inclined to think any better of the affair; this man Fairbairn was a stranger and when had a stranger brought them any good? (Nobody seemed to remember that Allan had been a stranger once and he was glad of that.) A fortnight later a paper was sent to big Alasdair, addressed to 'The Souming Officer', and everybody gathered to hear him read it out. Behind him, in his house, the new baby was crying loudly and he shut the door.

Lord Macdonald to the tenants in the Sollas townships.

The Drainage Inspector having remitted his report, we find that it is not in the general interest to lay out funds on the improving of the crofting grounds, on account of their heavy, wet nature and the many sub-divisions; but since the farms in Grenetote, Ahmore, and Oransay would answer to an extension of the drains and ditches, we shall make payable a wage of three pence per day (maximum of one shilling and six pence per week) for work done on those tacks, workmen to supply their own tools.

Further, since it has come to our notice that the late shortages have pressed hardly on the livelihood of the tenants and contributed to their arrears of rent, the wage so earned may be paid towards a passage oversea, the estate to find £1 for each pound earned at the work.

Patrick Cooper (Commissioner)
Donald Macdonald (Factor)
For the Estate

The ink was blurring and smearing in the blown drizzle. From the wet crowd a growl was rising, shot through with angry, unbelieving remarks:

'Slavery!'

'I will never work there.'

'What do they mean, arrears of rent, who is in arrears?'

'Tear it up, Alasdair!'

'Drive them out!'

Big Alasdair was looking towards Allan and Roderick McCuish, but there was nothing to be done; the paper had been snatched from his hands and was blowing away in pieces; children were fighting for the scraps and dogs were jumping on the children. A small wave of anger had gathered and broken. Maybe another would gather behind it.

'What is to be *done*?' Roddy asked the others in the evening. 'They have taken the best of the broad lands into their farms, outsiders have them now, and what is left for us?'

'Occupy them!' Archie MacLean answered him fiercely. 'Let the shielings alone this year – drive the herds on to the tacksmen's lands.'

'What good will that do?' Allan asked him. 'We would only lose the shieling pasture.'

'Reap their corn for them! Better than making pence digging their drains.'

'We would get little good of it until next season. The new man in Grenetote sowed only two fields in three, and they are patchy.'

While they talked, Cooper and Macdonald acted, or the Commissioner acted and the young factor dribbled the sealing-wax on to his letters, held his horse for him, and made eyes at Jessie over the rim of his wine-glass. Early in June a man in a new tweed coat rode into Sollas with Cooper beside him, and sent for spokesmen from the townships. Allan recognized him, it was Thomas Shaw, eldest son of the erstwhile factor, and here he was, Sheriff-Substitute for the county – once a family of spiders wove a tough web they clung to it forever. The man had clear hazel eyes like his father and his careful manner; as he greeted them and asked after people he had known, big Alasdair almost began to wish the father back again, at least he had been easier on them (or so it seemed looking back) than the old tusker Macdonald. After the civilities were over Sheriff Shaw took a packet of papers from his dispatch-case and served them all with notices of eviction.

If they come for us, we should not sit here, we should make a human chain, Allan said to himself. He rolled over on the flowery turf and propped himself up on all fours before levering painfully to his feet. Flo should be told what to expect, he thought, she should not be left to stagger forwards into the dark like so many of us.

'Suppose the case,' he started abruptly as they sat at the door in the gloaming, saving lamp-oil in the long sunset, 'of ten, eleven, twelve townships all up in arms against the laird. They flock against him in a little army of eight hundred or a thousand – '

'Any weapons?'

'No weapons – not at first. They gather round his place and demand that he signs a paper guaranteeing the ending of their grievance and no punishment, no vengeance when they have gone home again. Must the laird sign?'

'Och, I suppose he has no option. But surely he – '

'So away they go to their homes; now they are safe; he cannot hurt them all. But he knows, he is bound to know, that a few have done most of the talking – they only said what everybody knew but he must have some scapegoats. So he comes for them with his squad – '

'And they have weapons?'

'So do we, now, we turn our scythes and pitchforks into weapons, so that we can fight, but still we do not fight, the spokesmen are taken prisoner, he is carting them away and still we do not fight; we appeal to his conscience and he makes moral noises and carts them away, and we cut him off and make him stop and *demand* our people; we become very fierce and righteous, we will not stand for it any longer, and he sees the justice of our arguments and dazzles us with his teeth and while we are marvelling at the lustre of his dignity and the fine sounds of his language, *he – carts – them – away!*'

He could sense, without being able to make out the shading of her face, that she was angry with the story; she wanted to resist its logic. She had gone perfectly still, looking at the ground.

'They had only themselves to blame, in a case like that,' she said at last. 'Surely a thousand can always beat a handful? Unless the few have guns. And they will never come against Sollas with guns – will they?'

She sounded very young for a moment, wanting reassurance. But almost at once she was getting her dander up again: 'If Cooper tries to put us out, he will have to fight for every house. We never fought for the chief, but we will lose blood before we lose our homes.'

' "We"?'

'The womenfolk. Cooper has not managed to overpower his Jessie – no more will he get the better of us!'

As she looked almost wicked with relish at the thought of a set-to, he took a decision he had held back time after time for twenty years.

'Flo – you remind me of the women of Strathtay.' She looked mildly expectant, as though he was going to quote from a song or a tale. 'Far from here – on the other side of Scotland. But not so far from my old home. Because my language is a bit different from your mother's – you know that. It is because I came from Lochaber – more than sixty years ago...' He broke off as the years loomed behind him like a continent. 'Do you want to know?'

'Did you do some wrong thing?'

'Not in my own eyes. Or my friends'. How can I start to tell you? I have been secret for too long. Your mother was going to tell you, now that you can understand, but then she – ' His voice failed in his throat. 'I went... I went from Lochaber down to Glasgow and served my time as a joiner, and presently I got work in Perthshire, building a spinning mill. And then the government made an Act – the war with France was raging away – they needed men by the thousand. They were going to scour out the glens. And so – and so we stood up, and we made the lairds sign papers against the Act. And – Flo – here is the thing. How many young men do you suppose we saved?'

Quietness between them. Flo's face looked impersonal, as emptied of life as a bird's nest in winter. She glanced at him, then looked away across the darkened mass of water and waited for the end of his story.

'Not a one. We killed them. They say that hundreds were condemned to be transported for mobbing against the Act, and so they chose to go in the army, for fear of dying in Australia. So they died in France instead. Or Spain, or some other graveyard.'

'But you were not killed? Or transported?'

'I got off. I was never told why. They gave me bail and let me out of the prison in Edinburgh, in the winter – I was sick and stiff – I never felt so bad again till the year the potato rotted. So I slipped away, and went to Glasgow and changed my name to – various things, I heard they had made me an outlaw, because of course I was a desperate villain, I used to make people see reason and understand their rights. And so I drudged away in Glasgow for a while – I came over to Lochmaddy during the Treaty – and when at last I thought nobody would care any more, the wars had ended and the old kites in Atholl and Breadalbane would have died off at last, I sent a paper to Edinburgh and cleared my name. I never felt free to marry Mairi until that year, or you might have been born a good few years before you were...'

Why was he saying this? He had wanted to make her see how life dealt with them – how hard it was to stand against the rulers with their supple tricks, their deadly equipment. But Flo was taking her own message from his story.

'It is different now.' She sounded calm and sure. 'There have been no great wars for years. And we are not like meek cattle any more. I know you were not, but some of them must have been or they would never have let them cart you away. They will have to slaughter us all before we budge. And then who will grow their meat and wool for them? The MacDonald – the MacLeod – they are just drones.'

Looking at her, he saw his own ideas living again, and he blamed himself for letting old age undermine his hopefulness. But even as he took her arm and they went into the gloom of the house he was thinking, I was always split, between doubts and hopefulness; a hope is just a wish, and only a fool would expect the world to grant him that.

Chapter 16

1849

On 14 July a sheriff's officer called Macdonald, from Langass down beside Locheport, a tall gangling man with an embarrassed, raw-looking face, tried to serve notice of eviction, starting at the east end. Unluckily for him, Archie Boyd and Roderick McCuish lived there; they waited till he was well in among the houses and when he opened his mouth to read the piece on Archie's doorstep, Archie put on a respectful expression, Roderick gave the signal, and some of the lads and lasses, Flo and Roddy among them, stood up behind the dyke and let fly with stones. The hard crown of the officer's hat saved him but the stones were bouncing off his shoulders; he threw up his hands like a man with a swarm of bees at him, dropped his bits of paper, and ran for his horse.

They worked through his papers at big Alasdair's that night and found that they named every tenant in the townships.

Sunday was quiet. The Reverend Finlay Macrae got off his horse on the way back from his church; it was the last service before he went on holiday; he singled out the first crofter he saw, it was Peter MacLeod, and said he hoped there would be no bloodshed before they saw the end of 'this most unfortunate affair', and Peter MacLeod said he hoped so too.

On the Monday Allan and big Alasdair stationed Roderick McCuish's little brother Fergus and two of his friends as look-outs behind a dyke on the bare top level with Dunskellor. When they saw a little bunch of folk approaching along the Lochmaddy track, they ran the mile to Malaclete. They had recognized Cooper, walking his big black horse, and the 'bald man from the mainland' – that would be Thomas Shaw – and twenty more, strangers. But when they came nearer, several were recognized – they were sons of some of the Grenetote families who had gone away in 1843 and, so it was said, accepted small allotments on the moors beside

Locheport. Were they regretting having left this place with its fertile fields and hospitable people? The Malaclete folk did not ask them but drove them back with a storm of stones; Cooper and Shaw stayed in the rear like a pair of generals; Cooper looked furious, Shaw looked sick, but between them they failed to lead by example. That night at big Alasdair's they drank a little whisky to celebrate a good end to the second skirmish and Archie McLean tried to sing a stirring song by John McEwan of Houghgarry, about the regiment that Lord Macdonald had raised for the French war and paraded on the machair just past the Campbells' croft–

> 'Victory and blessing to the lads in their kilts…
> Strong in their manhood, bold on the battlefield…
> Standing or charging … er, eh … standing or charging…,'

Archie had lost his way and big Alasdair said it was just as well, John McEwan's own son Angus had been killed with the regiment in Egypt four years later and perhaps the old man was sorry by then that he had opened his mouth.

'And perhaps not,' Allan suggested. 'Once your kin have been killed, you can lose the pain of it if you sing loudly enough.'

'That was a sorry thing, bringing in the folk from Grenetote.' Roderick McCuish changed the subject. 'Did Cooper think they would fight harder because they envy us for holding on?'

'If he did, he was wrong,' said Peter MacLeod. 'A pack of bully-boys with not a brain between them. No wonder they let old Shaw diddle them out of their crofts.'

Allan and big Alasdair wondered if the families were taking it too lightly, revelling in the sight of Cooper with his tail between his legs. They got up before sunrise on the Tuesday and scolded the families until they went and lined the track three deep with heaps of sharp stones just behind them; the thing was turning into a little war; all they needed was a banner, and a skirl of shouts and jeers ran among the crowd when Flora, big Alasdair's daughter, and Flo and young Morag Matheson paraded along with three flags they had made out of widow MacQueen's old mourning dress. Since her baby's death in the year the potato rotted, Morag had turned bitter and quiet. Now she looked fit to wither the sheriff's officers with a look. The women planted the black flags in a line fifty yards east of Roderick's house, and when Sheriff Shaw appeared, by himself, with his twenty footsoldiers trudging behind him, the three women faced them and Shaw stood there looking like a cock that had lost its crow. The rain had started now, sifting down thickly from the west. Shaw was trying to shield his documents, and before he had got past 'I hereby give notice on this day of – ' Flo had drowned him out with a ringing speech.

'Mr Shaw – and Mr Cooper, if he is hiding somewhere – take your army with you and go out of here. This is our place – Lord Macdonald may have rights of ownership but we have rights of usage and occupancy' (she wondered afterwards where she got the words) and if you try to budge us, we will break your heads first, so spare us all the injuries and *get out of here!*' The passionate high note touched off the crowd; their cries swirled and screamed like gulls; Shaw was blenching under it and under the on-ding of the rain; his men were huddling, wishing themselves anywhere else, even on the driech slopes of Locheport. The last thing Shaw said was, You are in breach of the law, and I must warn – ' The cries drowned him out and he turned his horse, spurring to a canter through Sollas, and the children all along the road were flinging shingle at the backs of the bully-boys from Grenetote.

After that the families found it hard to sleep soundly. The days went by with no show of force from the Sheriff, no sign of Cooper. A few of the men walked over the hill past Kilphedder Cross to Baleloch to have a word with young Macdonald and see if he knew what his masters had in mind but there were only two of his ploughmen there, drinking and smoking by themselves while the cows munched at the green corn. Mr Macrae had gone off to stay with some of his grand friends on Skye, no doubt, but late in July he trotted into Malaclete and came up the path to big Alasdair's.

'Mr Matheson – and Mrs Matheson. I must not disturb the little one – I trust she is well? Yes, yes, yes… Difficult times, I am afraid – it has grieved me more than I can say to see the pass we have come to. That we should be fighting in the streets of our own township – yes, yes – and what will we gain by it all, I wonder? Mr Matheson, are we doing the right thing, do you think?' And he blinked repeatedly, his pale eyelashes flickering up and down as he waited for an answer.

People were gathering quickly; Allan and Flo had come up from the shore; Archie and Morag had come out of the house.

'Sometimes the right thing cannot be done,' big Alasdair answered him slowly, resenting the obligation to talk to the man. 'But is it right that we should be cleared from our own crofts?'

'No, no, no, not at all, of course it is not, it is a desperate measure, you know. But the estate is heavily in debt, that is no secret, and Lord Macdonald may well feel entitled to expect some recompense for his generosity in the famine –'

'Who was generous?' Morag interrupted him contemptuously. 'What we ate we earned.'

'Yes, yes, yes indeed, I am not saying you did not work hard.' Mr Macrae's eyelids flickered more than ever as he looked from face to face. 'But tell me now – do you see a decent life here for your families when there are so many mouths to feed on such a circumscribed acreage –'

'There is room enough along at Ahmore and Trumisgarry –'

'And on Grenetote –'

'We could plough out along the machair between the north and the east strands if we had leases like a farmer's –'

'I believe there might be room on Vallay, Mr Macrae,' Allan planted the point home, 'if you halved your glebe and let us make a croft.'

'An original idea, Mr Campbell' – the minister met his eye – 'but I believe the estate is quite well satisfied with my tenancy. I am sorry you have set your hearts against a removal; Lord Macdonald has been patience itself compared with some other proprietors. I fear for us all if the law has to take its course.'

Two days later the little lads on sentry duty saw a squad of men in dark blue uniforms marching in step along the plain of Sollas and ran to report.

'Soldiers or what?'

'A bit like soldiers.'

'Carrying weapons?'

'I think they had clubs – long white clubs.'

Flo and the women went at once to plant the flags across the track. The stones had heaped up by now into mounds and pyramids like shot. The young men were seething; Roddy and Archie would not wait behind the flags but went out in front as the police halted in a file four abreast with a sergeant leading them and a gang of estate men behind them. He shouted out commands and the policemen formed into a long rank two deep and stood easy. Rain blew over, making them lower their heads against it. People had arrived now from all the fields and houses; the women were standing with the younger children on the slope above the track, the men in a solid curve round the three with the flags, and Allan, Roderick, and big Alasdair had joined the two out in front. The parties eyed each other for a time, the policemen with their faces hardened over, the township folk looking from one to the other, wondering where they had come from, sizing them up (they were mostly big men with thick chests and shoulders), a bit daunted by the set of their faces (veterans were reminded of the troops in the line at Corunna and Waterloo). Here came the bigwigs, Cooper of course, two strangers, one of them talking busily to young factor Macdonald, and an officer – army? No, he must be a high-ranking policeman, in a fancy uniform. They reined in; the officer spoke quietly to the sergeant; Cooper stepped forward; a chorus of shouts greeted him; he held up his hand and as the shouts doubled he roared against the noise, 'Hear me now! You are already in breach of the law! This is the last time of asking – no force need be used – the householders with their families must comply forthwith with the orders of clearance' – the roar of voices rose in a gust – 'comply with the clearance and remove oversea. The benefits are clear – the estate will pay its share – you must pay the balance by selling me your stock' – he tried to say 'at a fair price' but the surge of noise rose like a wave with a wind behind it and he looked at the bigwig as much as to say 'You see, they are impossible.'

Peter MacLeod was calling out, 'We will not be moved, it is too late in the season, we cannot leave our crops standing,' and Allan, seeing the weakness of the argument – weak because it was an argument, nothing would do but outright resistance – roared out, 'We will not be moved' in his strongest voice, until he had everybody shouting it with him; the massed sound came down on the bigwigs like a cloudburst; you could see them flinch. Allan's own head was swimming, he wanted to lean on something, but when the chorus had sounded out a dozen times and was subsiding, he stepped forward a little and said in a carrying voice, 'Mr Cooper, and – who is this?' The bigwigs identified themselves, Sheriff Substitute Colquhoun, Mr Mackay, Procurator Fiscal – 'Mr Colquhoun, then, and Mr Mackay, you do not understand the case at all. Our place is here. Right is on our side. Move against us and we will meet force with force until you go back where you came from. You have your own place – go to it, and leave us in ours.'

Dogs barked at each other in the short silence after that. A four-year old called out 'Go away soldiers!' and the crowd nearest her laughed. Mr Macrae stepped forward and made a brief appeal: 'Good people – my people – please see reason – if you can join your friends and relations oversea, you will do well, I can promise you, and your children's children will live to build a new Sollas on Cape Breton Island.'

Archie McLean stepped towards him then and said in a choked voice, 'You are a Judas, minister – what did they pay you?'

A woman was weeping somewhere in the crowd; there was a stir and she stepped forward; it was Annie MacInnes from Sollas. 'We are ready to go,' she said, 'it will never do here.' Her husband stood beside her, looking at the ground. Their neighbours the Morrisons, followed by the Macaulays, came and stood beside them, like prisoners in the dock, or cattle in the sale ring. Macrae was waiting for any further offers while the women round the flags set up a chorus of derision, 'Off you go to Canada! off you go to Canada!' Allan and Alasdair were standing still, tense and silent; the enmity between them and the ranks of police was like a shadow cast by a thundercloud and Allan felt his chest tighten. The sheriff and the fiscal were conferring with the officer; Cooper and the factor were ignoring each other; the sheriff turned to the crowd and called out in a high voice, 'You see, now here are some reasonable people – they are only doing what is lawful. You must all follow suit now – I have the orders in my hand, every householder is named, and I promise you that the Superintendent's men will proceed with the clearance unless you remove now of your own free will.'

The policemen came to attention and raised their clubs, holding them upright. The men beside Allan reached for stones, and then the police were on them; bodies swayed and reeled in a knot; the white truncheons flashed; the police were lunging backwards, dragging at two men writhed like salmon, Roddy and Archie McLean, their wrists locked into handcuffs, chained each between two policemen. The other men surged forwards as the women screamed but they stamped to a halt as the police turned on them with their clubs high. The officer drove his horse across between the foremost crofters and his men and Allan felt, as he caught at Alasdair's arm to hold him back, the hot reek from the animal's haunch. Archie's voice yelled from somewhere in the posse, 'Save us! save us!' The police were trotting away in a close file, Archie and Roddy invisible amongst them, the riders keeping pace beside them, hooves chopping up the lazybeds, whips slashing down at the dogs.

The people looked at each other that night in a kind of trance. There was too much to say and all of it was useless. Flo cut the knot by saying,

'We should have saved Roddy and Archie – we should have saved them – the one thing to do and we let it go –'

Allan took her hands and said, 'They are only in the cells at Lochmaddy courthouse. Now we know their tactics, we can match them. We will go there and get them out.'

But she looked past him, looking for support among the others, and said again, 'We should have saved them.'

Alasdair said unhappily, 'They have heavy iron bars there and a high wall. You can hear the prisoners hammering at the oakum. It is like a barrack, or a fortress.'

'We can take MacRury's old files and chisels. You could break the doors down with your own hands, Alasdair.'

The big man looked uncomfortable. 'It cannot be done. And I have to go to Dusary tomorrow; the mill has offered me a hundredweight of meal if I fetch it myself.'

'Alasdair – they will be coming again tomorrow –'

It was the first time they had ever seen the big man angry. 'And what are we to eat? Flora needs all the milk, and the potatoes are done.'

Allan said carefully, 'The battle is not at Lochmaddy, it is here. Now, are we ready for them tomorrow? Flo, are we ready?' She looked at Morag, they both nodded, and then the group dispersed. Flo and Allan walked home silently, he wanted to speak to her, or her to speak to him, but their hearts were too gripped.

In the morning there was a mist shrouding the houses after the rain. The sea could not be seen. The police came out of the grey, two hours earlier than the day before. They lined the track and the ways between the houses, the bigwigs stayed mounted at the top end of Malaclete amongst the gang of estate men, and the gangling sheriff's officer from Langass went to the first door and knocked. Cooper with a policeman at his stirrup was looming just behind him. Archie Boyd opened his door and the man said to him, 'Notice to clear: will you go oversea on the terms offered?'

Archie looked along at Roderick McCuish's house. Roderick was waiting on his doorstep. Archie raised his face and said loudly, 'I will not be moving!' The man stood back, Cooper turned and signalled, and four men with clubs and tools came at a trot, shoved Archie aside, and went at the house like crows at a carcase. Furniture came flying through the door, stools and straw pallets, the frames of the beds, cooking pots, the spinning wheel, it broke up as it hit the ground, and then they were beating out the windows with a lever. Two more had climbed onto the thickness of the wall and were riving off the thatch with potato hooks and flinging it down into the faces of the crowd as they pressed forward. Archie stood stunned. Then he roared and went for Cooper but the bodyguard caught him, twisted him round, and held him with the truncheon barred across his throat. The sheriff's man had moved along the MacCuishes' and was saying into Roderick's stony face, 'Notice to clear: will you go oversea on the terms offered?' Roderick shook his head, very slowly, and put his arm across the door. Two men rushed him, barged him back into the house, and the crowd heard the smash and grunt of the struggle. Now the timbers were toppling outwards from the Boyds' roof, people jumped back, and the sheriff's man was at the MacPhails'. Eileen answered the door and said nothing when he put his question; her father was inside, sitting at the table, staring like a hospital patient. Men went in and began to throw out clothing and pots and sticks of furniture and the crowd gasped; there was old Morag, many of them had not seen her for years; the men tried to lift her on her mattress; she hit and scratched at them and they bumped her down onto the floor and dragged her out; she was gripping the side of the closet, the loom, the doorposts, her knuckles were white and her eyes were staring. That was her last effort; one of them cracked her hand with his cudgel and she let go with a high shriek of 'Murder! murder!' They dropped her on to the grass outside and she crept on all fours into the shelter of a dyke while the men tore out the roof.

Allan had got up at the first sounds from the far end. He was waiting with Flo at their door; she wanted to go out and rally the women but he said, 'We must defend this place.' The sheriff's man with Cooper close behind him stopped on the grass three feet away and rattled off his speech: 'Notice to clear: will you go oversea

'We will not be moved!' Flo shouted out and four men came at them with their clubs held across like bars, driving them back into the room. Water was flung onto the fire; it exploded in a burst of steam; they tore the bedclothes off; one of them began to swing at the frame of the loom with a heavy hammer. Allan lunged to grab him and the right-hand stave of the frame toppled onto him, hitting the side of his head, bringing him down. Blackness. A roaring noise like under water. Grass. He was lying on the ground, birds were cawing, a man came stooping out of the hen-house with a hen in each hand and thrashed them against the house wall, beating their heads to red rags. Another was riving at the hen-house walls with a shovel, throwing the turfs onto Allan's legs, burying them.

The township was stupefied. There was little movement except the frenzy of the bully-boys; then Flora Matheson rushed out of her door with wee Katrine clutched to her, shouting 'Murder! Murder! they are murdering the children!' Inside young Alasdair was locked in a wrestler's grip with a tall estate man. Alasdair was taller and he had the man round the ribs, they were cracking, the man was being bent backwards slowly while his mate bashed at Alasdair's head and shoulders with his club, making the blood stream. 'Murder! Murder!' The crowd was huge now; the neighbouring townships had swarmed round the black flags; Morag and Flora Matheson were guiding the people to the heaps of stones. As they began to fly, hitting crofters as well as policemen, the officer went part of the way up the slope and shouted out, 'There is no murder being done! Listen to the offer – the terms are reasonable – listen to the offer when your turn comes.' He turned down the hill; a stone caught him between the shoulderblades and then the air was all stones, volleys of them rattling against walls and bouncing off thatch; the police were holding their helmets on, cowering into shelter, while the estate men tried to get behind the police. Shouts from the shore. The Sollas women had arrived in force and were hurling big stones at Cooper's squad; they were too big and they fell short; children were scrabbling smaller stones out of the burn. The officer had gathered his wits now; he ordered his force into two sections, waited for the women to come at them, and sent his men against the side and rear of the crowd, clubbing them as they came past and chasing them back, battering at them as they panicked and tried to run past Malaclete on the seaward side. But as their blood got up dozens turned and fought and the Malaclete women rushed downhill to help them, taking the truncheons on their arms and shoulders, hitting back with shuttles, fork-handles, stems of sea-tangle, whatever they could find. Their weapons lashed and rattled off the men's helmets and then the clubs prevailed. Morag Matheson and Mairi Boyd were lying stunned among the pools left by the ebb, their scalps opened, their hair dark with blood.

When the officer saw the bodies littered among the drifts of dried seaweed, he blew his whistle and the police backed off slowly, their truncheons jabbing, keeping the women at a distance. The piles of stones were exhausted now and Flo screamed out in despair, 'Be manly Roderick,

Kenneth, Peter – stand up and fight!' A few shouted with her. It had no effect. People lay on their sides or crouched on all fours, breathing like driven dogs, staring, crying, bleeding.

Allan lay on the ground beside his house, half covered with a mess of turf and earth. Flo? Flo? Form a human chain, never swerve till we have cleansed the country, cripple his horse, big black horse, Mairi, watch your head, the head is coming out like a bruise, black sky, white hole at the zenith, reach it, swim swim swim towards it… He felt himself gliding uncontrollably, he made his eyes open and saw Flo's face and hair against the sky; she saw his eyes widen and his mouth open… Flo, a human chain and never swerve, watch your head, the club, Mairi, watch… Far away, into the glare at the end of the tunnel, on the other side of the house, a voice yelled out, 'Murderers! murderers! Come on and wash your hands in our blood!' And another voice, Agnes MacCuish's, 'Cooper! Cooper! May the devil come with his angels and sweep you out of here!'

The tide was well out now and jeers greeted Macrae as he jogged across the ford from Vallay on his grey garron. He conferred with Colquhoun and Cooper while a few stones flew down from the slope. Then he rode towards the crowd and held up his hand; was he going to say the benediction? 'Please hear me, my friends – no more bloodshed. Will four of you come forward and try to make –'

A voice called out, young Alasdair's, 'What are they paying you, Macrae?' A few more stones rattled down and Macrae looked as white as flour but still the police kept back in ranks and Colquhoun was muttering to Cooper, 'I will *not* exceed the writs – you are entitled to take possession but there is a question as to the ownership of the roofing timbers…'

Now Cooper made his final move. Four men went onto the MacLeods' croft, the man from Langass said his piece, the men went in, and then Peter MacLeod's mother was rushing from the house; she fell onto the grass and barked and howled like a dog while her goods showered about her; they heard Peter's wife screaming, 'Leave the roof above the loom – leave the roof –' The men were standing on the wall, hooking out the thatch and showering it down (but they left the timbers). Roderick MacCuish and Archie Boyd led a small group in a rush between the houses; the police left their ranks and chased them, flailing with their truncheons when they caught them up; the people nearest shook and hid their eyes as the clubs cracked; the men swung their boots and tried to close and wrestle but they were yielding, they were falling, and Archie and Roderick felt the handcuffs biting on their wrists. The police retreated in a tight bunch, dragging them like meat. A tenth house was gutted and then Cooper called a halt. Among the wreckage Flo was still kneeling down beside her father, lifting the rubbish off his legs; Morag, bloodstained, was helping her mother to shift wee Katrine's cradle and a few pots and a pallet to a neighbour's house; Macrae was moving about among the crowd, talking to the men, who listened with their eyes on the ground as he assured them that they could bring home this year's harvest, and stay in their houses till the spring, if they would sign a bond pledging themselves to leave the township.

When big Alasdair started down the hill on the committee road, his head crooked beneath his load, he saw the houses with their roofs gaping, goods heaped between them like jetsam after a storm-tide, and he heard a long plaintive wail like a funeral coronach. The women were keening and the sound passed along the shore, making a double echo among the steep hills behind the shieling.

Epilogue

On the morning of Friday, 3 August 1849, the tenants of the Sollas townships signed a pledge to emigrate to Canada when the estate decided.

On 13 September, at Inverness, Archibald Boyd, Roderick MacCuish, Archibald McLean, and Roderick MacPhail were sentenced to four months in prison for rioting and obstructing officers of the law in the execution of their duty.

In January 1850 Patrick Cooper gave the families a final warning to get out and a few months later young Macdonald was dismissed for 'inefficiency', James Macdonald resumed as factor, and word suddenly came that Cooper was bribing men with promises of land if they would form a posse to chase after young Macdonald and Jessie, who had eloped. A storm at sea forced the young couple to shelter on Harris, where Jessie's uncle held the girl, and her lover had to bring men from his father's place on Skye and rescue her at gun-point. While the young couple were entering on a new life in Australia, the Sollas families were still crofting, desperate to bring in one more harvest. In the autumn they were forced out into the wilderness near Locheport where they lived in huts of earth and turf, unable to fish or sow. Pneumonia and typhus decimated them; they perched there like refugees, watching their children's bellies distend and their limbs turn stick-like between the swollen joints, while back among the green and yellow fields of home James Macdonald had begun to farm the Sollas townlands as their sole tenant.

In 1852 the able-bodied male survivors among the refugees were told they would be given passages to Australia, provided they were married (Australia suffered from a surplus of bachelors). But the girls from their own townships were forbidden to wed on pain of eviction. The estate was determined to burst the last fibres of community and break the people's hearts. Just after Christmas 1852, plagued with smallpox and leaving their old loves behind, they sailed for Australia.

Roddy MacPhail would have refused the humiliating conditions and run away with Flo. But in the January of 1850, when he came back home from prison, he found that she had gone. Allan had been buried in December, somewhere on Dunskellor, but there are no lettered gravestones on the single dune above the machair; he could be lying underneath any of the thin, weathered headstones. A brown-haired woman called Flora Campbell was heard of during the Battle of the Braes on Skye in 1882, where the crofters organized a rent strike to win back their grazing and the police had to retreat under a barrage of mud and stones; and it is probable that her friend and comrade Morag Matheson was among the party who invaded Balranald and Balelone in 1884 and pegged out new crofts on James Macdonald's land.

In 1921, after two generations of the Land War, and after the Act of 1886 which gave the crofters secure tenure and took from the lairds the power to fix rents, the long kingship of factor Macdonald and his family was drawing to its end at last. In that year, in the biggest land raid in the history of the islands, veterans of the Great War laughed at the threat of prison, drove Captain James Macdonald's herds from Balranald, built themselves huts there, and started to plough. The people of Sollas, what was left of them, settled into new holdings beside the ruins of the family houses, digging their potato fields, sowing their oats, and grazing their brown cattle round the mound of Dunskellor, where the nameless grey headstones lean this way and that among the blue blades of the marram grass.